PRAISE FOR
MORNING IN THIS BROKEN WORLD

"*Morning in This Broken World* is a heartfelt take on the family we're born with, the family we choose, and the messy, beautiful intersections between the two. Katrina Kittle gifts us with an unforgettable protagonist, an endearing supporting cast, and a moving story about what it really means to call a place 'home.' The world would be a better (and dare I say less broken) place if it were filled with more novels like this one."

—Jessica Strawser, author of *A Million Reasons Why*

"Katrina Kittle's latest novel puts a moment in our collective memory into a context so comforting, so beautiful, and so hopeful that it is impossible not to look back on that time in a new light. *Morning in This Broken World* offers an emotional read full of heart-stirring highs and cathartic sorrows. I am buying stock in tissues before this novel comes out."

—Kelly Harms, bestselling author of *Wherever the Wind Takes Us*

"There are very few writers who can address the human condition in such a thoughtful and poignant way as Katrina Kittle. If you are looking to escape into a wonderfully diverse and entertaining world, this book is exactly what you are looking for as a reader."

—Angela Jackson-Brown, author of *The Light Always Breaks*

"*Morning in This Broken World* is a heartening reminder that even early in the COVID-19 pandemic, joy found a way to persist. Without contrivance or sentimentality, Kittle gives us a cast of characters that fight to be their best selves against terrible odds—both personal and global—armed with humor, hope, and the strength of human connection. This novel is in some ways an apocalypse story, and like the best of them, a powerful reminder of what we have to live for."

—Erin Flanagan, Edgar-winning author of *Deer Season* and *Blackout*

MORNING
IN THIS
BROKEN
WORLD

OTHER TITLES BY KATRINA KITTLE

MORNING
IN THIS
BROKEN
WORLD

KATRINA KITTLE

LAKE UNION
PUBLISHING

Published by Lake Union Publishing, Seattle

www.apub.com

Amazon, the Amazon logo, and Lake Union Publishing are trademarks of Amazon.com, Inc., or its affiliates.

ISBN-13: 9781662510113 (paperback)
ISBN-13: 9781662510120 (digital)

Cover design by Philip Pascuzzo
Cover image: : © wrangel / Getty

Printed in the United States of America

For Jason.
I love you. And I'm not bored.

THIS IS HOW A PANDEMIC ENDS, NOT WITH A BANG BUT WITH CICADAS
by Kathleen McCleary

We went underground this year
like the cicadas, burrowed deep,
huddled against roots, sucking
what little sustenance we could
from whatever we found.

The cicadas sing outside my window now.
And I swear the other sound I hear
is the crackling of millions of exoskeletons,
the shells we grew to harden ourselves
against our longing to be touched.

CHAPTER ONE

VIVIAN

March 2020

Vivian stared at the five amber pill bottles before her on the Formica kitchen counter. Well, what was she waiting for? She had enough pills, but did she have enough guts?

She'd been too afraid to do a computer search when she considered helping Jack die. Her handsome, smart-ass Jack. She'd stockpiled these painkillers from various procedures throughout the years—her hysterectomy, Jack's rotator-cuff surgery, her trigger-thumb surgery. She'd known if she'd decided to crush them up in pudding to help ease him out of this life of indignity, she'd have to be careful. There could be no search history in case there was an autopsy. She hadn't known: Did they do autopsies on Alzheimer's patients?

But Jack had passed. On his own. Her sharp sorrow had been mixed with relief that his confusion and pain were over.

And two days after he was gone, she'd finally researched: How much Oxycodone will kill a person?

She had enough.

These pills sang to her. For the month since he'd passed, through the blur of writing an obituary, planning his service, ordering death certificates, and making the thousand phone calls about life insurance, long-term-care insurance, and Social Security, the five pill bottles hummed a siren song to her. From their Ziploc bag inside the canister of cornmeal she never used (there wasn't even a working stove or oven in this Assisted Living apartment), their serenade rose, silvery, soothing, and full of promise. Sometimes the pills made her paranoid, when their harmony was so loud and others were in the apartment—aides checking on her, although she didn't need services; the cleaning lady; the head of social activities asking her to come to this concert or that trivia game; the director herself wondering if Vivian might like to return to the Independent Living dining room rather than eating alone in her apartment again. Vivian would tilt her head and study their faces. Did they truly not hear it? Were they just pretending?

What was stopping her, really? The love of her life was gone. The home they'd created together, their castle, their oasis, now for sale. Their daughter, their only child . . . well.

Vivian picked up one bottle and turned it in her hands, hearing the reassuring rattle.

Ann-Marie was gone, too.

She set the bottle down, and that same hand went to the buttons of her blouse. Two fingers slipped between the buttons and found the chickpea-size lump to the left of her sternum, at the top of her left breast. She rubbed her fingertips over it, as if it were a worry bead. There was this, too. Treatment and surgery? Alone? No, thank you.

She had friends. She had dear, dear friends. But nothing seemed to matter. Nothing seemed worth it. She'd just told this to her neighbors at the house, Steven and Drew, "the boys" as she called them. The boys had known and loved Jack long before his decline. They helped care for Vivian and Jack's house once they'd had to move to Sycamore Place, this sprawling, multistory facility chosen for its "continuum of care"—the ground floor full of luxury Independent Living apartments, the second and third floors for Assisted Living apartments, and the dreaded, locked-down top floor of Memory Care bedrooms, each floor with its own dining hall. When Jack passed, the boys were here that very day. But. But it wasn't enough. She felt like a burden.

How did people *do* this, for heaven's sake? How was she supposed to get up and go on with this sorrow hanging on her, dragging her down? The grief pinned her to her bed, left her unable to move for days at a time.

No, leaving this life was better.

Truly better.

If only Jack would give her a sign. Long ago, they'd joked that whoever died first would haunt the other, but so far, Jack had been a no-show, and frankly, that pissed Vivian off.

"I need a sign, Jack," she whispered.

Nothing. It figured. He'd always been hopeless at communication, at sharing his feelings.

She opened one bottle. She put a pill on her palm and tipped it into her mouth, swallowing it with the last of her coffee gone cold. Ugh. So she'd started it, then. With a sudden rush of energy, she turned to the fridge in the tiny galley kitchen and poured herself some ice water. There. Better. She'd need to take more than one at a time or this nonsense would last forever.

She poured a wee fistful into her palm, one skittering to the floor. She paused, wondering whether to pop the handful into her mouth before or after she searched for the one gone AWOL on the ugly tile floor—did she even need it?—when there was a knock on her door.

Shit. She shoved the handful of pills and all the bottles under the stack of newspapers and sympathy cards on her counter. She turned, heart racing, but when no one immediately entered, she knew who it was. Everyone else knocked once, then barged right in, the very thing that had rankled her most when they'd moved here.

The only nursing assistant who actually waited for a response was a lovely woman Vivian adored.

"Ms. Vivian? It's Luna. I have someone who wants to see you."

Vivian's heart lifted. Not just Luna but Luna *and* Wren. Wren. Lively Wren. This timing was terrible, but what was a half hour more?

"Come on in!" Vivian called, then grabbed a dishtowel and pretended to be wiping her hands.

Luna would know. Luna would sense something. Vivian braced herself for it. Luna was the best of all the aides who had tended to Jack. Jack's favorite as well as her own. Luna had treated Jack like the man he'd been once, not the man Alzheimer's had left behind. Vivian requested her and was always disappointed when someone else came in. But the poor woman couldn't work all the damn time. She had her own life, after all, outside of this place. And her own daughter.

That daughter, Wren, came through the door first. Her mother followed the girl's motorized hot-pink wheelchair. The eleven-year-old girl looked up at Vivian with gentle compassion. Oh, that face. Those round cheeks, bright eyes, and deep, long dimples. How much she looked like Ann-Marie as a child.

As Luna closed the door behind her—something other aides rarely did, leaving Vivian's and Jack's lives on display for everyone and anyone walking past, and, oh, did people gawk and stare here—Wren looked up at Vivian and said, "I'm so, so sorry about Mr. Jack."

"Thank you, Wren. I am, too."

Vivian bent to hug her, and the girl hung on, as she did, her hugs long and insistent. Vivian had the fleeting thought, *What if Wren had been with her mother and found me dead?* Good God, how horrifying.

After a moment, Luna rubbed her daughter's back and said, "Okay, sweetie."

But Wren only let go when she was damn good and ready. Vivian didn't mind one bit. When Wren released her, Vivian breathed deep and felt better than she had for days.

"How are you, Vivian?" Luna asked.

Vivian looked into Luna's deep-brown eyes. She knew. Vivian could tell Luna knew something was up. "It's been a hard day," she admitted. "After many hard days."

Luna reached out and squeezed her shoulder. "There will probably be more." The way she said it was a comfort, really, an acknowledgment.

Not that patronizing, insensitive, chipper insistence that "things will get better!" or "each day gets easier!" that made Vivian want to kick people in the shins, the simple sons of bitches.

Maybe not, though, Vivian thought. Maybe there would be no more hardness if there were no more days? The pills still sang to her from under the newspaper. Her hand rose to find the lump. When she realized she was seeking it again, she snatched her hand away and turned back to Wren. "What is this, Take Your Daughter to Work Day?"

Luna touched her daughter's shiny black hair with the gentlest of hands and said, "In our own sort of way, yes. Wren's school was canceled today. Someone tested positive for the virus. Have you been following that?"

Vivian nodded. "It's getting serious." Then she teased Wren, "Oh, so you're *stuck* with Mom today."

Luna and Wren both laughed but looked at each other with such adoration, Vivian's heart stuttered.

That song, though. That song was so insistent.

Luna joked, "I don't know how I'm supposed to get any work done with this little troublemaker along."

Vivian knew that was true. The apartments were already small, there were already so many wheelchairs and scooters around, that poor Wren was bound to be in the way and very noticed. Vivian wondered if Luna might even get reprimanded for bringing her here.

"Well, would the troublemaker like to stay here with me instead while Mom works?"

Wren's face lit up, but Luna said, "Oh, no, no, I can't ask you to—"

"Please."

Luna looked taken aback at Vivian's insistence. No, it was more like desperation.

Vivian smiled, tried to soften that hard edge of pleading that had been in her word. That song, it was just too damn loud. "I would honestly love it. I could use the company."

Luna regarded her a moment, assessing. She looked down at her daughter, who said, "Please, Mama? There's some worksheets and assignments I can get online."

"All right, then."

Wren made a little cheer and motored herself farther into the apartment.

Vivian and Luna stared at each other. "You're doing me a great favor," Luna said.

"And you're doing one for me."

Luna tilted her head. "You okay?"

"I will be now."

Luna held Vivian's gaze a moment longer, then reached past Vivian into the tiny kitchen and took a Post-it from the neon-orange cube. She wrote a number. "Please call my cell if you need anything. Or if she needs anything. Or if you're ready for her to go. Please call this number and not the nurses' station, okay?"

Ah, so she *was* worried about having Wren here. "Of course. But it's fine. We'll have a lovely time." She took a Post-it, too, and scribbled her own cell number. "This is mine."

"Thank you." Luna spoke with such sincerity. Just then, her radio squawked. "Luna? 310 is waiting for that wheelchair. How long do you think you'll be?"

They always called residents by their room numbers here. Vivian never understood if that was for privacy?

"On my way." Luna looked with great kindness at Vivian. "I stopped by to take Mr. Jack's wheelchair."

Ah, yes. So she hadn't come by just to see how Vivian was doing. And she hadn't come by just to try to find a place to stash her daughter for the day.

"Of course," Vivian said.

Luna kissed Wren on the cheek and told her to be good for "Ms. Vivian." Then she took Jack's wheelchair from its spot next to Vivian's blue reading chair, where Vivian had sat and held his hand as they watched TV or looked out the window. He always wanted to hold her hand. Hot tears burned, but she willed them back.

That wheelchair had been in her damn way, and she'd been irritated that no one had thought to come take it before now, as Hospice had come to take the hospital bed and the walker right away . . . but now that it was leaving the apartment, Vivian wanted to dive for it, to beg Luna not to take it, to say that she'd pay for it, that it comforted her.

But she didn't. She turned away as Luna wheeled it out into the hallway and then shut the door behind her.

Vivian wiped her eyes and willed herself not to shout, "Shut up!" at the pill bottles. A gauzy sensation floated through her, a slight dizziness she didn't understand. Then she remembered: the one Oxycodone was wisping into her system. She'd always been a lightweight with meds. She turned to Wren. "Do you want to get that schoolwork? I can get you on our internet." *Our.* Would she ever stop thinking of herself as a member of a couple, a team?

Wren scrunched up her face. "Not really." She hunched her shoulders. "I got that email from my language arts teacher. I hate language arts."

Vivian clutched a hand to her chest. "Oh, that breaks my heart. I would be the exact opposite!"

"I don't hate the *subject*," Wren said. "I only hate it because my teacher teaches it. She treats me like I'm stupid because I'm in a wheelchair."

Vivian went still at the blunt truth. "You are *not* stupid," she said, her tone fierce.

Wren smiled. "I know."

She did. No ego. No audacity. Just the acknowledgment of the truth.

"So what shall we do instead?" Vivian asked.

"I want to show you something," Wren said. "Can you get my backpack off the back of my chair, please?"

Vivian liked the way the girl always asked for what she needed clearly and simply, no simpering apologies or "Could I ask you a favor?"

"Of course." There were actually two backpacks. One smaller and black, tattered and worn, and a bigger one, hot pink and sparkly. The smaller one was draped over the pink one, so Vivian extricated it first. "This one?" she asked as she handed it to Wren.

"Oh! That's Mom's. She forgot it."

"Should I call her?"

"Nah, she'll come back for it when she needs it."

"Okay." Vivian held the black one by one strap while she unhooked the pink one. One arm of the pink backpack was stuck, and as she tugged it, she jerked the black bag, and its zipper slid open and spilled its contents all over the floor. "Well, shit!"

Wren giggled.

"Sorry!"

"I've heard worse, Ms. Vivian."

Vivian handed Wren the sparkling pink backpack, and the girl dug into it, searching for whatever she was looking for, while Vivian knelt to gather Luna's things she'd dropped.

Vivian's knees popped as she crouched, that shimmery vertigo swimming in her head. She grabbed the table for balance. She gathered up a lip balm egg, two tampons, a granola bar, some apple slices in a Ziploc, and a wallet. There were receipts, coupons, and other papers. Vivian didn't know if there was an order everything should go in, and she felt bad about just stuffing things back in. The backpack, now open like a clamshell, still contained some items, and Vivian was honestly only trying to figure out how to put the items back in with some kind of order when she saw an envelope tucked into a small pocket.

The pocket was too shallow for the business envelope, so two-thirds of it stuck out, visible. The envelope was bright yellow and stamped outside with Notice of Eviction.

CHAPTER TWO

Wren

Wren knew Ms. Vivian was sad. So sad, it scared Wren. Wren had been eager to spend time with one of her favorite people at her mom's work, but ever since her mom had left, Ms. Vivian had gotten weird. She seemed all nervous and twitchy and wasn't being fun.

Usually, she was awesome. She didn't act like an old person, even though she looked kind of old. She looked like that Jane Goodall lady who worked with the chimpanzees: tall, thin, with long white hair. Wren had read a book about Jane Goodall, and once Wren and Ms. Vivian and Mr. Jack had watched a documentary about her right here in this living room. Usually, Wren and Ms. Vivian would laugh together and take Mr. Jack outside into the sunshine. Mr. Jack liked to hold Wren's hand.

Until he forgot how to talk, every single time he saw Wren, he'd say, "Oh, sweet pea, what happened?" and gesture to her wheelchair.

The first time, Wren had said, "I have cerebral palsy."

Mr. Jack had been horrified and turned to Ms. Vivian with, "Why didn't you tell me this? What are we going to do?"

But Ms. Vivian had winked at Wren over Mr. Jack's head and said, "Oh, hon, she got hurt in a skiing accident. This wheelchair is just temporary. She'll be back on her feet in no time."

Wren had giggled and gone along with it. Mr. Jack had taken her hand and said, "Sweet pea, you have to be more careful." Wren's mom had taught her about her patients, the "residents," Mom always called them, with Alzheimer's and dementia, and how it was better to go along with them instead of correcting them. "If they think they're twenty again, what point is there in reminding them they're eighty?" Mom asked. "Let them believe what they want if it makes them happy. It's cruel to correct them over and over again."

Wren had asked her mom once, "What's that thing he always calls me? Is it French?"

Mom had tilted her head, that way she did when she was looking inside you and reading your mind. "What thing he calls you?"

"He always says something like, 'Oh, Am-or-eee.'"

Mom's face softened. "He calls you that? That's a name. Ann-Marie."

Wren felt something shift under her, like her wheelchair was on uneven sidewalk. "Who's Ann-Marie?"

"That's their daughter."

"What?" Wren had felt like Ms. Vivian had kept a secret from her. Why had she never explained the name to her? "They have a *daughter*? Why is she never there helping them?"

Mom frowned. "I think she passed away, sweetie. Don't you dare go asking about her."

Wren had a secret then. And she loved secrets. Secret passageways. Secret hiding places. Diaries with locks. Mr. Jack thought she was his daughter. Hmm. From then on, the few times she got to be in Mr. Jack and Ms. Vivian's apartment, she studied the photos. Wren did look like Ann-Marie. Same straight black hair. Same "apple cheeks," like Grammy, her mom's mom, used to call them. Same dimples. Like, they could be sisters. Or . . . twins. Like, maybe Ann-Marie was a secret other part of Wren? The part that had an able body?

So Wren created a game. When Wren was here and Mr. Jack was horrified to see her in a wheelchair, Wren told him a new story about how she got "injured." She wrote down new ideas in the journals Mom bought her. Ms. Vivian would laugh and nod, and Wrèn could tell she liked this game, too.

Once Wren told him she/Ann-Marie fell off a horse. Once that she fell off the stage in a dance recital. She fell while rock climbing, twisted an ankle hiking, and got dropped by her ballet partner in a rehearsal. All things Wren would give anything to have actually experienced, even the injuries, even the pain.

All things she would never do.

But she could do them through Ann-Marie. Sometimes, Wren wrote in her journals like she *was* Ann-Marie, the thin, athletic girl in the photos. She would write stories of her misadventures that had landed her in the wheelchair. This wheelchair was only temporary for Ann-Marie.

Ms. Vivian never told Wren about Ann-Marie or how she'd died. So Wren never told Ms. Vivian about the journals. Wren could have secrets, too. But Ms. Vivian always laughed and went with the injury stories. Ms. Vivian was fun.

Ms. Vivian always made the best of things, even when things were awful and embarrassing, like when Mr. Jack peed his pants outside one day. Ms. Vivian never acted impatient or mean. Wren felt awful, and she loved Ms. Vivian for being so nice to him. Wren had peed her own pants more than once because she couldn't move fast enough to get to the bathroom. She *could* use the restroom on her own, if it was accessible, but it was so much easier when her mom or her teacher's aide helped her. Falling was a big deal. She'd bashed herself up a bunch of times.

But now Ms. Vivian seemed so nervous. She kept asking Wren strange questions. She'd started with, "How are you all doing at home? How's your mom doing? Does she seem okay?"

That was weird. Ms. Vivian was the one whose husband had died. Ms. Vivian was the one who looked sad and tired. Wren should be asking about *her*.

"Mom's okay."

"What about your dad?"

Wren froze. "What *about* my dad?"

"Does he help your mom? When she's stressed?"

Wren lifted a shoulder. "I guess. He doesn't live with us anymore."

"Are they divorced?"

A noise came from Wren's throat, surprising her. "Separated?" It was a genuine question. Wren really didn't know, and both her mom and dad had told her not to worry about it, which Wren hated. If they wouldn't tell her *why* Dad had left, how could Wren do better and get him to come back? Why did Ms. Vivian want to know this? Wren felt exposed, like that turtle she'd seen on its back on the side of the road, like when Cooper said such mean things about Dad.

"What does he do? Does he work in health care like your mom?"

Wren shook her head. "He worked security at the airport."

"Worked? Past tense?"

"I don't think he does that anymore. I don't know what he does now. I haven't seen him this week." Something burned in Wren's chest. Her breath tightened to remember how her dad was supposed to spend the day with her a week ago. Maybe go to the zoo, or to RiverScape, or something, because it had been a bright spring day. But when he was an hour and forty minutes late, her mom had said, "Let's go," and taken Wren to the zoo herself. When Wren asked her later if her dad had called, Mom shook her head, pressing her lips together until they disappeared.

Mom didn't lie to her.

Wren didn't like feeling angry at Dad. For a second, she wanted to hurt Ms. Vivian for making her think about that day, but she didn't like that feeling, either. When Ms. Vivian said, "Does he have a job, though? Does he give your mother money?" Wren couldn't help it and asked her, "That's your daughter, right? In that picture?"

Wren already knew it was, but it was her turn to ask questions. She pointed to the photos crowded on the bookcase in the tiny living room.

Ms. Vivian's face did something really weird. Like, a bazillion emotions all moved under her skin at once. Wren recognized sorrow, anger . . . and maybe fear. "Oh. Yes. That's Ann-Marie."

"Did she come to the funeral?"

"There wasn't a funeral, really," Ms. Vivian said. "Jack and I are donating our bodies to the medical school."

That was super weird, and Wren wanted to ask lots of questions about *that*, picturing a stitched-together monster like in *Frankenstein* or something, but she wanted to stick to her own mission. "But there was a . . . a thing for him, right? Mom came to it."

"We had a memorial service."

"Did she come? Ann-Marie?" Wren wanted to find out what had happened to the girl.

"That was almost a month ago, right before we all knew how serious this virus was. Some people didn't come because of it, even then, but so many did, and I'm so afraid . . . I guess it's been long enough now. We would've known if a bunch of people got sick. There were so many crowded together that day, closer than we should have been."

"Did Ann-Marie come?"

Ms. Vivian narrowed her eyes at Wren. Wren could tell she wanted to say Wren was stubborn or something. But Ms. Vivian just said, "No," and got up from the table, moving for the kitchen. "I think I need coffee. I'm so sleepy."

"Is that why she didn't come? Because of the virus?"

Ms. Vivian stopped with her back to Wren. "No."

"What did she tell you?" Wren didn't know why she was doing this. But now she couldn't stop.

Ms. Vivian kept walking. Wren could still see her, because there was a big cutout square over the sink so you could see right into the kitchen. Ms. Vivian moved something on the counter and said, "I haven't spoken to Ann-Marie in six years."

Whoa. Wren realized her mouth was open. That was a weird way to avoid saying someone had died. Was she afraid to tell Wren? Did she think Wren was a baby and would cry or something? Ms. Vivian opened a cupboard and poured some water, and soon Wren heard the gurgle of a coffee maker. Ms. Vivian came back into the living room holding a bakery box. Wren tried to think of what to ask next, but Ms. Vivian said, "Okay, it's my turn again."

She set the box on the table and took off the lid, which made a sweet sugar aroma rush into the air. Wren saw cookies and cupcakes. Ms. Vivian dipped her finger in some chocolate cupcake frosting and licked it off. See? *That* was the cool Ms. Vivian. Mom would freak about that, like when Cooper drank straight out of the milk carton.

"Some friends brought these to me. Help yourself," Ms. Vivian said, pushing the box toward Wren, then taking another fingerful of icing from the cupcake she'd already messed up. "Now, tell me about where you live. What's it like? Is it a house or an apartment?"

"An apartment."

"What's the address?"

Wren told her, and Ms. Vivian started typing it into the tablet she used, where the font was so big Wren could read every word from across the table *and* upside down, even. "What are you *doing*?" she asked. "Why do you care where I live?"

"Because I care about you, and I want your family to be okay." Ms. Vivian's eyes shone like she might cry. Wren remembered Mom telling her that sometimes when people were sad and angry, they found different . . . what was the word she'd used? *Targets*. Like Wren: she'd been mad at her dad, but she'd been really mean to her mom.

Because her mom was there.

When Wren said to her mom, "The plan wasn't to spend another day with *you*," Mom had sighed and said, "I get it. I'm the easy target."

And Wren understood: Mom was *there*.

Wren could never lash out at Dad because Dad was never around anymore. And if she was rude or mean to him, like Cooper was, maybe he'd never come back.

Mom, though, would never leave them.

The whole thing was pretty unfair when Wren thought about it. She was rude and nasty to the person who was safest and the most reliable in her whole world. That sucked. *She* sucked.

So Wren took a deep breath and looked at Ms. Vivian's sad face and wondered if Ms. Vivian was being weird and pushy to Wren because Wren was here, the easy target. Wren wanted to ask so much more about Ann-Marie, but the sorrow and exhaustion on this nice lady's face made her change her mind. For now. "What about you, where you live?" she asked Ms. Vivian. "Are you going to keep living here?"

Ms. Vivian scraped more chocolate icing off that cupcake with her finger. "That's the plan," she said, but she didn't sound excited. "Not here in this apartment. This is Assisted Living, and I don't need assistance. We were here for Jack. But I'm on a waiting list for an Independent Living apartment here." She picked up the chocolate cupcake, licked the remaining icing off the top, then dumped it in the trash can behind her. "So often, the cake doesn't measure up to the icing."

Wren giggled.

"What?" Ms. Vivian asked, acting all innocent. "The icing is the part I like. I've decided I'm only doing what I like from now on. I deserve it."

Wren looked at the bakery box, and Ms. Vivian pushed it closer to her, as if reading her mind. Wren's belly pressed against her seat belt as she leaned over. She examined the cupcakes now in range and selected one with a cloud of vanilla icing with sprinkles. "Where did you live before you moved here?" Wren asked, wriggling and pushing herself back upright in her chair. She took a bite of the cupcake. Oh, man, that was good.

"We have a home not too far away. Our castle."

"Is it really a castle?"

Ms. Vivian laughed. "No, but we always called it that. I love that house. Everything we'd ever talked about wishing for or wanting in a house, this one had. If it didn't come with it, we built it ourselves."

Her face had totally changed. Wren looked at the happiness almost glowing from Ms. Vivian. "Like what kind of stuff?"

"I'd always wanted a fireplace, and I got a fantastic one. On the first cold night in autumn, I'd make a big pot of chili, and we'd eat in front of the fire."

Wren liked that image. She'd never had a fireplace.

"And I have the kitchen of my dreams. A great big island, all this counter space. So much light. The kitchen is always bright and sunny. I love to cook, and there are two ovens. We designed a bar where I'd always wanted one, because for parties, I never knew where to set up all the drinks . . ." She trailed off, and Wren saw Ms. Vivian was seeing those things right now.

Parties. Wren wondered what kind. Mom and Dad used to have Halloween and Christmas parties for all their friends. Cookouts in the summer with silly games, like even the grown-ups playing Twister.

"And Jack always wanted a library." Ms. Vivian said *library* in a mocking sort of tone, but Wren could tell she was just joking. "Floor-to-ceiling books, with one of those wooden ladders like in the movies. A great big leather reading chair. Holy Hannah, he loved that room."

Wren's eyes widened. She would *love* that. "What kind of books?"

Ms. Vivian raised an eyebrow. "Every kind you can think of. He especially loves mysteries. He collects rare books, too. First editions, autographed books."

Wren wondered if Ms. Vivian knew she was talking like Mr. Jack was still alive. She caught herself wanting to correct her, but she knew that would be mean. Besides, it wasn't like Ms. Vivian actually thought he was still alive, like how Mr. Jack had believed things that weren't true. It was a habit. A person was with you for so long, and it would take some getting used to for them to be gone. Like her grammy. Everything kind of fell apart when Grammy died. Way more than when Dad left.

"But my favorite thing, the most amazing thing, the reason we bought the house, to be honest, was the garden. I love to garden. The house has this beautiful backyard. When we moved in, it was all lawn, on a hill. What a waste. And now, oh my, *now.*" She stood and went to a crowded bookshelf, rummaging around, and brought out a photo album. Wow, that was old-school. Actual photographs, not just on your phone.

Ms. Vivian turned a bunch of pages and then put the book down in front of Wren. Ms. Vivian had taken before and after pictures of the yard. And wow, the after pictures of the garden. Wren made a sound. Oh. How beautiful and perfect. Like one of her favorite stories, *The Secret Garden.* She wanted to lose herself in this garden. It rolled downhill away from the house, then back uphill into some woods. It had, like, different levels and different rooms, if a garden could have rooms. Different places to sit, depending on the mood you were in. A cozy bench, half-hidden at the end of a gravel path. Arbors and arches loaded with flowers and leaves . . . and fruit? Were those grapes? The paths wound around, with hidden surprises. Statues of rabbits and turtles and even a ballerina. Birdhouses painted orange and blue and purple. A little pond. At least three birdbaths.

Was Ms. Vivian crazy? Wren would *never* leave a place so magical, so beautiful. She reached up for her necklace—the one Mom had bought her when the one her dad gave her for her birthday had broken—and was thrilled to find the clasp had moved to the front of her neck. She held the clasp and stared at a photo of Ann-Marie while she wished she could be in that garden. Then she moved the clasp to the back of her neck. Ann-Marie had lived in that beautiful house. Maybe Wren was *supposed* to be there? Mr. Jack thought so. How could Wren get Vivian to think so, too?

She looked up at Ms. Vivian. "Why don't you want to live there anymore?"

Ms. Vivian's face went blank. She looked over her shoulder at something in the kitchen; Wren didn't know what. When she spoke, her voice was different. Like a bunch of layers had been peeled away, and this was her real voice. "I'm afraid." It was the truth, Wren could tell. The kind of truth grown-ups hardly ever told.

Ms. Vivian stood and went to the kitchen. Wren watched her pour a cup of coffee, but she returned to the table without it.

"I stayed there one night, after the memorial service," Ms. Vivian said. "I thought I wanted to go back. We had a gathering there at the house, after the service. But it was . . . so lonely and awful there without him." Ms. Vivian whispered now. "It scared me, how lonely I felt. I was afraid of what I might do."

Wren reached out and took Ms. Vivian's bony, cold hand. Ms. Vivian squeezed her hand back and held on a moment. Then Ms. Vivian whispered, "Thank you, Wren. I needed that."

Wren wanted to tell Ms. Vivian how lonely she felt, too. How invisible. So visible and invisible at the same time. She was always in the way with this big, clunky wheelchair, taking up so much room everywhere she went. But people only looked at the chair. Never at her, never into her face. Only at the braces on her legs that kept her feet from turning in. Only at her thick, giant shoes. She knew she scared them. Sometimes, she knew she disgusted them. But she didn't want to say these words out loud, because then they became too real.

So instead, she turned the page in the photo book, looking at more scenes from the garden. A big swing. Glass flowers on metal stems. A section that looked like the woods, with a big log. A stump that looked like a gnome house with a door and a chimney. A fountain. Some plant trailing flowers in a birdcage hanging from a tree. Wren's whole body ached to be there.

"The house is for sale," Ms. Vivian said. "It officially lists today, this morning. People may be looking at it already."

Something dropped through Wren's body, like her stomach was falling. *No.* That was too sad. Too sad and awful that she should see pictures of this beautiful place but then never get to go there. She had to scoot herself back up in her chair.

Anger filled her. She didn't understand the anger, though. She should say she needed a minute to get her head together, like Mom had coached her the day she'd been so mad at Dad.

But instead, she let the anger take over. She pointed to the photo of Ann-Marie and asked, "Is she dead?"

Ms. Vivian flinched, like Wren had slapped her.

Ms. Vivian looked at the photo. Then she sighed a sigh that sounded like it scraped something out of her. She opened her mouth.

Before she could answer, someone knocked on the door, and they both jumped.

CHAPTER THREE

LUNA

When Vivian called, "Come in," Luna opened the door. Vivian stood, looking guilty and nervous. Wren looked at her, her expression suggesting she'd been caught doing something bad.

"Everything okay in here, ladies?" Luna asked, trying to assess the weird vibe.

They both nodded. Why were they acting so strange? Panic swooped in her rib cage, and she'd had too much of that feeling inside her today. And yesterday. And for the last week. And really, for way too long in general.

Vivian's sorrow scared Luna. The grief was thick, dangerous, and gnawing away at the woman. Every time Luna saw Vivian, she was thinner, more fragile, like a ghost of her former self, so much so that Luna had flagged Vivian with the director of nursing. Everyone on staff here was on alert for possible self-harm.

Into the awkward silence, Luna said, "I left my backpack on Wren's chair."

At that, Vivian flushed red. What the hell?

Vivian opened her mouth, about to say something, but then didn't.

"Is everything okay, really? She's not causing you trouble?" Wren never caused trouble, but something was causing palpable tension in here.

"Oh! No, no trouble at all."

"Are you doing your schoolwork, young lady?"

"I'm doing it now!" Wren reached into her own backpack on the cluttered table. Luna noticed the bakery box . . . and her own unzipped backpack, opened like a shell, with the yellow envelope blazing like neon. Oh.

Luna's own face flooded with heat.

"Your bag was unzipped," Vivian said. "Everything fell out. I think I got it all put back."

Wren opened her laptop, not paying any attention to this exchange, thank God. "What's your Wi-Fi password, Ms. Vivian?"

While Vivian told Wren, Luna zipped her backpack together. The letter had already been opened, of course, so she had no idea if Vivian had read it. Why would she have read it? Who *did* that? What kind of nosy, meddling—oh, who was she kidding? It said EVICTION right on the outside. Luna wanted to melt into the floor and disappear. She liked this woman. She believed this woman respected her.

The two women locked eyes over Wren's head as Wren opened the school website and looked for her worksheets. "Can I print?" Wren asked.

"Yes. It's wireless. The printer's over there." Vivian pointed.

Luna headed for the door and tipped her head for Vivian to follow her.

They stepped out into the hall, which was fortunately empty, save for poor Dennis, who wandered all day, taking his slow, shuffling steps, clinging to the wall banister, followed by his enormous—and enormously overweight—black-and-white cat, Ox. Dennis wouldn't care what these women said, and even if he did, he wouldn't remember it later.

Luna took a deep breath and kept her voice toneless. "Did Wren see it?"

Vivian shook her head. Good. At least Vivian wasn't going to pretend not to know what Luna was talking about.

"She doesn't know about this yet. Please don't say anything."

Vivian nodded and asked, "What are you going to do?"

"We'll be all right."

"That doesn't answer the question."

Luna regarded Vivian. She'd like to be offended, but that took too much energy. She was so exhausted. This was just one more stressor on top of a whole heaping mountain of stress.

"Let me help you," Vivian said.

Luna exhaled, feeling all her energy running out through her feet. "We'll be all right."

"Consider it a loan. I—it's just me now. I'll have Jack's insurance money soon. I don't need it. You can take your time paying me back."

Luna held up a hand, but it only made Vivian talk faster.

"Please. You helped me so much. You helped Jack. If I could make something easier for you, won't you please let me repay the favor? *Please*."

Luna's radio crackled on her belt. "249 needs assistance. Who's available?"

Thank God. Luna answered, "I'm on my way." She shouldered her backpack, the letter burning through the bag into her skin. She looked up at Vivian, into the woman's piercing blue eyes. Just an hour ago, this woman had seemed hollowed out and breakable with her sorrow. A new energy now pulsed through her. "Thank you. But we'll be all right."

Sylvia, the day nurse, wheeled her medicine cart down the hallway, parking it outside the dining room, just a few doors down.

Luna looked at Vivian again and knew Vivian understood that they couldn't talk about this, any of this—not Wren taking classes in Vivian's apartment, not the letter—right now.

Luna sucked in a breath like she'd been held underwater as she walked away. Why, why, why? Why was everything spiraling out of control? The work of holding it all together, of appearing calm, depleted her. She wasn't sure why this part mattered so very much. Who cared if Vivian knew about the eviction? It was none of her concern. Luna and her children were not Vivian's problem, nor was Vivian Luna's problem. But truly, why wasn't she grabbing that woman around the knees and saying thank you?

Because Luna never accepted help. She didn't need help. She'd been raised by her iron-willed, resilient, hardworking parents to be strong and self-sufficient.

And how's that working out for you?

Shut up! She wanted to hiss it out loud. She could just hear Cal saying this to her. Cal, who wouldn't hesitate to take Vivian's money.

What good did this do? This wallowing in past bad decisions? There was only forward; only what happened next mattered. She walked to the stairwell and paused there in the blessed silence.

Get it together. Get it together. These residents deserve your best while you are here. Be present for them. Luna leaned on the metal stair railing. She breathed in and breathed out, making each inhale and exhale last seven seconds. *Focus.* She would figure this out. She always did. She would provide for her children, which was the most important thing. Later, she would take Wren to her PT appointment and work on finding them a place to stay. But for now, she was here. And she would be present for these people who depended upon her.

She went down one flight of stairs and walked toward 249. This job was a blessing in more ways than one. The work consumed her while she was in it, providing distraction from the anxiety that had become a constant buzz.

She reached apartment 249 and knocked. She heard Miss Florence call, "Come in!" None of the doors were locked in Assisted Living, but Luna couldn't imagine how that lack of privacy wore on someone. Privacy. Huh. Like having someone read her mail? *Focus on Miss Florence.* The tiny woman, who reminded Luna of a Chihuahua, with her big brown eyes and ferocious spirit, smiled at Luna. "Oh, good. I was hoping it would be you. You're my favorite."

"Oh, now, I won't tell the others you said so," Luna teased.

"The others don't know what they're doing."

Ah, there's the sharp Chihuahua bite.

"Let's get you all dolled up to face the day, shall we?"

Miss Florence could do most things on her own and was fiercely independent. Luna knew how it must irritate the woman to need help with the most private of acts, like Luna's daughter did. Miss Florence loved a shower, and some of the other aides didn't want to do showers more than twice a week. Showers could be hard work. The risk of falling was high, and that was a nightmare, a constant possibility with Wren that terrified Luna. But Luna herself couldn't imagine doing without the warm water on her skin.

Miss Florence, being the skinny little zero-body-fat being she was, kept her apartment heated like a sauna. Luna, who had some body fat to spare, found it unbearable but tried not to rush the woman. Not during this. *Be present.*

Being so close to the woman's veiny, mottled skin; her sunken ribs; tiny, shriveled breasts; the faint body odor of her never failed to strike Luna. This was what made all humans alike, all equally vulnerable: these strange, wondrous, exasperating bodies. These bodies that could betray us so. Luna held Miss Florence and guided her twiglike legs over the two-inch lip into the shower. Luna lowered her onto the plastic shower seat and turned on the faucets. When Miss Florence approved of the temperature, Luna switched the water to the shower, stepped back, and closed the shower curtain, saying, "I'll be right here if you need me."

She'd just seen the woman naked, after all, but everyone needed these fleeting moments of privacy. Miss Florence was capable of scrubbing herself and washing wherever she wanted to. The woman kept her hair in a buzz cut that made life easier. Some of the women here clung to their fussy hairstyles.

As the woman hummed and washed herself, Luna stood still and breathed. She'd watched other aides pull out their phones at every single second of free time like this, but Luna refused to do that. Her rule was to be present and focused on each resident she served. But standing still allowed the anxiety to swirl around her again. What the hell exactly was she going to *do*? She sucked in a breath again, like a gasp, and realized she felt like she was drowning.

"You all right?" Miss Florence called.

"I'm all right." Good Lord, the woman had heard her over the water. *Get a grip. And you are not all right. You are not all right at all. Pretending isn't going to make anything go away.*

A sudden image came to her of how she'd pretended her father wasn't sick when she was a little girl. How she didn't acknowledge his loss of hair and weight, how she didn't ask questions when her parents told her he had another doctor's appointment. How she just pretended he was fine, that it would all be okay.

It didn't work.

He'd died. Luna had been in no way prepared for it. She wondered now if her father had ever tried to talk to her about it. Surely he'd known he was dying.

Thank God Miss Florence said, "All right. I'm finished," and spared Luna her memories of being shell-shocked and dazed at her father's funeral. Luna reached in to shut off the water, and Miss Florence sang, "Oh, that was heavenly," as she did every single time.

Luna helped her towel off and lotion herself, inconspicuously doing a skin check—scanning for sores and rashes—and taking discreet peeks at Miss Florence's privates, which were prime areas for infection. Early detection was key.

She helped Miss Florence dress and put on jewelry, which was too difficult with her arthritic hands; then Miss Florence surprised Luna by hugging her. "Oh, bless you, child," Miss Florence said. "I don't know what I'd do without your kindness. I hope you know what it means to me."

Luna had to fight not to burst into tears.

After that, she helped toilet and dress Mr. Larry, who rarely spoke to her, so she hummed the songs he played on his radio to fill the void, then helped her friend Cachè shower feisty, scrappy Louise, who never wanted to shower, bathe, or change her clothes and who cursed them with a mouth fouler than Luna had heard on her son's friends. She and Cachè busted up laughing at the creative strings of obscenities Louise threw at them.

When they left Louise's apartment, Cachè handed Luna a Reese's Cup from her pocket and unwrapped one for herself. "We earned this."

"Stop giving me these. They're my kryptonite."

Cachè laughed and said, "Just another month to baseball season!" They'd go to Dayton Dragons games, where they'd shell peanuts until their thumbs were sore. Luna latched on to that image, to good traditions, to a promise of a future when things would be okay.

Luna then found wandering Dennis, escorted him and his giant cat back to his apartment, and supervised a sink bath and a change of clothes. Ox rubbed against her shins, as if thanking her.

She helped seven other residents dress for the day and helped another clean up after an accident before she had a break. She'd been almost dreading the break because she knew what she must do, what she must face.

She rushed outside, into the sharp March air, where snow flurries fell on the crocuses and daffodils of the landscaped grounds. Her phone pinged with a text: her best friend, Danielle. A photo they occasionally sent back and forth to each other of a card that read, "You are doing a freaking great job." Luna half sobbed, half laughed. Danielle always knew when she needed that message.

Danielle had already offered to let them stay with her and her daughter, Birdy, her son's best friend, but there was no accessible entrance to her house, and the only bathroom was on the second floor.

Luna jogged up the hill to the employee parking lot and got into the van equipped to lift Wren's wheelchair. Another text pinged in: Wren's PT was being indefinitely stalled because of this virus. Damn it. Luna knew the cancellation made today temporarily easier—one less ball to juggle—but it was also devastating. The physical therapist said she'd be in touch with alternatives soon.

Luna forced this news out of her head. She was dealing with the needs of this day like triage.

She didn't have time to stall or psych herself up, so she just tapped on Cal's number. *This is futile. He won't help. He can't help.* She knew he'd want to. He always meant well. But he'd never get his act together in time.

She shook her head and fumed at herself for this. *Pathetic.* But she had to know. She wasn't sure what she'd do if this didn't work. So she had to try.

As the phone rang, she didn't know what she wished for, to leave a message so that she'd have longer to pretend or have him actually pick up.

"Hey, babe."

His voice startled and annoyed her, but she stuffed the annoyance down. She needed help. When she said his name, her voice wavered. *Damn it. Do* not *cry.* "Your check bounced."

"Shit." Cal said the word like it deflated him, making it last until the air ran out.

"We're getting evicted."

Silence.

She waited, determined to make him come up with something, *any*thing.

"You can't cover it?" he finally asked.

Luna's face flamed here in the van even with the snow flurries on the windshield obscuring her view. Those flurries yanked her without warning back to herself at eight, watching *The Nutcracker*, mouth open with delight, squeezing her mother's hand. Luna shook herself. How had she completely lost herself as an adult? "You know I can't pay the rent without your share."

"Babe." He sounded gentle but impatient. "Maybe you shoulda thought of that before you asked me to move out."

Luna closed her eyes. She would not apologize for that, never in a million years. "We made an agreement. You said you'd pay your share, for the kids."

He made an exasperated sound, then coughed. "And I did. You know I don't have a job."

She leaned her head on the steering wheel. He'd had a good job at the airport. They'd been doing fine. But when his car broke down, he couldn't afford the repairs, and his twenty-minute drive turned into a two-hour commute by bus. When he was late to work a fifth time, he got fired.

"If you won't let me use the van, what am I supposed to do?"

"You *know* why you can't use the van." She hated that she needed to explain their daughter's safety to him, time and time again. The van needed to be where Wren was. Available to Wren. *Reliably* available for Wren.

"I don't know what you want me to do."

She always had to explain everything to him. She wanted a partner who'd know what to do, who'd take the lead one damn time and not leave her feeling like she had *three* children. "What can you give me to help hold off the landlord? We've got to scrape enough together to make him stop the eviction. I need your share."

Cal laughed. "I'm not magic, babe. If I could just conjure up money, I woulda done it way before now."

"What can you give us?"

"Nothing. I don't have a job."

She slammed the heel of her hand on the steering wheel. "Ask your brother."

"I'm not doing that. He's already letting me sleep here."

"These are your children. Where are *they* supposed to sleep?"

At least he had the decency to pause. "Look, I'll talk to Ricky. The kids can sleep here. I'll find someplace else. Until you figure something else out."

Luna closed her eyes and exhaled. Why was it always on her, the figuring things out? "How are we going to get Wren into that apartment?"

"Oh, shit."

How could he do it, time and again, forget Wren's needs? Was he just pretending she didn't have a disability?

"We could carry her up," Cal said. "We can do that."

Luna wanted to cry. They might have to. The wheelchair could stay locked in the van. She could sleep in the van, but she couldn't ask Wren or Cooper to do that. Oh God, how had it come to this? She was not this kind of person! She'd always worked hard, saved her money, paid her bills on time. How could she paddle so hard and still not keep her head above water? She sucked in a breath again.

"Luna? Babe? You okay?"

"No. I'm not okay. This is horrible. Our kids don't deserve this." *Do not cry. Do not cry.*

"Hey. Hey, now. Listen, I'll tell Ricky the kids need to sleep here. If it's just that, just crashing at night, that'll be okay, all right?" He paused to cough again, and she frowned. Could he not be bothered to move the phone before hacking into her damn ear? "I know you'll figure it out. You always do. I gotta go, babe. Text me when you all are heading over, okay?"

You'll figure it out. You always do.

It wasn't a compliment. It pissed her off. He had no idea at what price she always figured it out. And she was sick of figuring it out alone.

Okay, so they could stay at Ricky's. But only at night. The kids would be in school during the day . . . but it was Thursday, and what about the weekend? And what about this virus?

She leaned her head against the headrest and forced herself to remember him the day they met, at a block party in the neighborhood where their mothers lived. He'd been playing the upright bass in a three-piece rockabilly band with Ricky and one of their friends. The Trailer Trash Cats, a blatant rip-off of the Stray Cats, but surprisingly good. He'd spun that bass and winked at her from the makeshift stage, seeking her out after he finished playing. She tried to remember how her heart had fluttered, how sexy he'd been. She missed those fun days, watching the Fourth of July fireworks from kayaks on the river downtown, dancing in the rain at RiverScape, picnics in the MetroParks.

She shivered, here in the van. She'd known when she called Cal not to expect anything. So the fact that the kids would have shelter was *something*, right?

Who the hell was she kidding? It wasn't enough. She'd hoped, when they separated, that he'd miss her, that he'd work on himself to win her back, but she'd been prepared to go it alone. She'd hoped, but she hadn't held her breath. She'd gotten used to doing things on her own.

She snorted. He'd actually suggested, when she told him she wanted time apart, that maybe they needed another baby.

She sat upright. The last thing she needed was to fall asleep out here and jeopardize her job. She couldn't remember the last time she'd gotten a real night's sleep.

The windshield had fogged up. She shivered. She wanted nothing more than to lie down here and fall asleep. Sleep for days. But she couldn't. "No rest for the wicked," her mother had said. Was she wicked? She'd tried hard not to be.

Luna had just opened the door when her phone pinged in her hand. Then again. She looked. Two messages had arrived simultaneously.

The first was from Sycamore Place and at first, her heart clutched, but she looked at the time and knew she was still within her break; she had not been gone too long. She opened it and saw it was an official text, the sort that went out to everyone on staff. Emergency meeting today at 1:00 p.m. regarding new protocols and policies with the COVID-19 virus.

A bit of fear sparked through her. This thing was real and getting worse.

But she was used to juggling many balls, and 1:00 p.m. was still two hours away. Put that fear away and focus on one thing at a time: the next text.

Cooper.

Oh God. Oh no. There was no way to know what this might mean. News from her son in the middle of the day was never a good thing. Her mind spun with possibilities: Was he being suspended again? Or expelled? Arrested? She willed her breath to calm.

But the horror was a different kind, not any of the scenarios she'd imagined.

A cop just put a red sign on our door. we have 5 days to move our stuff. And power just got shut off.

CHAPTER FOUR

COOPER

Cooper stood in the dark apartment and tried to breathe. He went outside again and looked at the red sign slapped to the door. The cop had been nice enough, but he wore a face mask, which had kind of freaked Cooper out. When Cooper told the cop his mom and dad weren't there, he was afraid the cop would ask him why he wasn't at school, but he just pointed to the red sign on the door. "Look, you're not allowed to take this down, right? Once this red tag goes on, you've got five business days to pack up and leave before what's called a setout."

Cooper's mind had filled with a buzzing sound.

When Cooper didn't speak, the cop went on. "That means a bailiff will come supervise while your landlord has a crew move your stuff out to the curb. You want to make other arrangements before it gets to that. Move your stuff to a new place yourselves. You don't want a setout to happen, right?"

The cop looked at Cooper, waiting for something.

"Look," the cop said. "Call your folks right away. You don't want your stuff out on the curb for everyone to see. Maybe in the rain, right? Make a plan; take some action."

Cooper didn't know what to say.

The cop stared at him. "How'd you get that black eye?"

Cooper touched his cheekbone. "Basketball," he lied. "Got an elbow in the face."

The cop gave a little smile. "I'm sorry this happened to you all. Good luck."

Then he walked away.

"My sister is disabled," Cooper said. But he said it to himself, too quiet for the cop to hear him. When the cop was in his car, Cooper said, "Where is she supposed to go?"

This three-bedroom apartment, even though the front door opened to the parking lot like some cheap motel, was ground floor. And spacious, with wide doorways and an accessible bathroom. Wren could roll right in. They even had a disabled-person parking spot that everyone knew was for Wren and nobody else parked in it. Everybody liked Wren.

Five days? Okay. A lot could happen in five days. The whole world could end in five days. Could it? Please?

Cooper dreamed about the apocalypse, the zombies coming, the aliens, the nuclear winter. The big freeze from climate change. The End of Days, maybe, that his mean grandma Rainie—his dad's mom— always talked about. But he'd never loved the pandemic stories, movies like *Contagion* or *Outbreak*. Oh, he watched them, but they kept him awake. Probably because they were the most likely to happen. And they showed how humans were the worst. They turned on each other. They stole; they hoarded.

When Cooper first started hearing about this novel coronavirus, he felt a thrill of hope, not fear. Here it finally was, the end of the world, thank God.

The CDC said they were overdue for a pandemic, after all. Pandemics happened every hundred years. When they said on the news that the virus could "overwhelm the medical system in China," Cooper saw images in his mind from movies, like people lined up on cots in school gymnasiums. He felt bad for those people, but he also hoped it got here. And fast. His dream was for schools to close so he didn't have to face the relentless harassment and exhausting dread of staying on guard.

No one seemed to be paying attention to the danger. And if somebody said, "Are you hearing about this virus in China?" they'd say such racist bullshit. Like, there was some exchange student from China they called "Jackie Chan" in one of Cooper's classes, because no one could be bothered to learn to pronounce his real name, which wasn't even a hard Chinese name—Yiting Zhu—and when the kid was absent for two days and the teacher asked about him, some dipshit girl said, "Wait. Isn't he from China? What if he has that virus? Oh my God." Like Yiting was going to get it simply because he *was* Chinese.

That clueless twat was why he wanted the apocalypse stories he loved to be real. So people like that, who'd had everything handed to them, would have to do without and learn what kind of courage it took to take on a single day in this country if you weren't wealthy. Or healthy. Or white.

And then the power had gone out in the apartment. Before he texted his mom—why worry her when she couldn't do anything about it yet?—Cooper made his feet move, and he walked outside. As he passed the other ground-floor apartments, he heard televisions, saw lights. No one else's power was out. It was only their apartment's power, not a glitch in the whole complex.

Back in the apartment, he felt paralyzed. He wanted to go get high with Birdy somewhere and disappear. What the hell were they supposed to do? "Make a plan; take some action," the cop had said. He leaned his head against the living room wall. All his mother did was take action. The poor woman never slept. Couldn't she get a fucking break?

He wanted to cry. He really wanted to let loose and wail, for a hundred reasons he'd kept caged inside, but no. He straightened up and took a deep breath. *Crying is for sissies. You a sissy?* he imagined his dad taunting.

Fuck his dad. Cooper hauled off and hit the wall. *Ow.* That was stupid. He rubbed his scraped knuckles. This was all Dad's fault. How was Mom supposed to do all this herself? Cooper was glad his dad was gone. His own life had been more peaceful. But he'd welcome Dad back with open arms and put up with all of Dad's judgment if it meant Dad was here helping Mom, paying his fair share.

Another deep breath. "That's not going to happen," he said into the quiet apartment. True quiet. No hum from a fridge or any other appliance. Stillness.

He closed his eyes. *Make a plan; take some action.* Could they just stay here? With no electricity? Just a coupla days to get ready? They probably had candles somewhere. Mrs. Martin, the nice old lady Cooper helped out for money, she had candles. He could ask around. But he looked out the window at the snow flurries beginning to drop from the dark-gray sky. The apartment was already cold. With no heat? *Shit.*

He lifted blinds all the way for the light and watched the slushy wet snow plop to the pavement and cars. The slush stuck to the windshields but evaporated on the blacktop. Cold seeped through the cheap window, but closing the blinds made it impossible to see.

Anger bubbled in his chest. How had his mom let it go this far? Why hadn't she said anything? C'mon, to get evicted, didn't you have to be late on your rent more than once? It was only a couple of weeks past the first.

In his bedroom, he opened the curtains so he could see and pulled out the stash of money he had wadded in a sock and stuffed down in the winter boots he hadn't worn in a couple of years. He didn't need another excuse for kids to give him shit. Just thinking that made the bruise on his cheekbone throb to life. His scraped knuckles itched to punch Brett again.

Cooper knew exactly how much money he had, but he counted it anyway: $512. Even. Plus the change he kept in the shoebox on his dresser. There was probably at least $100 in there.

This money was mostly from his job working concessions and cleanup at the Cineplex. Crap money, but every bit helped. He watched Mom scrape and save and work so hard. He made dinner out of popcorn and those nasty-ass hot dogs whenever he could, to make the food at home last longer. The rest of the money was from helping people here at the apartment complex. Cooper'd get up early on snowy/frosty days and scrape people's windshields for three dollars. Nobody had garages here. He'd printed up little flyers on a computer at school and stuck them into mailboxes, telling people to text him. The three dollars added up. One morning, he made thirty bucks. A couple of people gave him a five and told him to keep the change. But one guy was a dick and texted him but never paid him, even when Cooper went knocking on his door. See? People were always standing by to screw you over.

He thought about the Vicodin in Mrs. Martin's medicine cabinet. He'd asked Tommy at the movie theater and knew he could sell those for twenty dollars each. The date on the bottle was old. He'd counted them, and every time he was in her apartment, helping her unload groceries, or put up her Christmas tree, or anything she needed, he counted them again. She didn't take the pills, probably didn't even remember she had them. He even hid them in the back of the cabinet, to see if she mentioned missing them. The last thing he wanted was to steal pain meds from an old lady who'd only ever been nice to him and his family. But if the pills were just sitting there, maybe he could swipe them. He could make about $300 just from that bottle.

Before he had a chance to talk himself out of it, he snatched up his phone charger and walked to the rental office. The heat embraced him as he walked in. He wasn't sure if he was relieved or pissed that it was Misty at the desk instead of Carl. He hated that asshole Carl. Carl had told Cooper's mom once that she was never getting a security deposit back because Wren's wheelchair had ruined the carpets.

Misty was on the phone and waved to him with her gross fake nails. While she was busy, Cooper plugged in his phone to charge.

"Hey there, Cooper," Misty said in a fake sad voice and pouty face that told him she knew about the red tag. "You okay? I'm so sorry. I told Carl to give you all another month."

Cooper shrugged. "Hey, if we make a payment, can we stop the eviction? I have about seven hundred dollars."

He hated the way Misty's eyes lit up. He shouldn't have given this away. "Oh, hon, it's too late to stop the eviction, but you know you gotta legally pay that rent. Whatever you can, anyway."

"But you'd still kick us out?"

Misty's pout intensified. "It's not like that. We can't let people stay for free."

"We just want an extension. My mom's only behind one month, right?"

"Oh, hon, no. You'd just get a warning after one month."

What? "So how many months does she owe?"

Misty chewed her lip and tapped those creepy fake nails, with the stupid white polka dots in the green polish. "Oh, Cooper, hon, this is between your parents and the—"

"I live here, don't I? I'm being forced to leave. Along with *my sister.* My sister who uses a wheelchair. Who needs a ground-floor apartment. How much?"

Anger flashed in Misty's eyes, but only for a split second. She then returned to that fake pouty look. "Your folks are behind three months."

That wasn't like his mom. That wasn't like his mom at all.

Misty tapped her gross green nails on a computer and read to him, with smug self-righteousness, "She only made a half payment in January. Your dad wrote a check for the full amount for February— really late, by the way—but the check bounced. And here we are in March. Nothing paid."

Dull red swirled in Cooper's vision. His dad. What a loser. January was when she'd asked Dad to leave. He bet Dad was supposed to pay half the rent.

"Does my mom even know that check bounced?"

"Um, *yeah.*"

The way Misty said it made Cooper want to punch her. He'd like to pick up that laptop and smash all her fingers and nails with it.

Misty just kept talking, not realizing the danger she was in. "So, now there's late fees for all three months. And the bank fees for the bounced check. So you could apply your seven hundred dollars toward that." She smiled as if this were all so perfect.

Cooper tried to remember what the school counselor had taught him after his second suspension for fighting, or, more accurately, for *defending* himself from a bunch of assholes. Mrs. Gross knew what the bullying was *really* about, and she was pretty cool to talk to. He breathed. He counted. "When they start after you," Mrs. Gross had told him, "don't speak. You don't have to speak. *Think* first. Ask yourself: What do you really want?"

What did he want? He wanted his mother to be okay. For his mom and his sister to have a warm, safe place to sleep. Because of Mrs. Gross, he asked himself: Would calling Misty a stupid twat help him get those things?

He ground his teeth together, bent, and yanked his phone from the outlet. Then he walked out without speaking to her.

"Hon, I'm really sorry!" she called after him.

"Stop calling me hon, you evil bitch," he said back, not yelling but totally loud enough for her to hear him.

He stalked toward the apartment, wanting to break every window on the way. The red notice on the door enraged him. There it was, shining like a traffic light so everyone who lived here could see what losers they were.

He slammed the door behind him. The apartment was already chilly. There was no way his sister could stay here.

Even though he hated asking the man for anything, Cooper made himself dial his dad's number before he could change his mind. *What do I want?* Focus on that. Staying focused meant not yelling, not calling his dad a deadbeat, terrible piece-of-shit human.

The phone rang and rang. No surprise. With any luck, his dad had found a new job and was out earning money to help them. Yeah, right. Cooper wasn't going to hold his breath. The ringing continued, and Cooper wondered whether to bother leaving a voice mail, not wanting to leave a permanent record of him needing something from this man, when his dad picked up, blindsiding him.

"Hey, Coop, what's up?" His dad sounded breathless and wheezy, and that sound of his dad panting caused a flashback in Cooper's brain: an image of hiking with his mom and dad and little Wren strapped to Dad's chest. Climbing a steep hill at Sugar Creek. That was the day they saw the family of red foxes.

"Coop?"

Cooper shook himself back to this cold apartment. "Hey, man," he plunged right in, "we're getting evicted, and we need your help."

His dad coughed, then said, "Your mom already called me. You all are gonna sleep at Ricky's for a few nights."

Oh. Cooper should've known his mom was on it, that she had some kind of arrangement already figured out. But . . . "How are we gonna get Wren up there?"

"We'll carry her," Dad choked out before starting a coughing spell.

Cooper recoiled and held the phone away from his head. Damn. While he waited for his dad to stop coughing, he thought about carrying Wren up those narrow stairs at Uncle Ricky's and how much she'd hate that. Then he thought: there's no way in hell they could carry her motorized wheelchair. So that meant once she got up to Uncle Ricky's place, she'd be helpless, stuck wherever anyone put her. She'd need to be carried into the bathroom. His face burned on her behalf.

Dad still coughed. Cooper exhaled and realized he could see his breath now in the apartment.

Dad stopped coughing but still panted, as if catching his breath. "Damn, man," Cooper said. "Doesn't sound like you're up to carrying much."

Dad maybe laughed, but it sounded like a wheeze. "I'm sick as a damn dog," he said.

An alarm bell went off in Cooper's head. "What's going on?"

"Just a cold. Headache that's killing me. Chills. This cough."

A painful silence stretched through the phone.

"Uh," Cooper said, "have you been to the doctor?"

"Can't afford it." His dad's words were sharp enough to cut.

"Dude. You might have the virus."

His dad didn't respond.

"Dad? Seriously. This is no joke."

"I'm fine. That's all happening far away. In China."

How could he be so stupid? Had he not turned on a TV? Cooper knew he sure as shit hadn't *read* anything. "Um, *no*. It's here. Every college in the state has sent everybody home. It's a big deal, and you should—"

"Jesus, enough. You sound like a scared little girl."

And there it was. That had taken, what? Two minutes? Dad started coughing up a lung again, and Cooper didn't care. He hoped Dad did have COVID. He hoped Dad ended up on a respirator and died. They'd all be better off. They sure wouldn't be *worse*.

When Dad stopped coughing long enough for him to be able to hear, Cooper said, "Does Mom even know you wrote that bad check? Did you give her any warning?"

"Son, you are out of line."

"Did you even think about what this would do to Wren?"

"Your mother's the one who ended things," he said. "She wanted me to leave."

"Oh, like it's all Mom's fault?"

"You. Are. Out. Of. Line."

When Dad started coughing again, Cooper hung up.

He texted his mom.

Then he went to his room and packed up his own stuff in two duffel bags he had. He packed his clothes, both dirty and clean. His cookbooks and novels. A really cool collage Wren had made for him for Christmas last year. The *Food & Wine* magazines he'd stolen from Wren's doctor's office lobby—he liked to look at the beautifully arranged pastries and cakes in spacious kitchens before he fell asleep.

He checked his phone. Nothing from Mom yet.

He went to Wren's room to pack up her things. He found a gym bag to use.

Next, he went to the storage closet and pulled out their two good suitcases. Once those were full, he started putting things in trash bags. There was a new box of bags under the sink.

There, in the kitchen, the panic rose within him, like a bird trapped behind his ribs. This was too much stuff. But they couldn't leave any of it behind. They'd need it. How could this fit into their van? Whatever place they found to stay, they'd need a storage unit for the furniture and that would cost money plus they'd have to move the furniture and who was supposed to help them and Mom's back was already always hurting from the old people she had to help in and out of bed and on and off the toilet and then she had to do the same thing for Wren at home and they were all going to starve to death and die under a bridge and his sister and his mom deserved so much more than that and how did this even happen?

His vision swirled with white sparkles, and he feared he might faint. He recognized that he was hyperventilating. He sat on the kitchen floor and put his head between his knees.

Why do you have to get so hysterical, like a girl? Dad's voice taunted him.

His phone pinged in his pocket. *Please be Mom.*

But it was a text from the Cineplex. They were closing for the next two weeks.

There went twenty hours of pay.

His phone pinged again. What would it be this time? Airports closed? Martial law?

Mom. Warmth spread through his arms and legs.

I'm on my way

Good. Mom always figured things out.

CHAPTER FIVE

VIVIAN

Vivian enjoyed Wren's company. The girl's bright, lively chatter lifted Vivian and helped, along with the coffee, cut through the drowsy heaviness of the Oxycodone. Most importantly, Wren made the remaining pills stop singing in the kitchen. The relief this quiet provided Vivian surprised her. Would Jack be disappointed she wasn't coming to join him? A strange pang shot through her, and she knew he'd be horribly disappointed that she was coming too soon, before her time. His judgment burned her. *But, Jack, you don't know what it feels like, to be left behind. To be left without you.* She'd been without the complete Jack long before his physical self was gone, too, but she missed even the bewildered, forgetful shell of Jack unbearably. She'd loved him even then. And since he now couldn't be bothered to haunt her, what else was she supposed to do?

Her phone rang, startling her. Wren was bent over a worksheet, the tip of her tongue protruding with concentration, so Vivian headed off to the bedroom to avoid disturbing her. It was Terrence, her Realtor, and a heavy sludge of dread filled her. When she answered and pulled the bedroom door almost closed behind her, he was chipper and manic.

"Great news, Viv!"

She winced and wanted to slap him. No one but Jack called her Viv.

"We had *forty-seven* people come to the open house. We've received seven offers. And one of those offers is *fifty thousand* over the asking price."

Vivian's eyes filled with tears.

"This is fantastic news," he said. "Just fantastic. But I could let the others know, see if anyone counters even higher. I wanted to run that by you. Or do you want to just accept this?"

His preference was perfectly clear. More money! More! But she didn't *need* all this money. What on earth would she even do with it? If only Luna would let her gift her some help.

"Viv? Are you there?"

"Yes," she croaked out, surprised by the closing of her throat. "Let's see what the others do."

"Atta girl!"

She didn't want more money, but she wanted more time. More time before this was a done deal. But *why*? Why was she reacting this way? She'd made up her mind. The floatiness of the one pill she'd swallowed waved around her. Was she being wishy-washy?

Jack was never indecisive. To the point they sometimes argued about it. "It must be exhausting," Vivian remembered snapping, "to *always* be right!" But, God, she missed that maddeningly smug assurance when dementia stole him from her. That was one of the first signs for her, her first red flag of worry: his new uncertainty, his blinking wariness, like he was balancing on the edge of a cliff, about the simplest of things he'd done a thousand times, like how to turn on their alarm or how to operate the propane grill.

Terrence said some other inane things, reminding her of a cheerleader, and when she hung up, she sat on the bed and dissolved into tears.

She hadn't cried much when Jack died. Her throat would close up and her eyes would burn, but none of this ridiculous sobbing of the past few days. What on earth was wrong with her? When he'd passed, she felt depleted. The final months caring for him were brutal in their exhaustion, and she'd doubted herself every hour. Was she doing right by him? Is this what he would want? Is this what he deserved?

She curled into a ball on her bed. She grabbed the pillow that had been his. She breathed deep, catching the aroma of his shampoo, his skin, his self.

"Ms. Vivian?"

Wren peeked from her wheelchair through the two-inch crack in the door.

"Oh, I'm sorry," Vivian said, wiping her face. "Did I disturb you?"

"No! I had to go to the bathroom. What's wrong? Why are you crying?"

Vivian sat up. "Do you need help? Should I call your mom?"

"No, I can do it. You have handrails and a high toilet. Why are you crying?"

"Do you know what? I'm not really even sure. I'm just a mess, I guess."

Wren pushed the door open wider and leaned in her chair to peer at Vivian. "Who called you? Was it bad news?"

Vivian barked a short laugh. "No. It's 'fantastic news!'" She mimicked Terrence's fervor, but that made Wren frown. "It was my Realtor. A whole bunch of people want to buy our house."

"You're selling your house?" Wren's eyes flashed with something like panic.

"Well, yes."

"Why?" Wren looked like she might cry.

"What's the matter? I *told* you I was selling the house."

Vivian watched an odd transformation take place in the girl's face. Her fear morphed into cool nonchalance.

Wren shrugged and said, "I really wanted to see your garden, is all."

"Oh! Well, we could still do that. We have time."

"Really?" Wren asked, in that tone Vivian remembered well from when Ann-Marie was her age. That tone that meant, *Don't lie to me. I'm holding you to this.*

Vivian took a deep breath. Was she lying? That could be arranged, right? To be safe, she said, "If it's okay with your mom, you and I will take a field trip."

The girl smiled, but the smile didn't reach her eyes. She rolled to the bathroom, closing the door behind her with expertise.

Vivian remembered when she'd returned home and stayed overnight, after the memorial service, after all the guests invited back to the house had left, after the boys—wonderful Steven and Drew—had walked home, the last to leave. The house had taunted her. Each room whispered memories. She'd been nervous, jumpy in ways she hadn't been since . . . the break-in. But memories of the burglary weren't what scared her that night. What horrified her was the dead quiet, the absolute emptiness of everything. She could find no point to living without Jack. She'd paced the halls like some strange ghost trapped among the living. The house whispered to her: Each day would be endless. Each day would be a year, each night a century.

That was the night she thought of the pills.

She'd gone back to the house five times since that night. Always in daylight, never to stay. The garden pulled her there on those strange warm winter days Ohio gave, the tease. She'd lost herself in garden cleanup for the listing. Oh, she paid someone to mow, to shovel, to look after basic home needs, but she didn't trust the garden to anyone else. She fed the birds, pruned, and cleared out the dead winter brush. Every time she went, she dreamed of never returning to Sycamore Place, of just staying in her home. Of pretending she hadn't lost Jack already.

But then night would fall. And the whispering started.

She created a garden book, a map of everything planted there, with directions of how to care for each plant and shrub, when and if to prune and deadhead, how much to water, to mulch, to fertilize. When a plant first appeared each spring and what it would look like when it first emerged. Warnings such as that the hibiscus was always last to arrive and you'd always begin to believe it was dead before the long green fingers of new shoots rose from the soil, making it the perfect place to plant tulip bulbs. The tulips would be spent by the time the hibiscus surfaced.

Jack had called the garden her sanctuary. But really, *he* was her sanctuary.

She didn't want to stay at Sycamore Place, as the staff here were encouraging her to do. They'd taken such good care of Jack, and for that she was profoundly grateful, but she was far from needing their services herself.

And what if she bought a different house and the whispering followed her?

No, in either place, she would be without Jack. So she could sell the house and pretend she would stay here because she'd known she *wasn't* staying here.

She wasn't staying, period.

And chances were, even if she didn't swallow the pills, she wasn't staying long. Her fingers slid between her shirt buttons and found that lump, her worry bead.

The commode flushed. After a moment, she heard the sink run and wondered how difficult it was for Wren to reach the faucets from her chair. When the girl rolled back into the hallway, Vivian heard herself say, "Hey, why don't I talk to your mom about you coming here for your online classes for a little while? You know, just while your school is closed."

The pills in the kitchen shrieked, "Chicken! Liar!"

Wren grinned.

"And then we can maybe go to the garden more than once."

A knock on the door half startled, half annoyed Vivian, especially when the door opened before she could answer. "Vivian?" a woman asked.

"Coming." Vivian didn't bother to disguise the irritation in her curt voice.

Vivian squeezed past the wheelchair and walked down the hall to face Priscilla, the social director, who wore a blue surgical mask. Priscilla held a clipboard, and even with a mask on, it was clear how nervous the woman was.

"We're checking in with everyone about new policies and protocol here at Sycamore Place because of the virus. May I come in and go over things with you?"

Vivian thought about saying no. For no other reason than a fierce contrariness had taken hold of her since Jack had died. Instead, she shrugged.

Priscilla did an almost comical double take as Wren rolled herself into the room. "Oh! And who is this?"

"This is my friend Wren. She's been cheering me up."

"Oh!" Priscilla seemed to flutter even when she stood still. "Isn't that . . ." Priscilla turned to Vivian and stage-whispered, "Isn't that Luna's daughter?"

Vivian laughed out loud at this rude absurdity. "Wren's not deaf. Her hearing is just fine."

Priscilla's face flushed red above her mask.

Wren's voice was cheerful. "Yes, Luna's my mom."

"Oh. Well. This is—this is very unusual."

"Wren is my guest. I invited her to stay with me today. I enjoy her company very much."

"Well, that's not—" Priscilla looked at her clipboard as if searching for a script. "You can't have guests in your apartment right now. That's part of the new policy. Because of the virus. Here. Let me just—" And she handed Vivian a sheet of paper, which she then began to read aloud.

Vivian wanted to snap, "I can read, thank you," but the words jumbled behind her teeth as she absorbed what was on the list. Effective immediately, Sycamore Place was considered closed to all outsiders. No visitors allowed in the lobby or in apartments. The dining rooms were closing after tonight and instead, meals would be delivered to residents' apartments.

The walls drew closer. The pills began a steady hum for the first time since Wren had arrived.

All activities were suspended. No bridge, no trivia, no game nights or live music. The movies scheduled for the building's two cinemas would be streamed to the residents' televisions on the Sycamore Place channel. Residents were not to leave the premises except for medical appointments. If residents did leave, they had to quarantine for fourteen days upon return. If family or friends brought groceries or other supplies, they must be left in the lobby, and a staff member would deliver them. All residents must wear a mask outside their apartments.

The pills increased their volume.

"We are providing each resident with five masks," Priscilla said. "We encourage you to try to order more, as well. And we have hand sanitizer for you." She placed them on Vivian's table. Her fussiness seemed to fall away, and her body language softened as she turned to Vivian. "Look, we know this won't be popular or pleasant. But we want to keep you safe; that's our very top priority. We'll get through this together. We will."

Vivian nodded. The rules made perfect sense. They were sensible and practical.

But these rules, right now, also would kill her, and she knew it.

"This all makes sense," Vivian said. "I appreciate the actions you're taking."

From Priscilla's eyes, Vivian could tell not all residents had reacted this way.

"Okay, then, if you'll sign right here to show that you agree to abide by these rules until you're notified otherwise."

Vivian did. She watched Priscilla wipe off the pen when Vivian handed it back.

Priscilla looked at Wren, then back to Vivian. "Your friend will have to go now."

"Well, I do understand the new rules, but with such sudden notice, Wren doesn't have transportation or anywhere else she can go just now. Surely you understand."

Priscilla hesitated. "Well. Yes. But no more visits after today."

"Right." *I just signed the damn thing, didn't I?*

Priscilla handed Wren a mask, too. "You should both wear these today, okay?"

That seemed ridiculous to Vivian, as they'd already been together in this small apartment all morning, but in silent understanding, both she and Wren donned their masks.

"Wash your hands a lot. And don't touch your face," Priscilla said. "It's nuts how much I touch my face now that I'm paying attention to that." She paused and then said, her voice gentle and real, "We'll get through this. We have to be diligent, though."

When she left, Vivian took off her mask. Wren did, too.

"So I won't be allowed to do school here," Wren said.

Vivian shook her head. "And I won't be allowed to have any company." She'd be trapped here, in this apartment, trapped with memories of Jack. The facility had to keep them safe. She admired their quick, decisive action. But . . . but the timing. The timing would not work for her.

So take the pills.

"And I can't do therapy. My PT and OT are canceled."

Vivian wondered how many appointments a week the girl had.

"I can't do school at home. Cooper texted me that the electric's been shut off."

Vivian's stomach dropped out. "Who's Cooper?"

"My brother."

Vivian hadn't known Luna had other children. "How many siblings do you have?"

"Just Cooper."

Vivian had once had a cat named Cooper.

"He's fifteen. He's mean and bossy."

Great. Just great. Vivian could not stay here. "Take the pills. Just take the pills," the bottles wailed. But no. The floatiness fell away, and her mind sharpened with urgency. No. There had to be a way to make this work. Jack always told her, "Trust your gut, Viv." Step one: she went to the kitchen, to the little Post-it note with Luna's number on it. She texted Luna, taking her time, pecking out one letter at a time, envying the way she'd seen Wren and other kids in the building fly over their tiny screens with their thumbs. With the new policies here because of the virus, I have a plan that will work for all of us. Please call me.

Vivian looked at the clock. It was nearly dinnertime.

Step two: pack your things. She went to the main closet and retrieved both her suitcase and Jack's. She stopped a moment, considering all the trips they'd taken, all the times Jack had packed this suitcase for adventure: Sedona, Breckenridge, New York, Paris. She carried both cases to her bedroom. There were very few things she actually needed. The house was still fully furnished, staged. Oh, Holy Hannah, Terrence was going to kill her. She packed her clothes, her toiletries, dumping them into the cases. She felt so . . . free. What she *needed* wasn't material at all. What she needed couldn't be put into a suitcase.

Vivian wrapped some photos and a photo album into some sweaters, tucking them in among her underwear. She put the strongbox of important papers and files into the suitcase as well.

She headed into the kitchen to grab her very favorite coffee mug. Wren was talking to someone on the phone, and she heard her say, "Okay. Okay, Mom. All right. I love you. Bye."

Vivian froze, looking through the cutaway hole at the girl. Wren turned her face to Vivian's and said, "That lady? The one who gave us the masks? She got my mom in trouble. Mom has to come get me now. I'm not allowed to be here."

Rage bubbled in Vivian's chest. "That tattletale *bitch*."

Wren's eyes widened. Then she giggled. "She really is, isn't she?"

"Yes. She is. So what did your mom tell you to do?"

"She and Cooper are on their way to get me. They packed most of the stuff we need in the van. We *were* going to stay at Uncle Ricky's with my dad, but for some reason, now we're not."

Vivian's stomach fluttered. "So where are you staying?"

Wren's face pinched in panic. "Mom says she has a plan. But I don't know what it is. And I heard Cooper telling her he couldn't find a handicapped-accessible hotel room."

Oh, sweet Jesus, what these people had to go through.

"Mom kept saying, 'Don't worry. I have a plan,' and Cooper kept saying, 'Stop telling her that. There is no plan.' I think Mom was crying. And maybe . . . what if we really don't have a plan?"

Vivian stood up straight. "She has a plan. We made one together. Why do you think I was packing?"

Wren's face lit up. "You're going with us?"

"Yep. Gather your stuff."

"Wait. Are you allowed to just *leave*?"

"Of course I am."

Vivian texted Luna again. She was tempted to use voice-to-text to be faster than her slow, old fingers, but she didn't want to risk Wren hearing her. She texted: You DO have a plan. You're coming with me to my house. It can be just for tonight, but hopefully it will be longer. I can't stay here with these new rules. And I can't stay at my old house alone. There's room for all of you. There's a ramp & elevator. We'll meet you out front.

Oh God, would Luna do it? *Please, Luna, please.*

To seal the deal, Vivian sent: Wren is excited to see the garden. Manipulative? Yes. Did she care? Not one rat's ass.

"Where's your coat? Were you wearing a coat when you got here?"

"My coat is wherever Mom signs in."

Vivian donned her mask and ran down the hall to the nurses' station. No one was there, but in an alcove behind the desk, Vivian lifted one tiny, puffy pink coat from its hook.

She jogged back down the hall to her apartment. She helped Wren on with her coat, surprised by how muscular and thick the girl's arms felt. Vivian threw on her own coat and finished shoving her mug and the bag of coffee beans into the second suitcase. She paused, looking at the pile of papers. The pills. Did she leave them? Take them with her?

She swept up the entire stack of papers with the pills underneath and shoved it into the suitcase, then latched it.

Wren's phone pinged. "They're here."

"Tell them we're on our way." Vivian snatched Jack's pillow from the bed and tucked it under one arm. Before she shut off the lights, she turned to look at the apartment, taking a moment to register: this was the last place her Jack had been alive.

She didn't bother locking the door behind her. No one locked doors here.

I'm going home. I'm going home.

The hallway was uncharacteristically empty. As they waited for the elevator, Vivian was delighted to see Ox, the giant black-and-white cat who belonged to addled Dennis. Why that man wasn't in Memory Care was beyond her, but she adored both him and his loyal cat. Ox entered the elevator with them, which made Wren giggle. "Where are you going, sir?" Wren asked the cat, who answered with a solemn, "Mrp."

The elevator opened onto a crowded main lobby. Vivian's pulse quickened, but she picked up the tone. Most people were at the front desk complaining. Vivian said to Wren, "Follow me."

She watched Ox wind his way through the crowd, sure enough homing in on his human, wrapping himself around Dennis's shins, distracting him, and leading him away from the fray. Vivian walked into the crowd with deliberate purpose, and no one paid them any mind at all. Good. Vivian had long ago learned that if you acted sure, no one questioned you. "Pretend you know what you're doing," Jack used to say, "and doors will open."

"Excuse me," she murmured, parting the crowd. She worked her way to the sign-out book, which sat alone and ignored at the edge of the front desk amid all the complaining, fearful voices. Vivian wrote her name, the date, and "Going home" under the space for her destination.

Wren still looked stressed. "Won't, like, an alarm go off or something if you leave?"

"No. Stop worrying. That only happens with Memory Care residents. They wear bracelets that set off alarms." She eased through the crowd, making a path for Wren, remembering how Jack had to wear his alarm on his ankle because he fretted with it constantly on his wrist.

She reached the front doors and hit the handicapped button. She grinned behind her mask.

Wren rolled out after her, and they walked down the ramp into the falling snow.

Wren pointed to a tan van. "There they are."

Pretend you know what you're doing.

The van's side door opened as they approached, and an unpleasant-looking young man with a black eye got out. He scowled at Vivian but said, "Hey, Wren."

He lowered a ramp, and Wren rolled into place. The boy turned his back on Vivian and bent to thread belts through Wren's wheels, affixing her safely in place in the middle of the van. Ingenious. Vivian saw the van was stuffed full with garbage bags and suitcases.

Luna got out of the driver's seat and walked around to Vivian. Holy Hannah, she looked like a different woman than the serene woman who had left her daughter with Vivian that morning. Luna had clearly been crying, her eyes red and puffy, her mascara smeared. She looked smaller, defeated, like she'd aged a decade in one day. "Vivian, I—" she began, but Vivian cut her off.

"Here's the address—put that into your GPS. Or just follow me. It's not far at all." She handed Luna the Post-it with her address printed on it. *Pretend you know what you're doing.*

Luna opened her mouth, but no words came out. She looked at the Post-it and the ink beginning to smear in the sleety snow.

Vivian patted her arm. "Why don't you just follow me?"

Luna's shoulders slumped.

"Mom," the scowling boy said, his word a challenge.

Luna nodded.

Good. Good. Vivian hefted her own suitcases and headed for her car. *Pretend you know what you're doing, and doors will open.*

Oh, please let her know what she was doing.

She grinned again, picturing herself like a Cheshire Cat behind her mask. Oh, Jack would approve. She was heading home.

And surely, she wouldn't hear the house—or the pills—whisper with this much company surrounding her.

CHAPTER SIX

WREN

As Mom followed Ms. Vivian's car, Wren's heart raced. *I made this happen. I'm magic.* She had wished for this, and it was coming true. She felt more powerful than she ever had in her life. She knew in her heart the power had something to do with Ann-Marie, and she sent a little mental *thank-you* to her. Ann-Marie's spirit was guiding her; she could feel it.

Wren could not wait to text her friends this news. She couldn't help it and sang out loud, "We're going to live with Ms. Vivian, and I get to have a secret garden!"

Cooper made a growling sound in his throat. Why wasn't he happy?

Mom said, "We're just staying tonight." Her voice reminded Wren of a wrung-out washcloth.

"And *then* what?" Cooper may as well have spit the words, they were so hard, so full of bite.

Wren's chest went heavy. Why did Cooper have to ruin everything?

They followed Ms. Vivian's car in silence for several minutes. Wren tried to make sense of the tension in the van. "This is going to be way better than Uncle Ricky's," she said.

No one answered.

"Why'd you change your mind about staying there?"

Nothing. Wren *hated* when they ignored her. She asked, "Will Dad come stay with us?"

Cooper whipped around. "Why would you want that piece of shit to come stay with us?"

"Cooper!" Mom said. "That's enough." But her voice had no energy.

"This is all his fault," he said. "He's the reason we're following some stranger in the middle of the night to God knows where."

Wren looked at her phone. "It's only seven thirty."

"That's not the *point*," Cooper said. "We don't even know her. She's one of Mom's *patients*. She could be crazy. We don't know what she wants from us. She could—"

"She's not a patient," Mom said. She turned, following Ms. Vivian's car. It was hard to see through the dark and the murk of the snow, but the houses were getting big in this neighborhood.

"Resident. Whatever," Cooper said.

"No," Mom said. "Her husband needed services. She didn't. She was never my patient."

"Why are you mad at her?" Wren asked. "She's helping us."

"I'm not mad at her. I'm mad at Dad. If it weren't for Dad, we wouldn't have to rely on some lady we don't even know."

"I know her." Mom's voice was quiet. Tired. Usually, she didn't let Cooper speak this way.

"She wants something," Cooper said.

Wren rolled her eyes. Cooper ruined everything.

"She's just being helpful," Mom said.

"People just don't do that. Everybody wants something. And now, because of Dad, you're going to owe her. Like you don't work hard enough already."

Mom reached over and pushed Cooper's hair behind his ear. She didn't even take her eyes off the road. Wren didn't know how she did that. Or *why* she did that. The gesture was Mom's *I love you* move. Why was she being nice when Cooper was being a butt?

Wren saw Ms. Vivian brake, turn on her blinker, and pull into a long driveway. Mom followed. Wren leaned forward to see the house through the windshield.

"Holy. Shit," Cooper said.

Wren was shocked Mom didn't comment on his language.

Wren looked at the house, all lit up, lights on inside, too. It looked like something out of a movie; it was so big. As big as one of the buildings in their apartment complex. Only the whole thing would be theirs. *I'm magic! I made this happen!*

Ms. Vivian hopped out, grabbed one of her suitcases, and said, "The ramp's back here."

Cooper helped Wren out, and in the cold dark, she craned her neck to look up at the house. *We are going to live here!*

Mom and Cooper dug around for some of their bags, and pretty soon, Wren was rolling up the ramp to the back door. When she went through that door, she was in the biggest, cleanest kitchen. Like something from a magazine at her doctor's office. Six of their apartment kitchens could fit in this one. She realized her mouth was open.

"I'll show you your rooms; then I thought we'd need some dinner," Ms. Vivian said. "Have you eaten? I know Wren and I haven't."

Mom and Cooper shook their heads. Wren noticed their mouths were open, too, and she was glad that Cooper finally looked impressed.

"This kitchen," Cooper said, so quietly Wren could barely hear him. She grinned.

"I'll order pizzas," Ms. Vivian said. "That would be fastest. What do you like on your pizza?"

"Mushrooms," Wren said.

Mom shot Wren a look. "Don't go to any trouble. Please. And we have money."

Ms. Vivian waved her hand. "Tonight is my treat. We'll figure out a system for groceries tomorrow, but for tonight, please let me get it."

Wren was shocked to see her mother burst into tears. Real tears. Like, back-shaking sobs. Ms. Vivian wrapped her skinny little arms

56

around her. Ms. Vivian was taller, and her chin was right on top of Mom's head. She held Mom, rubbed her back, and said, "It's been quite a day. Everything is going to be all right."

Cooper looked furious at this and slammed his bag down. Why was he so mad? Wren shook her head at him. *Don't ruin this,* she mouthed, but he couldn't tell what she was saying.

"Let me show you your room," Ms. Vivian said to Mom. "The kids'll be fine for a few minutes." She opened a drawer and said, "Here," putting a pizza menu on the kitchen island. "Pick what you want. I'll be right back."

When they were out of sight, Wren said, "Why are you being such a jerk?"

"I'm sick of everyone saying it's going to be okay. *How* is it going to be okay?"

A bolt of fear shot through Wren's chest. "You're always telling *me* things will be okay."

He snorted. "It's what you say to little kids. It's not *real.*"

She felt her limbs stiffen. Stress made the CP worse. She straightened her legs out in front of her, and she slid in her seat, caught by the seat belt.

She saw Cooper notice this. "Hey. I'm sorry. It was a really shitty day, okay?"

Now she wanted to cry.

Cooper patted her legs. "Bend your knees. Put your feet on your footrests."

She pushed herself back upright. She did what Cooper coached.

Cooper picked up the menu. "What do you want besides mushrooms?" he asked.

Wren couldn't stop grinning when Ms. Vivian showed her to her room. It had a desk and its own bathroom. The doors were wide enough for the wheelchair, the toilet was high with handrails, and the shower! The shower was walk-in and had a seat. This was made for Wren.

"Why do you have all this?" Cooper asked. At least he didn't sound mad this time, just bewildered. They'd only ever seen a walk-in shower at a hotel once.

Ms. Vivian sat on the edge of the bed and traced the flower pattern under her finger. She watched her finger instead of looking at them. "We built it for Jack's mother to live with us. I loved that woman. She had Parkinson's disease. It ended up she wasn't here very long before she passed away." Ms. Vivian kept tracing the pattern on the comforter. "Jack and I thought it would be perfect for us when we got old and decrepit. But . . . well, Jack wasn't here very long, either." She slapped the bed and stood with fake energy and cheer, Wren could tell.

Cooper's room was upstairs, next to Mom's, and Ms. Vivian's was downstairs, next to Wren's, down a hallway from the kitchen. Wren thought maybe somebody else lived here, like a butler, because Ms. Vivian kept talking about "the master," but then she realized that was what Ms. Vivian called her bedroom. Weird.

Cooper asked Wren, "You won't be creeped out, sleeping alone so far away from us?"

She hadn't thought about that. "Well, I am *now*."

"There's an elevator," he said. "In a *house*."

This house was made for me. I brought us here. Ann-Marie brought us here.

The elevator was right off that amazing kitchen. Wren rode it upstairs with Cooper to see Mom's room, but Ms. Vivian came out and closed the door behind her. "Let's leave your mom alone for a bit, okay? She'll join us later. Are you ready to order pizza?"

Wren nodded. But she didn't like the way Ms. Vivian sort of blocked Mom's door.

Ms. Vivian rummaged in a bag she'd dropped in the hallway and held out a credit card. "Here. Go ahead and call if you want."

Wren froze. So did Cooper. Neither of them reached for the card.

Ms. Vivian stepped toward Cooper. "Go ahead. I'm sure you're starving. I'll be down in a minute. I like anything on pizza. Even anchovies. But be sure to get something you know your mother wants."

She stepped so close to Cooper that he had to take the card, and then she picked up her bag and headed into "the master."

"I told you," Wren whispered. She liked being right. She liked knowing something first before he did. Ms. Vivian *was* a good person.

They took the elevator downstairs, but as they entered the kitchen, two men walked in the back door. One man, who looked like a younger, *way* cuter version of her science teacher, Mr. Wu, called out, "Hello?" before he saw them.

Wren stopped her wheelchair, her chest stuttering.

The cute man said, "Oh," as he looked at them. He cocked his head funny, reminding Wren of her mom. The other man was white and bigger, taller, stockier. Wren didn't know why, but she felt like she'd been caught doing something wrong. Cooper stepped in front of her, and she was glad.

"Hello," the cute man said, friendly enough. "Um, could I ask who you are?"

"Who are *you*?" Cooper shot back.

"We're Vivian's neighbors," the bigger man said, not as nice as the first one. "She asked us to keep an eye on the house, so we'll ask you again: Who are you, and what are you doing here?"

"Ms. Vivian invited us," Wren said. Her voice sounded too high and scared.

"Oh?" the friendly one asked. "Is that your van outside?"

Wren nodded. "Our mom's."

The two men exchanged a glance that alarmed her.

"Is your mom here, too?" the scary big one asked.

Wren nodded again. "She's upstairs."

The scary big one stepped forward, right across the kitchen island from Cooper. "What's that you've got there?"

Cooper tossed the card down, holding up his hands. Fury radiated from him.

"She wanted us to order pizza," Wren said.

The scary big one picked up the card and showed it to the friendly one, who looked much less friendly when he saw it. The formerly friendly one said, "Where did you get this card?"

Cooper lifted his chin. "She just gave it to me. Told me to order pizza." Wren's heart broke. She saw that he'd be accused of stealing it. That's how Cooper's luck always went. She knew he looked like some kind of criminal or robber with his bruised eye.

"How many people are upstairs?" the scary big one asked.

"Why?" Cooper asked. Uh-oh. The fury was gonna bust out.

Wren wheeled closer. "Just our mom and Ms. Vivian. She really did give us the card. You could ask her your—"

"I'm going up there. Vivian!" the scary big one called, heading toward the stairs and elevator behind Wren.

But the formerly friendly man grabbed his arm and said, "Wait. We don't know what's happening up there. Maybe we should call the police."

Wren's heart lurched.

"Whoa," Cooper said. "Why would you call the police?"

Everything felt like it was going fast-forward in the wrong direction.

Thank goodness at that moment, Ms. Vivian came trotting down the stairs. She brought her happy energy into the kitchen, and it swooped out ahead of her like a breeze. "Are the pizzas on the way?" she asked as she came down the hallway. Then she called out, "Drew! Steven!" like they were her favorite people on the planet.

Wren watched Ms. Vivian pick up on the bad energy in the room. She froze, looking at everyone's faces. She looked at Wren, then back at the men. "What's wrong?"

"Is Ann-Marie here?" the scary big one asked.

"*What?* No!"

Alarm bells vibrated in Wren's knees and elbows. *Ann-Marie?* The possibility of Ann-Marie had caused *this* reaction?

"Oh, no. No, no. Nothing like that," Ms. Vivian said. "Oh, boys, I should've called you."

Wait. Wait. Ann-Marie is alive? What?

"I'm so sorry," Vivian said. "Of course you thought—oh, hell, I mucked this up royally. These are my guests. Wren, Cooper—I'd like you to meet the best neighbors in the world. This is Drew and Steven. They live in the house on the hill above us. It was probably too dark for you to see it, but their deck looks over my garden."

Wren watched the men. They relaxed a little but didn't look happy. And her mind swirled with Ann-Marie. They thought Ann-Marie was alive. And they thought she was *dangerous.*

The silence in the kitchen got really awkward. Cooper glared at the men.

"Which one is which?" Wren asked. "Which one is Drew and which is Steven?"

The big scary one said, "I'm Drew."

She put on her best, brightest smile. "Hi, I'm Wren."

"Hi, Wren. I'm Steven," said the friendlier cute man. He was really, *really* cute.

Cooper still glared. Ms. Vivian said, "And this is Wren's brother, Cooper. Cooper, did you order pizza?"

"No. They thought I stole your credit card."

Oh, Cooper. Wren felt bad for him, but he never knew when to shut up and let something go.

"Look, Cooper, I apologize," friendly, cute Steven said. "It's just we had no idea anyone was going to be in the house, and we were worried about Vivian. That's all."

"This is all my fault. Cooper, I'm so sorry," Ms. Vivian said. "And, boys, forgive me. I should've called, but it's been a whirlwind, and things happened so fast."

Everyone made noises of reassurance, but Cooper didn't budge. Ms. Vivian touched his shoulder, but he flinched away. *Don't ruin this!* "Cooper, please know they didn't suspect you as much as they were looking out for me. These guys are my guardian angels, and they always have my back. The house is supposed to be empty, so it's good they came over. What if someone *had* been robbing me?"

Cooper lifted one shoulder. That was all they were going to get. Wren hoped they took it.

Into the weird silence, Cooper's stomach growled. Like, really growled, like a dog in the room with them. Everyone chuckled. Well, not Cooper. His face turned red. But everyone else.

Ms. Vivian held out a hand for the credit card, and Drew handed it back to her. She presented it to Cooper. "Would you still do the honors?"

But he shrugged again and said, "Nah. That's okay."

Cooper, why are you such a jerk? But Ms. Vivian acted like it was no big thing. She asked Drew and Steven if they wanted to stay and eat, and Wren could tell they didn't want the pizza at all, but they didn't want to leave. They wanted to know what was going on. Wren recognized it because she felt it, too. There was a mystery here, and she wanted to solve it.

Steven ended up calling for the pizza and using his own credit card, even though Ms. Vivian gave him hers. They fake-argued about it in a way Wren had never seen grown-ups do.

Cooper went upstairs, but Wren was too interested to leave. Ms. Vivian offered "the boys" cocktails, and they agreed to those way faster than they had to the pizza. At the end of the kitchen, Ms. Vivian opened a cupboard full of all kinds of beautiful bottles that looked like potions. Ms. Vivian mixed up magical combinations like a Good Witch and handed them to the men in weirdly shaped glasses. She apologized for not having anything but water for Wren to drink, but Wren didn't care and thanked her all the same, hoping to make up for Cooper.

"We'll get groceries tomorrow," Ms. Vivian said.

"Don't go to the store," Steven said. "Order them. It's too dangerous right now."

Ms. Vivian pursed her lips, and Wren recognized the expression. It meant Ms. Vivian was going to do whatever she wanted.

They talked small talk, all of them, and the boys asked polite questions. Wren knew they wanted to ask Ms. Vivian what the hell was going on, but they couldn't as long as she was there. She hated that. She couldn't snoop or spy with a big old motorized wheelchair, and she really, really wanted to eavesdrop. She hung in there with the conversation for a bit, asking them questions, finding out that cute Steven was a dentist and had a clinic called Reality Bites, which was a weird name. Drew owned a flower shop called Bloom, and she thought it made a funny picture that a giant, tough man liked flowers.

Eventually, she said she needed to charge her phone and wheeled all the way down the long kitchen, almost into the living room, and plugged it in. She then opened a game and halfheartedly played it, the volume low but loud enough for them to hear it, so they'd think she was distracted. She wanted to text her best friends, but she needed to pay attention. She knew the grown-ups would start real talking soon. People underestimated her. Something about being in a wheelchair made you not count, and if you were looking at a phone, then you may as well not even be in the room. She may not be able to be stealthy, but she was still a spy.

"So how long are your guests staying?" Drew asked.

"I'm not really sure. Hopefully a long time."

"Wait," Steven said. "But the house sold, right?"

"I changed my mind."

There was a long, weird silence. Wren made sure to make some sounds on her game.

"I'm not selling," Ms. Vivian said. "You're stuck with me."

"Oh my God, that's awesome!" Both men hugged her, and they seemed so happy at this news. They weren't faking it. Wren was good at being able to tell when people were faking it.

"Terrence will hate me for it," Ms. Vivian said. "I suppose I should call him now. I'm not kidding you when I say this day has been a whirlwind and this all *just* happened. Oh God." Wren glanced up to see Ms. Vivian rubbing her temples. "He'll be furious. And you know what?" Ms. Vivian lowered her voice. "I give exactly zero fucks about that."

Drew and Steven laughed. Wren tried not to grin.

One of the guys sniffed, and Wren risked another quick glance. Steven wiped an eye, and his voice was all choked up. He was crying! "I am so happy you'll be here. God, I'm so happy." He reached across the island and took Ms. Vivian's hand.

"What changed your mind?" Drew asked. "You were so determined. Don't get me wrong—I'm overjoyed. I'm just curious."

Wren was afraid to look up in the quiet that followed. Ms. Vivian must've gestured to something, or maybe she said something really quiet that Wren couldn't hear. Then she said, "I told you . . . I couldn't be here alone. And now I'm not."

"You wouldn't have been alone," Steven said. "We're right—"

"It's not the same. I know, and I love you for it, but you're not *here*, in this house. The house . . . the loneliness, the memories, it all talked to me, okay?" She sounded a tiny bit angry and maybe a little embarrassed. "And what it said was scary. It made me scared. Of myself."

"Oh God, Vivian," Drew said. And then they all leaned close and whispered so low, Wren couldn't hear them again. What did that mean? Scared of herself? Wren sensed movement, and when she looked up, all three were standing in a group hug. All three were crying. Wren figured she should pay attention to them now; no one would believe her if she didn't notice this.

"Are you okay, Ms. Vivian?" Wren asked.

Ms. Vivian turned her head, her cheek against Drew's shoulder. "I'm okay now." She crossed the room to her and kissed her on the head.

This was way better than staying at Uncle Ricky's. But still. She missed her dad. Would he be sad that they were staying in such a cool place without him? Maybe she could convince Ms. Vivian to invite him here, too.

Wren saw car lights down below the kitchen in the driveway. "Looks like the pizza's here!" she said. She was really hungry now, her stomach grumbling.

Wren texted Cooper: Pizza here. Tell Mom.

Steven went outside to greet the delivery person. He came back in just as Cooper entered the kitchen. Only Steven didn't come back with any pizza. He came in with two police officers.

CHAPTER SEVEN

VIVIAN

What on earth? Vivian took in the two uniformed police officers, one man, one woman. She looked to Drew, but he appeared as flummoxed as Steven.

The boy, though, Cooper, looked betrayed. And furious.

Wren looked scared.

"This is all a huge mistake," Vivian said before the officers had even opened their mouths. "The boys must've called before they realized what was going on. It's a false alarm. I'm so—"

"We *didn't* call," Steven said. He turned to Drew. "*I* didn't."

"*I* didn't call! I was standing beside you the whole time. When would I have called?"

"Vivian Laurent?" the woman officer asked. She had enviable cheekbones and honey-blonde hair pulled into a tight bun.

"Yes, that's me. But there are no intruders. Everything is fine."

"Intruders?" Officer Cheekbones repeated. She exchanged a glance with her partner.

"I told you this address was flagged," the male officer said.

"She invited us!" Cooper said. "She practically made us come here!"

"Who made you come here?" the male officer asked.

"She did!" Cooper pointed at Vivian.

Vivian did not like the way this situation was spiraling out of control.

"She asked our mom to come here, to her house," Cooper said. "We didn't do anything wrong." He glared at Steven and Drew.

"Where *is* Mom?" Wren asked her brother.

"She's asleep."

Vivian held up her hands. "Let's leave her be." Vivian made her voice warm and loving. Yes, her address was flagged, but that had nothing to do with her current situation. Did it? Did they know something? The entire situation with Ann-Marie was recorded as a "heads-up" if ever a call to the police came from this address. She wasn't sure if hope or dread flared strongest within her.

Vivian turned again to Drew and Steven. "Did you call the police?"

"No!" they said in unison.

Well then. Vivian turned to the two officers. Their faces were stony, not revealing a thing. "Shall we start again? How can I help you?"

"Ms. Laurent," Officer Cheekbones said. "Could you explain why you left Sycamore Place earlier this evening?"

Wren gasped.

Oh. That. Vivian wanted to roll her eyes. Wren had been certain Vivian couldn't just walk out of her own accord, and Vivian was damned if the girl hadn't been proven right.

Vivian made sure she smiled. "I left Sycamore Place because I *chose* to. I can come and go as I please. Well, that is, until they outlined their new COVID-19 regulations. Those new rules were why I chose to leave there and return here to my own home."

The two officers looked at each other again. Officer Cheekbones nodded. Vivian liked it that the woman seemed to be in charge.

"The people at Sycamore Place were very concerned about your well-being," Cheekbones said. Her voice softened. "They know you're grieving. They were worried. When you didn't go to dinner and you weren't in your apartment, they were alarmed about your safety."

"My safety? I signed out. I told them where I was going."

"Well," Cheekbones said. "Your sign-out destination felt a little . . . cryptic to them."

"Or, actually, more alarming," the male officer said.

Vivian frowned. "I said I was going home." She opened her arms to indicate "here I am."

Cheekbones sighed. "Ms. Laurent. I think the people at Sycamore Place consider Sycamore Place your home. They worried that 'going home' meant something else."

Vivian couldn't process this for a moment. She blinked.

Officer Cheekbones, seeming to sense her confusion, said—so, so gently it embarrassed Vivian—"They'd raised a concern about you at a staff meeting. They were simply scared for your well-being."

With the realization, Vivian's face flooded hot. They *knew*? Someone knew she was considering . . . that? Did they know about the pills? Her emotions teeter-tottered. She let anger be heavier than her shame. Anger felt safer, more solid. "Raised a concern?"

Cheekbones said, "Yes. The staff feared you might . . . self-harm. They know you're grieving."

Vivian hated the way this woman officer said *grieving*, like it was some activity she was indulging in temporarily, like fasting or doing a detox. Vivian burned to drive back over to Sycamore Place and let them have it . . . but . . . but it was true, it was true, it was true. They cared enough to send police searching for her? Potentially to stop her from going through with it? Resentment competed with gratitude.

More headlights flashed across the kitchen windows.

"*That* would be the pizza," Vivian said, her voice a bit too jovial for the circumstances.

"I'll go try this again," Steven joked. He stopped before the officers. "I mean, am I allowed . . ."

"Yes, of course," Cheekbones said. When Steven exited, Cheekbones said, "This is just a welfare check. They were *very* worried."

Vivian pressed a hand to her sternum, aware of the lump there under her skin. "I'm so sorry to have worried them. I thought signing out was enough—oh, I was so thoughtless. I should have spoken to someone."

Shame slammed down its end of the teeter-totter.

"I'm going to call them and let them know you're fine." Cheekbones pulled out a phone as Steven came back in carrying five boxes of pizza.

"What the hell did you order?" Drew sounded angry, but Vivian knew he was teasing, trying to break the awful tension. "It's practically a pizza per person."

"Would you like some pizza?" Vivian asked the male officer. "Clearly, there's plenty."

He said, "Sure." Vivian saw the disdain in Cheekbones's eyes as she waited on the phone.

Vivian tried not to listen as Cheekbones began talking to whomever answered. Drew and Steven opened all the pizza boxes on the kitchen island and handed out plates. Steven moved one of the barstools so Wren could ride right up to the island.

Vivian heard Cheekbones say, "No, she's just fine. She's at her house having a pizza party with some friends."

Vivian turned away, mortified. They cared. Of *course* they cared. How could she have just fled like that? Did she really think no one would notice?

"I'm an asshole," she said. The room went quiet. Everyone looked at her. "That was such an asshole move."

She reached for the officer's phone. "Please. May I speak to them?"

Cheekbones handed it to her.

"I am so, so sorry," Vivian said, not knowing who exactly she was speaking to.

"What the hell, Vivian?"

Em. Her favorite receptionist. A tall, willowy young woman who always seemed like she'd look more at home on a model's runway than at an assisted-living community.

"We were terrified." Em's voice caught, and Vivian realized Em was crying. Crying with relief that she was okay.

"I'm sorry. It was all so crowded and chaotic, and I was so thoughtless and rude. Please forgive me. I just couldn't stay. Not with the COVID rules. That apartment would suffocate me. Please. Please tell everyone I'm sorry. I'm mortified. Truly."

Vivian watched Cooper reach for pizza and put it on his sister's plate.

Everyone at Sycamore Place had been so good to her. They'd been so good to Jack. They'd been aware of her sorrow. "Someone really thought I'd . . ." Now she couldn't even say it, although this morning she'd swallowed an Oxycodone, ready to do it.

"You're so sad, Vivian. We just care. Luna brought you up in a meeting about a week ago. I know we've seemed distracted with all this virus stress, but we *care* about you."

Luna had noticed. Of course Luna had.

"I'm an asshole," Vivian said again.

"You really are," Em said. Then, thank God, she laughed. "But I'm really glad you're okay. Listen, thanks for letting me hear your voice. I'm sure someone will follow up with you later about your plans and your apartment and all that, but for now, everyone will be so relieved to hear you're okay."

"Thank you. Oh God. *Please* tell everyone I apologize."

Vivian handed the phone back to Officer Cheekbones. "Eat pizza. Please."

Cheekbones laughed but declined and said she needed to write up a report, insisting it was protocol. The male officer scarfed three pieces while Cheekbones filled out her paperwork. "You said there's a woman sleeping upstairs?"

"Yes," Vivian said. "You don't need to talk to her, do you?"

She shook her head. "I just need her name."

Vivian gave it, and the officer wrote it down.

"So," Cheekbones said, "the individual who's flagged with this address? She's not a part of this—" The officer gestured to include the motley crew eating pizza.

"Oh. No. Not at all." That teeter-totter again. This time, relief competed with the sharp bite of disappointment that never failed to surprise her even after all this time.

"Anything new to report on that front?" Cheekbones asked.

Vivian saw Wren listening, the curiosity shining from the girl's face.

"No contact at all for about six years," Vivian said. Ann-Marie had never, ever stayed away so long before.

"Do you want the flag to remain?"

Vivian paused.

"Yes," Drew said. "I think it would be wise."

"Oh, Drew," Vivian said. "She's dead." Vivian took a deep breath and made herself say it. "She's likely dead." She tried not to think of the dead Jane Does her private investigator had found. In unmarked graves. But if it meant peace for Ann-Marie, then . . .

Drew looked at Officer Cheekbones and said, "Leave it."

Vivian appreciated that the officer ignored him, waiting for *her* response. Vivian nodded her approval. Not because she believed but because she'd already worried these boys enough tonight.

The officer put her hand on Vivian's shoulder. Her grip was warm and firm. "I'm very glad you're okay."

"Thank you." But Vivian knew she wasn't okay.

Vivian closed the door behind them. For a second, she stood, looking out the back-door window, at the driveway and terraced garden, wondering if Ann-Marie had ever been here and Vivian hadn't known it. Vivian liked to think she would sense her daughter, that she'd somehow know she was near. But she knew that was foolish.

"Ms. Vivian?" Wren called to her. "Come eat pizza."

Vivian turned with a smile. She'd be okay *for now*. The pills' song was distant and muted.

She'd see how long she could make that last.

CHAPTER EIGHT

WREN

Ann-Marie might not be dead. Wren's mind whirled with this amazing new knowledge. She hoped they could stay here forever, no matter what Mom said. She knew that's what Ann-Marie wanted. She knew it was what was meant to be.

Cooper didn't say much, but at least he stayed downstairs with them and didn't take his pizza to his room. Ms. Vivian and the neighbors mostly talked about the virus.

Drew said, "I don't know if this will be as serious as they're making it out to be."

"That's the problem," Ms. Vivian said. "If they act quickly and nothing happens, they look like Chicken Little alarmists. If they don't act, and it gets terrible, history will judge."

"Doesn't this happen every other year?" Steven asked. "Swine flu, Ebola, bird flu? It's always Chicken Little. I have to close my clinic because hospitals may need our PPE."

Wren wondered what PPE was.

Then her brother piped up. "The CDC says we're overdue for a pandemic. A real pandemic."

Everyone looked at him, and no one spoke. *Great. Just great. Thanks, Cooper.*

"Last time was in 1917 and 1918," he said. "The Spanish flu. It happens every hundred years. Or around that. Through pretty much all of human history."

Wren wanted to kick him. Or scream at him. *Why, why, why. Freak.*

"Have you studied this?" Steven asked.

"Not in school," Cooper said. "Just, I read about it. I think it's interesting."

"It *is* interesting," Steven said. And he didn't even seem to be faking it.

"They certainly started taking it seriously at Sycamore Place today." Ms. Vivian told Drew and Steven the new rules. "I admire them for the caution. But listening to her tell us made me claustrophobic. I thought I'd suffocate if I stayed." Ms. Vivian smiled at Wren. "So I'm not trapped there alone in that awful apartment where my Jack disappeared."

Her words made Wren wince, but Ms. Vivian giggled after she said that. She swirled her glass, making the ice clink, and Wren wondered if Ms. Vivian was drunk. Her dad sometimes got drunk. But when he was drunk, he didn't giggle. He got quiet and sad and talked about how the universe needed to give him a break. Ms. Vivian giggled again. "Terrence is going to kill me."

Drew picked up his own glass and said, "Fuck Terrence."

This made Wren giggle, and both Drew and Steven looked mortified. "Sorry," Drew said.

"Oh, please," Wren said, waving her hand, trying to sound like a grown-up.

"I'm scared about my mom having to work there," Cooper said.

And just like that, all the giggling was gone. Cooper could suck the happy out of any room.

"What's your mom do?" Steven asked.

Wren tried to beat Cooper to it—she wanted to be part of this conversation, too—but she was too slow, mostly because she was distracted by this new fear that her mother was in danger. The thought made her feel like she'd forgotten to charge her wheelchair and was stuck somewhere.

"She's a nursing assistant in Assisted Living," Cooper said. "And she doesn't make enough for what she does. That job is *hard*."

Shut up, Cooper. Jeez. Mom had helped take care of Mr. Jack. He was going to hurt Ms. Vivian's feelings.

But instead of looking hurt or mad, Ms. Vivian said, "It *is* hard. And I'm in awe of the people who do it. Especially those who do it as well as your mother. She took excellent care of my husband. She always treated him like an actual human being. I'm so grateful."

"Wait," Drew said. "Luna? Is their mom Luna?"

Ms. Vivian nodded.

Wren felt warm all over, like someone had hugged her. They knew her mother's name. "Do you know her?" Wren asked.

Drew said, "No. I mean, I met her once, when we visited. But mostly from what Vivian said about her. Luna was your favorite, right?"

"By far," Ms. Vivian said. "Thank God there are people who do this job like she does."

"But they don't get paid enough to risk their lives," Cooper said. What was his deal? "Or their family's lives. Wren is at risk."

Wren felt her face go hot. Now she wasn't just stuck, she was nude and trapped right in front of these people. "I am not," she snapped, knowing she sounded like a baby.

"Wren," Cooper said, talking to her like she was a moron. "You have cerebral palsy."

Like she didn't know that!

"You're immunocompromised already. If you get this virus, it could kill you. Why do you think we couldn't stay at Uncle Ricky's tonight?"

"Wait. What does this have to do with Uncle Ricky?"

Cooper looked like he was in front of an oncoming bus. Wren could see his "oh, shit," like it was a cartoon bubble above his head. He said, "Nothing," really fast. "Forget it."

Steven cleared his throat. "Is your uncle sick?"

Cooper shook his head but looked down at his pizza.

"Then why did you say that?" Wren demanded. "Why couldn't we stay at Uncle Ricky's?"

"Because we got *this* great offer from our new savior." His words hit sharp and nasty.

Ms. Vivian's face hardened. "Cooper. Is your father sick?"

Cooper nodded.

"What?" Wren said. "Why didn't you tell me? Does he have the cora—that virus?"

"I don't know!" Cooper sounded angry again. "But he was coughing a ton. He has a fever. And he's not taking it seriously. He hasn't even gone to the doctor."

"He can't afford it!" Wren said, mimicking the words she'd heard him say. "He can't help it."

"Wren," Cooper said. "He knows about this virus. He knows about the symptoms. He worked at the *airport*! He knows all that, and he still thought it would be okay for us all to sleep there in Uncle Ricky's apartment. He thought it would be okay for *you* to be there." Wren could feel the rage radiating from him. He shoved his plate away.

Silence fell in the room. Wren hated this. She hated Cooper. She knew that didn't make sense. But she hated Cooper for telling her this. For making her dad seem so clueless.

"Did you see him today?" Ms. Vivian's tone warned Cooper he could not lie.

Cooper shook his head.

"Did you go to that apartment?"

Cooper shook his head.

"Did your mother go there?"

"No. She was going to, and I made her call him instead. To hear him for herself."

Wren couldn't believe it when Cooper started to cry. She stared as his face twitched and turned brighter red. He sucked in a huge breath, and Wren could tell he was trying to get ahold of himself. He whispered, "When—when we couldn't go there, she sort of . . . fell to pieces.

I—I never saw her like that. I—I was . . ." He swiped under his eyes like there were bugs on his face.

Into the awkward silence, even though Cooper had been rude to her, Ms. Vivian said, "Your mother helped my husband and me, and"— she gestured to the house around them—"and I have plenty of room for you. I'm not your 'savior.' You're also helping me. More than you know."

Cooper didn't look at her and didn't speak.

He stayed that way, not eating, not talking anymore, while Ms. Vivian and the guys argued over the leftover pizza. Wren helped pick out the kind her mother would want most—mushrooms, sausage, and banana peppers—and after the guys talked about helping get the rest of the stuff from their old apartment the next day, they left, carrying two boxes full of assorted pizza slices.

Ms. Vivian turned after she locked the door. Her face was kind and full of love, and Wren's grammy flashed into her head again. Not Grandma Rainie, who had too many rules, but Grammy, her mom's mom. God, how she wished for Grammy. But Grammy was gone. Everything was gone. Her mom was falling apart. Her dad had the virus. They didn't have a home. She was at risk. Her limbs stiffened with anxiety. She wanted her mom. What was her mom even doing upstairs?

"I need to wake Mom up," Wren said.

"No," Cooper and Ms. Vivian said together.

"She needs to help me get ready for bed!"

"I'll help you," Cooper said.

Wren wrinkled her nose. She opened her mouth, but before she could say anything, Cooper said, "Wren. Please. Mom had a really bad day. Let's let her sleep. I can help you tonight. It's okay. She didn't forget about you, I swear. She set an alarm so she'd wake up to help you . . . but I turned it off. She's . . . Please. You saw her crying. We need to leave her alone. Just this one time."

Ms. Vivian came to her and cupped the top of Wren's head. Wren drank up the touch.

Cooper could be awesome when he really tried hard. Wren knew he looked out for her.

But then Cooper lifted his head and asked Ms. Vivian, "So, those guys. Are they, like, faggots?"

And the look on Ms. Vivian's face changed. She looked like she smelled garbage.

Cooper always ruined everything.

CHAPTER NINE

LUNA

Luna slept for fourteen hours straight.

When she woke in the strange bedroom, fear darted through her veins like a school of tiny panicked fish. She remembered yesterday. The snow. The eviction. The power off. Her son, trying so hard to save the day. Her husband, willing to expose them all. The nasty phone call from the office about collecting Wren from Vivian's apartment.

Wren. Wren! Luna bolted from bed and out of the room, flying down the stairs. She burst into the kitchen where Vivian was speaking to a man she didn't recognize, and they both turned to her with alarm on their faces. Luna didn't see her children anywhere.

"Well, there she is!" Vivian said with forced cheer.

"Where's Wren? Is she okay?" Good Lord, how had Luna slept so long?

Vivian came to Luna and guided her back into the hall and the bottom of the stairs. "She's just fine. The kids wanted to let you sleep. Cooper has been helping her."

Relief flooded through Luna. She looked down at her braless, T-shirted self. She was in her underwear! She caught her breath and was grateful Vivian had led her out of the man's view. "Thank you. I'll be down in a minute."

Vivian squeezed her arm. "You take your time."

Luna climbed the stairs and remembered that moment in the van. The darkness. Outside *and* in. How for the first time in her life, she'd had no clue what to do. She was out of options. And then that text from Vivian.

She'd slept for fourteen hours. Fourteen hours? She'd just relinquished her children to Vivian's care and surrendered.

She'd surrendered.

She'd never done that before.

When was the last time she'd slept like that? She'd sunk into a sleep so deep, with no dreams or insomnia. The last thing she remembered was texting Danielle, telling her where they'd ended up. Danielle had texted back: THANK GOD

Earlier yesterday, Danielle had been exasperated, asking, "What the hell is wrong with you?" when Luna had called to tell her about her situation and Vivian's offer. "Why wouldn't you accept her help? Why aren't you saying, 'Yes, please. Thank you'?" Luna hadn't had an answer for her, at least not one Danielle approved of. That's just not what Luna had been taught. She'd find a way herself, just like her mother had.

But here she was after all.

As Luna's brain released the panic over Wren, she registered an amazing aroma from the kitchen she'd just been in, something yeasty and buttery flooding her brain with memories of her mother's baking.

She blossomed into true awake awareness. She worried about the stuff at the apartment. Where would she put it? Could she and Cooper manage all of that? How many trips would it take? And Cooper should be in school. This shouldn't be his problem.

As stressed as she was, gratitude filled her for this chance to refuel for a minute before the hamster wheel spun again. She picked up her phone. Danielle had texted her this morning, and Luna hadn't even heard it. Luna typed, I slept 14 hours!

Good for you! You deserve it!

Did she deserve it, though? Luna felt like she'd failed somehow.

She went into the bathroom. Her heart twisted to see Cooper's mouth guard and his bathroom kit here on the sink. He'd seen her at her worst, at her darkest, and she hated herself for it. No kid deserved to know that their mother had led them to the brink of homelessness. He was so angry at his dad, but she'd seen that anger shift last night. Cooper also blamed her. And why shouldn't he? She'd naively believed that if she worked hard and did her best, everything would work out.

She was as bad as Wren, with her wishes and magic.

Luna washed her face. She didn't need to shower, as she'd taken a hot bath last night when they'd arrived. Their current apartment didn't have a bathtub. Who was she kidding? They didn't *have* a current apartment. They had no home to speak of. She mentally listed the day's tasks: collect their belongings (but take them where?), list places she could store things (maybe in the basement of Sycamore Place?), search for food banks, apologize to Priscilla and make sure everything was okay on that front, search for libraries or cafés open where Wren could access the internet and do her schooling, help Wren do her PT.

Luna's rested, grateful state had stuttered and faded during this inventory. For a moment, she had trouble drawing breath. She braced her hands on the sink edge and breathed in deep through her nose, exhaling through her mouth. *Keep it together. Keep it together for your kids, damn it!*

She patted a bit of concealer under her eyes. She looked better today. Last night, she'd barely recognized the cadaverous face in the mirror. She applied lipstick and pulled her long black hair into a ponytail. Not terrible.

She dressed in sweatpants, a long-sleeve T-shirt, and a pink zip-up hooded sweatshirt. Casual enough for hauling stuff around all day but also fashionably casual. She loved that she got to work in scrubs, as it was far cheaper than keeping up with "real" clothes for a professional setting. Plus, the scrubs were forgiving with her generous figure.

Scrubs. *Damn it.* She also needed to do laundry today. She needed clean scrubs for work tomorrow. When would she find a time and place to do *that*? She slid down the bathroom wall and put her head on her knees. She couldn't keep up. She was drowning, failing in every possible way. She longed to crawl back into that bed and sleep for another fourteen hours.

Keep it together. You can do this. You always find a way.

She braced herself, heaved herself to her feet, opened the door, and went down the stairs toward the lovely aroma and the now-angry voices. This time, Luna looked at the man Vivian now argued with. He was bald and wore a blue suit a little too shiny for her liking, with round red glasses.

The man said something about a contract, but Vivian turned away from him toward Luna, cutting the man off. Luna admired the move and felt warmed by Vivian's genuine smile.

Vivian surprised Luna with a hug. Luna feared she'd burst into tears again. The hug fueled her. Lifted her. *You can do this.* Vivian held her by her shoulders and said, "You look so much better. More like yourself. There's coffee. And cinnamon rolls and fruit salad from the neighbors."

Good Lord, Luna was hungry. "The cinnamon rolls must be what I smell."

The bald man cleared his throat. Too loud and fake.

"Coffee?" Vivian said, ignoring the man.

"Yes, thank you, but I need to see the kids. Where are—"

"Ah, of course. Wren is in here, at school." Vivian walked to a doorway at the end of the kitchen, and they peered into a sunny little sitting room, where Wren was set up at a table. Luna watched the laptop in front of her daughter, the little Zoom boxes filling the screen, the connection clear. Wren wore headphones, so Luna couldn't tell what was being said, but Wren laughed at something and wrote something in her notebook. Sunshine flooded the cheery room.

Wren was engaged, so Luna backed away. She faced Vivian. "Thank you."

"This is tricky, this online business," Vivian said. "I don't like it. The teacher certainly doesn't like it. But I guess it's the best they can do under the circumstances."

"Vivian, please!" the man said from the kitchen. "We need to resolve this."

Vivian walked back into the kitchen ahead of her, saying, "It's resolved. I told you. I changed my mind."

Luna looked into the dining room and wondered where Cooper was. He hadn't been in his room, had he? Should she go upstairs? But Vivian called, "Come get breakfast. Don't mind us."

Good Lord, this woman was fierce. She had no idea what they were arguing about, but Luna loved that Vivian showed no signs of deference to this pushy man.

He started in again, and Vivian held up a hand to stop him as she told Luna, "Cooper's school is closed. For real. I called and checked." *Well, well, she knew Cooper already.* "They're not set up to be online yet. They hope to be in a couple of weeks. Right now, he's downstairs in the laundry room. He wanted to do laundry for you."

Oh, her complicated little shit of a compassionate boy. Luna poured herself some coffee.

"Look, Terrence, I don't know what else to tell you," Vivian said. "I am sorry to have wasted your time. That was never my intention." She sounded sincere. "I changed my mind after much soul-searching—"

"We had a verbal agreement."

Vivian made a "psh" sound. "Please. I am truly sorry. I plan to make certain you are compensated, but I have to say, I feel less and less inclined to do so the longer you harass me."

"Do you know how much money you stand to make?" he asked her.

"And how much *you* stand to make in turn? Terrence, listen, because I'm tired of this conversation: There's a global pandemic going on. Yesterday, I faced the reality of going into total lockdown, trapped for God knows how long in the apartment where my husband died.

I. Changed. My. Mind. I'm truly sorry it inconvenienced you, but my intent was not malicious."

"You could live anywhere with the money from this sale. I could help you find—"

"We're done. You can go now."

Terrence stared at her, shaking his head. He gathered up some papers. "When you're ready to leave this place, don't call me. I'm never working with you again."

With no anger whatsoever, Vivian said, "Fair enough. But this will be the last place I'll live."

Something about the way she phrased that chilled Luna's blood.

The man left, slamming the door too hard and stomping down the ramp.

Vivian turned to Luna and nodded at the coffee mug she held. "Do you take cream or sugar?"

Luna laughed out loud. "You are a force of nature, Ms. Vivian."

"So I've been told." Vivian opened the fridge and put a container of half-and-half on the kitchen island. "Sugar's there." She pointed to a pretty little yellow sugar bowl with a lid.

Luna poured the cream into her coffee, coffee she could tell from the aroma alone was the good stuff, the really good stuff. She took a sip. Heaven. *You can do this.*

Vivian topped off her own coffee. "That man is a pompous ass. I don't know what I was thinking, believing I could give this place up." She looked at Luna and said, "Thank you."

"Thank *me*? I should be thanking you."

Vivian shook her head. "I couldn't live here alone. I tried. It's too soon. It's too much. It scares me. I . . . I'm not even sure I should say this, but . . . I . . . almost . . . Yesterday, I was going to . . ." She stopped and waved a hand, as if dismissing the subject.

Luna wondered what Vivian had been about to say. She'd watched this woman grieve herself too thin, too gray-skinned in the weeks since her husband passed. Vivian wasn't doing well, and everyone at Sycamore

Place had been too busy with the virus to notice. That's why Luna had brought it up at a staff meeting, and everyone had agreed to keep an extra eye on her.

"Oh my goodness," Vivian said. "The last thing I want is for you to feel held hostage by a needy old lady. I just want you to know you're helping me."

"Well," Luna said. "You've been so kind. But we can't stay."

Vivian scooped a cinnamon roll onto a little saucer. "And why is that?" she asked as she microwaved it for eight seconds.

"Well. Because. *I* need to provide for my kids. We need our own home. I can't just use you. Or—or—be a charity case." Her parents, those proud, fierce workers, would be ashamed. She'd feel that shame from their graves. Her mother had always given to others. "There's always enough to share" had been her motto. Luna had never once seen her *take*.

Vivian set the warm, oozing cinnamon roll down in front of Luna, along with a glass bowl of fresh fruit salad. Blueberries. Raspberries. Kiwi. Peaches?

"You are not using me. You didn't ask me for anything. I offered."

"But only because you saw that eviction notice. You felt sorry for me." Luna took the first bite of cinnamon roll. Before Vivian could answer, Luna said, "Oh my God. That may be the best thing I've ever put in my mouth."

Both women laughed.

"Did you make these? This morning?" She looked around the kitchen. Surely she hadn't left and grocery shopped already?

"Oh, hell no. My neighbor Drew made them and brought them over, with fruit, coffee, and cream this morning. The kids met him last night. He and his husband, Steven, had pizza with us." Vivian's voice grew too chipper and bright. "And listen, I thought you should know. Cooper did ask me if the neighbors were—" She paused. "I don't even want to say it. Don't want it in my kitchen. But I feel you should know. He asked if they were *faggots*."

84

Luna froze, face ablaze. "Oh God. But—that doesn't make—I mean, I think—" She wanted to crawl under the table. "In front of them?"

"No, no. After they left. He was fine while they were here."

Luna exhaled through her nose. "I'll kill him. That's his father talking. Or actually, his father's mother's *church*." *Why would he say such a thing? Especially after all the fights with Cal?* She knew in her heart who her brave boy was, and for him to have said that broke her heart. "I'm so sorry. I really hope you called him on that."

"Oh, hell yes. We had a little come to Jesus, I assure you."

"And he . . . responded to that?"

Vivian smiled. "Let's just say I left him no choice."

Luna waited, then wasn't sure if she was relieved that Vivian didn't elaborate. Instead, Vivian pivoted to, "Look, because of you I get to be back in my beloved home, but not alone. You're giving me noise and purpose and energy and joy. Why not ride out a pandemic together?"

Luna didn't know what to say to the hard stuff, so she asked, "Is it a pandemic now?"

"Yes. The CDC made it official Wednesday."

Two days ago? That felt like two years with all that had happened. Luna looked at this regal, sad woman. "You saved us last night."

"And *you* saved *me*."

Luna reached a hand across the kitchen island. Vivian took it and squeezed. They both said, "Thank you," at the same time, then laughed.

"Mom! You're awake!" Wren rolled into the kitchen. "You slept *forever*."

"I know. I really needed it. I feel like a new woman." And she really did.

Wren, though, looked stressed. Shadows loomed under her eyes. Her hair was a mess. Her arms didn't raise and reach in a way that allowed her to do her own hair. Oh, poor Cooper had done the best he could.

"Have you talked to Dad?"

Damn it. Luna's face warmed as she realized she'd not once thought of Cal this morning. She was a horrible person. Her shoulders felt heavy. Did she have to add that to the list of impossible tasks today? Taking care of Cal? Still?

"Is he okay? Cooper said he has the virus. Is that true?"

At that moment, Cooper popped into the kitchen from a door beside the refrigerator. "Mom. You're up." He made a teasing face at her and mimicked her own words, "When you sleep that long, you're letting the day get away from you."

She laughed and held up her hands as if guilty.

"Mom!" Wren said. "Is Dad really sick?"

Cooper met Luna's eyes and shrugged. He mouthed, *Sorry.*

"I think he might be," Luna said, stroking her daughter's hair. "His symptoms were too troubling for us to stay there last night."

"I texted him this morning, but he hasn't answered me," Wren said.

Cooper muttered, "So what's new?" at the same time Luna thought, *Surprise, surprise.*

"Shut up, Cooper," Wren said. "No wonder Dad doesn't want to live with us!"

Luna's heart wrenched. That wasn't fair. *She* was the one who had asked him to leave. But a cowardly part of her didn't want Wren to know that. "Wren." Luna used her warning voice. "You're tired, and you're not being thoughtful. That was a hurtful thing to say."

Cooper, thank God, kept his mouth shut.

Luna was embarrassed for Vivian to have witnessed this, but to her surprise, she saw the woman was no longer in the kitchen. She'd slipped away like a ninja.

Wren was wound up, though. "Can he come stay here with us?"

Luna shook her head, all of her good, restful feelings of strength and confidence sliding down a drain around her feet. "No, hon. *We're* not staying here."

"Why?" Wren wailed, almost in tears.

To her surprise, Cooper looked angry. "Why?"

"Because we're not freeloaders, okay? We pay our way in the world and don't owe anybody anything." Luna's words sounded paltry and stupid. "Ms. Vivian was kind to help us, but we can't just *stay* here indefinitely."

Cooper crossed his arms over his chest. "So where are we going, then?"

Luna sat at the kitchen island, her breath tight again. "I don't know yet. I'll figure it out."

You always do, she told herself. *You always do.*

Until last night. She'd failed last night.

Vivian wandered back into the kitchen, as casual as can be, and set a cardboard box on the kitchen island. "These are things the Realtor wanted me to hide away while he showed the house. Signs of life and personality. The house was supposed to be generic." She began to lift framed photos and other items out of the box and place them in spots around the kitchen. Luna saw a photo of Vivian's daughter.

Cooper saw it, too. "Is that *Wren?*" He frowned and shot a look at Luna, as if to say, *See? I told you this lady was a serial killer.*

Vivian laughed and said, "No. That's my daughter. Don't she and Wren look alike? My husband thought Wren *was* Ann-Marie."

Cooper held the frame and looked from the photo to his sister. "That's . . . creepy."

Wren beamed, then blurted, "Ms. Vivian, can we stay here with you?"

"Wren!" Luna said. "That is not polite." She turned to Vivian. "I'm sorry."

"No apology needed," Vivian said.

With challenge in his voice, Cooper said, "My school's going online, too."

Luna's head swirled. Cooper didn't have a laptop. Even if the school provided one, she couldn't afford bandwidth for them both to take class on the same internet. Cooper could go to Danielle's and take classes with Birdy, but that wasn't a viable option for Wren.

Into her silence, Cooper said, "And wherever we go needs to be ground floor. And have a handicapped bathroom. And be—"

"I am well aware of your sister's needs." Her voice was sharp.

"Your mother knows what's best for you," Vivian said. "And she has a plan."

Luna felt gratitude that Vivian had backed her up. Even if it was a lie.

As if he read her mind, Cooper said, "Oh yeah? What plan?" She hated that sneering voice.

She lifted her chin. "I'll ask you not to use that tone with me."

Like a little shit, he said in a mock-sweet voice, "Pray tell, good mother, what is your plan for our well-being and safety?"

Vivian cleared her throat and shot a death glare at Cooper.

To Luna's amazement, Cooper wilted under that glare. "Sorry," he muttered.

Luna made eye contact with Vivian. Vivian's icy blue eyes gave her strength. In an even, calm voice, Luna said, "Ms. Vivian has been generous enough to invite us to stay here while we look for a home of our own. That way, there's no rushing around or panic to the search. I can take my time and really find what's right for us, not just what will do."

Vivian nodded, as if they'd actually discussed this.

"This is kind of a crazy time, with the pandemic. People are nervous, and rightfully so. So we're guests here for a short time, thanks to Ms. Vivian's generosity."

Luna hated how relieved both her children looked. Damn it. How would they ever return to the kind of apartment they could afford after living in this damn mansion?

"Please don't think of yourselves as guests," Vivian said. "For as long or as short as you're here, I want you to feel at home."

You're not helping, lady. The longer they stayed, the more awful it would be to leave. But Luna thought of the bath, the bed, the sleep. Just for a while. Just for a while was all right.

"Okay." Luna smacked her hands on the kitchen island, once, like a judge's gavel. "Young lady, when is your next class?"

Wren looked at the clock over the double ovens. "Now. But, Mom, what about *Dad*?"

"We'll talk about him later. You need to get to class."

"But is he all right? Does he have the virus?"

"Honey, I don't know that. We'll call him later. Now, go."

Wren whispered hateful things under her breath, but Luna knew when to pick her battles. She was on shaky ground right now, and she knew it. At least Wren went, thank goodness.

"So. You, young man. Thank you for starting laundry."

One corner of his mouth lifted in his grin. He was stingy with his grins, so when he doled one out, she always felt like she had received a gift. "*Starting?* It's finished. It's even folded."

How could he be such a shit and then turn around and be so amazing? Luna's eyes burned like she might cry again. "Thank you, sweetie. Thank you." The hamster wheel felt like it rolled at a pace she could keep up with today. That hardly ever happened in her life. "And thank you for helping your sister."

He shrugged. "I didn't have to do much. You saw that bathroom."

"She didn't shower, did she?"

"No. I wasn't . . . I didn't think . . . And she—she said she'd wait for you."

"That's good. Thank you." The rule was that if water was involved—and therefore the risk of slipping—Wren couldn't do it alone. The fear of falling was far too terrifying. "Since you don't have school, I guess you're stuck moving stuff with me. I'm going to see if we can store it in the basement at Sycamore Place."

She saw Vivian and Cooper exchange a glance. "Actually," Cooper said. "If you can wait until after two today, the neighbors said they'd help us."

"And you can put your things in the garage," Vivian said. "For as long as you need to. I sold Jack's car, so one half is empty."

Luna knew she should feel grateful but instead felt weighted down. This was all too good to be true.

"*If* that's okay with you," Vivian said. "Just another option."

"One guy has a delivery van for his flower shop," Cooper said. "So we'd have two vans and could probably get everything with one trip."

"Well." Bitchiness rose up inside her. "Sounds like you all have everything taken care of. Any other plans I should know about?"

Katrina Kittle

She hated herself for the confused look on Cooper's face.

"Mom? What's wrong? I was just trying to help."

"You don't have to do any of this," Vivian said, but Luna sensed the "what the hell is your problem?" in the woman's tone. And seriously, what *was* her problem? She thought of Danielle scolding her yesterday.

Luna sighed. "Sorry." She meant it. "I'm—I'm not used to this."

"Having help?" Vivian asked.

Luna snorted a laugh. "I guess. It feels very weird, very wrong. Which makes no sense. It should feel right . . . but I'm wary."

"Too good to be true?"

Holy shit, the woman read her mind. Luna laughed to hide her discomfort.

"I get that," Vivian said. "But there's no hidden agenda here. I swear. You'll love Steven and Drew. They're great guys." Luna saw the look Vivian shot to Cooper.

Luna nodded. *She* had to have the plan; *she* had to be in control. She'd never trusted anyone else to help. Everyone but her own mother had always let her down. Over and over again. But, with the panic deadline on a place to sleep gone, everything felt manageable. The hamster wheel was just a steady, purposeful walk. She didn't even have to be out of breath.

But . . . that felt very strange and unfamiliar. The day stretched out before her. The tasks to accomplish actually felt doable.

She made sure Cooper had schoolwork he could do, and as she left the kitchen, he was asking for another cinnamon roll. She'd love to put some weight on him. As she walked away, she heard him asking, "Drew *made* these? He didn't buy them?" and heard Vivian's laughter.

Vivian hadn't laughed in a while that Luna had seen or heard. Her grief was visible, had been palpable in that apartment. Okay, so maybe they *were* helping Vivian. This could work. For a while. For the weeks or so until they got this virus under control.

In her room, aware that she already called it "her" room, Luna checked her phone where she'd left it charging. No calls or messages from Cal. She called him back but got his voice mail. "How are you feeling?"

she asked. "Let us know how you're doing, okay?" It pissed her off she had to check on *him* after the darkness and exhaustion of yesterday. All during their marriage, it had never been her turn to be taken care of.

No. That wasn't fair. She made herself remember how he'd tended to her and doted on her during her pregnancies. Massaging her feet. Singing to her belly. Going out at 2:00 a.m. to get the salt-and-vinegar chips and Reese's Cups she craved.

Oh, how she'd craved her mother's canned pickled beans. Her mom brought over a jar a day in the last month before Wren's appearance. That month before Wren arrived three months early.

Focus.

She texted Ricky the same message, Just wondering if Cal's okay. Let me know if you get a chance. Thanks. She added a heart emoji. Ricky had always been nice. He'd known the sort of man his brother was and had tried to warn her. "You could do so much better," he'd said. She remembered being offended at the time.

She then called and officially discontinued all the utilities she paid at the old apartment: their internet, the gas, the water, and the trash. She canceled the renter's insurance. She pulled out the little Post-it from last night, with the address Vivian had written down, and she went online and put that in as a forwarding address on the post office's website. She took the time to thoroughly read yesterday's messages from both Wren's physical therapist and her occupational therapist and their instructions on how to help Wren with therapy. They both said they hoped they'd figure out how to do video sessions.

She called Sycamore Place and apologized to Priscilla for yesterday, explaining that she'd had an emergency with her son and she hoped she wasn't too short or strange on the phone when Priscilla called her.

"In no circumstance," Priscilla said, "is it okay to ask a resident to *babysit* for you."

Luna bristled but knew to play the game. "Vivian asked to see Wren. She wanted to see Wren. That had been arranged long before the situation with my son. They've become friends. I think Wren really cheers her up, especially now. Vivian's been very depressed."

Priscilla paused, and Luna couldn't tell if the woman believed her. "Well. That's very unusual. We don't encourage that kind of relationship with the residents."

"I understand. I know Vivian doesn't think of herself as a resident. She says often she only moved because Jack needed to. She's been very blue, which is understandable, so when she asked to see Wren, I didn't hesitate."

"Well. I guess it doesn't matter now anyway because of this COVID-19. Your daughter won't be allowed to visit, if and when Mrs. Laurent moves back to her apartment. And I sincerely hope you had nothing to do with encouraging Mrs. Laurent to leave."

"Oh, no. No. Of course not."

"It's a bit troubling to us all that you were at her home last night."

Luna's blood chilled. How did she *know* that? Luna decided not to disclose that she was still at Vivian's, since she already teetered on thin ice. "I didn't mean to break any kind of protocol."

"All right. As you know, it's busy around here. I'll see you tomorrow." And then, as if remembering how to be a human, Priscilla asked, "Is everything okay? With your son?"

Luna paused. "Oh. Yes. Thank you." She had said it was a family emergency, after all.

"I'm glad to hear it."

When she hung up, Luna wondered what Priscilla would've said if she'd known where Luna was calling from. Were they angry with Vivian for leaving? Would they approve of Luna staying here? Oh God. She couldn't lose her job over this.

The hamster wheel squeaked as it picked up speed.

Luna's phone buzzed in her hand. She looked down at a text from Ricky: Took C to ER early AM. They kept him. Won't let me stay.

CHAPTER TEN

COOPER

A neon-pink sun barely peeked over the horizon. Cooper rode along to the grocery store with Vivian even though Steven and Drew had told her not to go. His mom insisted he call her Ms. Vivian, but Vivian herself had said—in front of Mom—that they didn't need to. Wren, the little suck-up, still called her Ms. Vivian in front of Mom, but not when Mom wasn't around.

Dad had been in the hospital for two days. Cooper wondered if he'd die. Would that make life easier for Mom?

Would it make life easier for him? He hated that he thought this way. He did not like those thoughts. But all he could think was, *That asshole invited us—including Wren!—to come sleep in the same apartment with him!* He hoped Uncle Ricky wouldn't get sick.

Would Cooper get sick going to the grocery store? Would Vivian?

Vivian had done a grocery delivery the day after they arrived, and she'd been all bitchy over everything that had come, saying shit like, "This is not a substitute!" and, "Look at the state of these apples!" and, "Did they run over these bananas with their car?" Plus, the whole time she was ordering online, she was complaining, so he wasn't surprised when she pretty much hated everything that arrived. He figured Vivian was used to getting everything she wanted. Must be nice. But she'd been super polite to the old couple who actually delivered the groceries and had even given them a tip even though the tip was already built into the cost. He'd tried to show her that, but she said, "It just doesn't feel right."

When Vivian had asked him to "accompany her" this morning, he felt like he had to say yes. He'd been doing everything he could to get points with her after his stupid-ass thing about Drew and Steven. Man, she had handed his ass to him over that. And he knew she meant it and wasn't joking. "Make no mistake," she'd said. "Civilized, enlightened people do not use such slurs. If I ever hear you insult those fine men again, you are out. Out on your ass. Do you understand?"

"Yes, ma'am," he'd said. He had no idea where that came from, that *ma'am*. But he was determined not to ruin this like he seemed to ruin most things. He didn't know if she'd kick out his mom and sister, too, but no way would he jeopardize this current situation.

The thing was, he knew exactly why he'd said it, and the botched, moronic move was so stupid, it still made him want to vomit. He didn't even tell Birdy about it when they'd FaceTimed. He was too ashamed for her to know it. Birdy was brave enough to be out at school, and she might not forgive him even if he *tried* to explain it. Cooper wasn't an idiot. *Of course* he knew it was a slur, an asshole thing to say, but he'd said it as some way to try to win Vivian over, and it had backfired. Big-time. He'd been using it as a cue, a way to show her he thought like she did. Or obviously how he *assumed* she did. A rich white lady was probably conservative, right? But he'd only said it to try to get points with her, *not* because he believed it. Not at all. But how did he explain that to her without sounding like a spineless pussy? How did he explain that his dad and Grandma Rainie had tried to make him believe no intelligent, useful person had any respect for people like Drew and Steven? Even though he *knew* that was bullshit. He *knew* it. And yes, Vivian had been polite and even loving to those guys, but maybe she'd just been being PC, like his dad said everyone had to be today. Whatever. It had just walked out of his mouth without permission, and he'd regretted it even before she'd turned that blue-eyed fury on him and ripped him a new one.

There was lots more to this old lady than met the eye.

Vivian pulled into the grocery store parking lot. A line of people stood outside the front door. "Well. I don't like the looks of that," she said. "Hop out and find out why they're waiting."

Cooper hated talking to strangers but got out of the car without a word. He approached the line with his heart pounding. They all looked at him with fear in their eyes. That was weird. Most of them wore masks, so Cooper took his out of his pocket and put it on. "What's the line for?" he asked.

One guy said, "Line starts back there."

Cooper's shoulders tensed. "Yeah. I see that. I'm not trying to cut. I just wanna know why you're in line."

"They just opened," a woman said. "They're only letting a certain number of people in at a time."

"I thought they were open twenty-four hours," Cooper said, looking at that very statement printed on the window.

"Not anymore. They disinfect the whole place overnight."

Another man said, "But the first hour is only for people over sixty. You can't come in now."

"I *got* it. I'm just *asking*." Cooper turned away. "Jesus."

Back in the car, when Cooper relayed this to Vivian, she shook her head, squinting at the line. "Well, hell. I'm not going in there with *that* bunch."

She drove instead to the Dunkin' Donuts drive-through. She got a coffee with cream and a chocolate-glazed doughnut. He ordered a milk and a chocolate-glazed doughnut.

"Just one?" she said.

He felt challenged but only shrugged. She turned back to the speaker and said, "Make that a total of four chocolate-glazed doughnuts and one chocolate-iced cream-filled."

She handed the bag to him and didn't say a word when he ate them all on the way back to the grocery store. She actually seemed pleased. Cooper was always hungry. Always.

She parked way in the back of the lot. She backed in so she could watch the door. She sipped her coffee and turned on the radio news. Except it was a whole different vibe than the TV news his grandma Rainie watched. This was NPR, the announcer said. Nobody screamed or interrupted each other. They all took turns and sounded like they were talking in the library or church, even.

Grandma Rainie was his dad's mom. Dad. Tension pinched Cooper's shoulders. This COVID thing was no joke, even though Dad had texted his mom yesterday saying it "was no big deal" and that "everyone's overreacting." Why couldn't his dad get sicker? Get really scared so he'd take it seriously? School closed, his dad in the hospital, no visitors allowed, the line at the grocery store. This was like Cooper's apocalypse movies come to life. "Be careful what you wish for," his mom always said to him.

What did he wish for? He didn't even know. Vivian had asked what he wanted to do with his life. The question gave him goose bumps. No one had ever asked him this before. He'd said, "Survive," then worried she'd think he was being a smart-ass. Maybe what he wished for was finally coming into focus as a possibility. He couldn't stop thinking about Steven and Drew. Okay, especially Steven. But the two of them, too. A real *couple*. Like, a team.

Vivian turned off the radio and said, "No one's gone in for a long time. Let's go."

He expected her to move the car, but she hopped out and started to trek all the way across the parking lot. There were tons of spots open up close, but he wasn't going to say a word. Cooper pulled his mask back up over his nose.

"Well, son of a bitch!" Vivian said, stopping. "I left my mask in the car." She walked back.

He liked the way she cussed. She cussed like she'd always cussed. Sometimes old people used profanity and you could tell they were aware of it, that it was unfamiliar in their mouths. Not this lady.

When she returned to where he waited, he had trouble keeping up with her. Those long legs were fast. He was used to walking with Mom, who was like this miniature person. Or with Wren. But Vivian stopped again, almost making him run into her, right before the entrance, looking at a big semi that had just pulled up. "Now, what do you suppose is in that truck?" He swore joy and anticipation radiated from her.

"Um, groceries?"

She rolled her eyes. "Cooper, you lack imagination. Groceries get delivered in the back. Whatever's in this truck is going out front. *Outside. It's March.*" She stressed these words like they were clues. What the hell?

He shrugged.

She sighed as if he'd disappointed her, then said, "You'll see when we come out."

Cooper was determined not to be the reason his family had to leave. He loved how his mother had seemed these past few days, how she had time to sit and talk with them, how she'd laughed last night over dinner. She looked prettier. She seemed . . . lighter.

"Want me to push the cart?" he asked once they were inside.

"Thank you."

Cooper didn't go grocery shopping often. Mom grabbed stuff on her way home from work and usually just a few things, like the ingredients to make one or two meals at a time. Vivian pulled out one of the giant carts. He took it from her and followed. She had a list, like a legit, old-school list written on paper. She marked things off with a pen as they shopped.

She spent a lot of time in the produce. Cooper loved the produce section. He thought the fruits and vegetables were beautiful. He'd shopped with his father once and commented on a pile of tomatoes, all different shades of red, plus yellow and orange, saying they looked like gems. His Dad had thwacked him on the head and said, "You want people to think you're a pansy?"

His phone pinged. A text from Wren: Dad is leaving the hospital today! Yay!

Disappointment slugged him in the stomach. Was he really disappointed? What did that say about him? He didn't want his dad to be right, that the virus was no big deal.

Cooper heard a recorded sound of thunder. What the hell? A mist of water sprang forth from above the produce. He watched, intrigued, as it sprayed the bell peppers, leaving them glossy, and left pearls of water on the broccoli.

Vivian paused before the peppers and sighed. "Aren't they just like art?"

She didn't wait for his response. It surprised him that she noticed that beauty.

He tried to shake away thoughts of his dad, but a memory flashed into his brain of standing on a chair, cooking with his grammy. She'd tied one of her aprons under his armpits, and she let him help her paint the batter for lumpia—he'd brush the batter into a square on the hot pan; then Grammy scraped it off with a spatula and filled it with chopped beef, carrots, and onions. But his dad came in and said, "Huh-uh. No way," and untied the apron.

"Oh, don't be foolish, Cal," Grammy scolded.

"Nope. You're not turning my son into some sissy."

"He's helping make dinner."

"That's women's work."

Rage boiled in his veins, remembering. How arrogant and insulting. His dad never helped with any meal. Never even cleaned up after. That was all on his mom. How the hell was he even eating without her? What woman had he suckered into cooking for him?

He couldn't remember what Grammy had said. She was too quiet and nice to start a fight in front of the kids, but he didn't think she was the sort to just take that insult without reaction.

"What do you like best for breakfast?" Vivian asked, snapping him back to the present.

"Oh, whatever's easy. I usually had Eggos."

The top of her nose wrinkled, like when he'd said that shitty thing about those guys. God, why, why, why had he been so stupid, so chicken? "Those frozen cardboard waffles?" she asked.

"They're not . . . really cardboard."

She tilted her head. "Do you *like* them?"

He shrugged. "They're easy. They're what my mom brings home."

"Have you ever had a waffle that was *not* an Eggo?"

"No, ma'am." Damn! Where did that *ma'am* keep coming from?

She narrowed her eyes. "Stop calling me that. You make me feel old."

He wanted to say: "You *are* old, lady."

"Would you like to try a waffle that is not an Eggo?"

"Sure."

"All right, then."

Actually, he would *love* to learn to make a waffle from scratch. One like in the magazine pictures, with strawberries and whipped cream.

They continued shopping. He'd seen her with Mom last night, making this list. He'd slipped out of sight in the hallway and heard them argue about the money. Mom insisted on paying their way. Vivian had reluctantly taken her cash.

Cooper swore they were going up and down every aisle in the store. A store that was eerily deserted. They turned a corner and both stopped. The shelves in the entire row were empty. He saw Vivian look up to the sign above the aisle. PAPER PRODUCTS. TISSUE.

Kleenex, toilet paper, paper towels. All out. He thought of that scene in *Contagion* where Matt Damon and his daughter tried to shop, but the stores were mostly depleted, and people fought over what was left. Cooper looked at the bare shelves. He swallowed.

Vivian shook her head. "I think we are about to learn a great deal about ourselves," she said. "And it's not going to be pretty."

As if to prove her point, a woman in tie-dyed yoga pants wheeled her cart into the aisle like she was in a race and said, "Seriously? Are you kidding me?" The woman looked at Vivian and said, "Do you need toilet paper?"

"I was going to buy some, yes."

The woman pointed toward the front of the store. "There are people in line buying *three* twenty-four packs! Three!"

When Vivian didn't respond, the woman raced off, like the store was about to close.

Vivian watched the woman sprint away. "I don't think the American personality is very well suited to sacrifice." She stared at the barren shelves a moment, then said, "Look at this. It's downright apocalyptic."

"Did you know 'apocalypse' means 'a revealing'?" Damn it. He did it again. Shit just left his mouth without permission. He thought of his counselor, Mrs. Gross, and how she was always telling him: "Think before you speak."

But Vivian cocked her head. "I didn't know that. That's very interesting."

And he could tell she meant it; she didn't say some rude, dismissive thing about being a nerd like his dad would. God, why couldn't his dad have gotten sicker? Again, he shoved away that wish. He didn't want to be that person.

Vivian began walking again but said, over her shoulder, "That's really perfect. Because it does reveal so much about us. Drew said that yesterday, when he was at Costco, they had an employee guarding the toilet paper so families only took one pack at a time. And those are forty-eight rolls!" She sighed, as if weary. "Who would've thought that when the end came, we'd be fighting over toilet paper? Sweet Jesus."

At the end of the aisle, he expected her to turn left and continue their progression through every aisle in the store, but she turned right and said, "I'm sorry. I know you must be bored out of your mind, but the state of those shelves is making me reconsider some purchases. We need to backtrack."

"It's fine. I'm fine," he said. Had he been acting bored? Was his body language giving off a bad vibe? He followed her to the ramen section, where only three packets remained.

She took only one. "I will not be that asshole," she said. She grabbed some pasta, which was also nearly out, and some boxes of mac and cheese. Vivian picked up the biggest jar of peanut butter he'd ever seen, six big cans of tuna, and several cans of soup from the paltry selection left on the shelves. He was curious, but when she put four giant jugs of drinking water on the bottom of the cart, she said, "In case people continue to be idiots—and I'm certainly not holding my breath that they won't—I need to restock the apocalypse pantry."

A jolt of energy shot through him. "For real? You have an apocalypse pantry?"

"I do indeed. Fortunately, it's almost spring, and we're heading into garden season. If the food supply gets royally screwed because of this virus, we'll be eating well at our house."

A weird thing happened inside him when she said *our* house. He felt warm, grateful, and relieved, but he also felt angry. Who did she think she was? His family wasn't her little charity project. Plus, he knew she wanted something in return, and he couldn't figure out what it was. *Stop it. Stop it.* "What do you really want?" Mrs. Gross would ask him. He shoved all those weird feelings away. "Are you, like, a Doomsday Prepper or something?"

"Oh God, no. I just love the movies. And I think people are stupid. That's all."

She wandered off, and he pushed the crazy-loaded cart behind her. Cooper had never in his life seen anyone buy this much stuff at once.

"I love apocalypse movies, too."

"Well. We have that in common."

No way. What movies was she thinking of? He couldn't imagine her watching the same stuff he liked. But she seemed full of surprises so far. And he needed her to like him and let them stay. He needed to make up for the stupid, stupid thing he'd said. He was an asshole.

The lines to check out were long.

Cooper looked down the store to the self-checkout area. That's what his mom always used.

"I usually use self-checkout," Vivian said, following his gaze. "But we have an awful lot of produce, which is a pain in the ass to check out. We can be patient. This is a big haul."

Damn right it was. The bill came to almost $300, and it gave Cooper a queasy feeling, but Vivian didn't blink. She just swiped her card as if it were nothing. It made him almost hate her.

When he pushed the cart outside, she seemed crazy excited. She said, "Yes!" and pointed to where the truck had unloaded a bunch of brightly colored pots of little flowers. "I knew it!" He was confused when she sped right past them all the way to the car about five bazillion miles across the parking lot. They unloaded all the groceries, but when he opened the door to get back in the car, she said, "Nope, not yet! Bring the cart," and started sprinting back the five bazillion miles. What was with her walking so damn fast?

By the time he caught up with her, she already had trays of flowers in each hand. "The pansies are back!" she sang.

He froze. He looked around, expecting to see the people she referred to.

"They are my favorite flower." She set the trays into the cart.

Oh. He was glad he wore a mask to hide the heat in his face.

"I just adore them. They're the harbingers of spring. A sign the long, dark winter is over."

He leaned his elbows on the cart and tried not to picture his dad. That expression when Dad looked at him sometimes, that look like he smelled garbage. But Vivian had the same look that night he'd said that awful thing. Confusion swirled through him.

He watched her peer at every little flower, choosing, examining them. Sure, they were pretty, their colors totally saturated like a photo filter, orange and purple and golden yellow. The palest shade of blue.

She brought two more trays to the cart. "I have no idea why their name has become synonymous with weak or fragile. These flowers are tough little cookies. They can be covered in snow or even frozen through, and they'll bounce right back. The way people use their name boggles my mind."

He had no idea he was going to say it. The words flew out of his mouth in that way he hated, the way he just blurted shit that got him in trouble. "My dad called me a pansy."

Vivian stopped. She looked at him. She really looked at him. He couldn't read her eyes, and her mask covered her face. But he held her gaze. "Well," she said. "He must have meant you were tough and could withstand difficult conditions."

He thought he might cry and felt really alone and small. "I don't think my dad knew that stuff about pansies. I think he thought . . . something else."

Cooper pictured Steven again. His high cheekbones. How neat his hands and fingernails were. His lips when he smiled. His lips when he didn't.

Vivian continued to stare at him with those predatory bird eyes. She pulled down her mask and said, very clearly, "Then your father is an ignorant ass."

She tugged her mask back in place and marched back into the store to buy her flowers.

He smiled behind his own mask as he pushed the cart back inside behind her.

CHAPTER ELEVEN

VIVIAN

Vivian sat in the Breast Center waiting room at the Cancer Care Hospital. She'd brought *Station Eleven*, an apocalypse novel she'd been inspired to reread after talking with Cooper.

Vivian had once had a cat named Cooper, but she hadn't told Luna or Cooper this. Cooper the cat had had raggedy, matted orange fur and a bloody face when she scooped him out of the gutter on Cooper Street. She and Jack had been out looking for their daughter, and it had felt so good to care for something, to comfort something, to give the cat shelter, warmth, food, and protection, all the things Vivian so longed to give to Ann-Marie. The boy Cooper shared some traits with the cat Cooper. Both were prone to unprovoked hissing, both wriggled away from affection, both came predisposed to expect threat and challenge. Not to mention they were both runt-of-the-litter skinny and looked ill-kempt and rumpled.

Vivian checked her watch. It was now seven minutes past her appointment. She both wanted a nurse to call her name and wanted a nurse never to call her. The waiting room was empty, save for some peppy posters telling her that cancer was just a chapter in her life, not the whole story. She rolled her eyes. Her mask made her hot and nervous, and she fought her urge to take it off. Why was she even here? Still trying to please everyone, at her age. Ridiculous. She should've kept this to herself. Her fingers slid between her shirt buttons and found the lump again.

Cooper the boy was tall, too lanky. Vivian knew he'd grow into himself, but right now, he looked like a twig you could break over your knee. Vivian knew he hated that about himself.

Just like Ann-Marie, whose body, when she was twelve, had fallen suddenly out of sync with who she thought she was, with breasts, hips, and sweaty armpits all at once, while she still played with dolls.

We *all* feel so alien. Just like her own new life as a widow. Widowhood didn't match who she thought she'd ever be, sniffing her husband's old pillowcase every night.

Vivian made herself pull her hand from the chickpea-size lump.

Why the hell was she thinking about Ann-Marie so much lately? Those thoughts only added another layer of misery to her emptiness. Vivian was busier, it was true, and she loved the noise and life in the house, but she was never not aware of the pill bottles in her bathroom. Some days they were silent, but most days they hummed. At least they didn't sing arias like they used to.

Vivian's face burned behind her mask when she remembered almost confessing her plan to Luna. What a lot of audacious pressure to put on a person: you give me reason to live. For the love of God, how could she pile that stress on an already exhausted, depleted woman?

Vivian wanted this family to stay. She would never, ever mention it and would never try to talk Luna out of it if Luna came to her one day and said she'd found a place to move, but having this family here, and knowing they would be here tomorrow, was the only thing able to quiet those pills' song. Vivian caught herself worrying the lump again. Why hadn't she kept her mouth shut about it?

Well, really, she had, for a long time. While caring for Jack, there was no time to care for herself. Her own appointments were disruptions to his routine, his happiness. He was terribly fretful when she left him alone, and he'd long stopped being manageable to take out into the world with her. Sweet Jesus, the dementia had made him lose whatever filter he ever had, once asking her, in a louder-than-conversational voice, "Do you think that's a man or woman?" of a person sitting across from them. Vivian had quickly handed the poor person a card that read, "Please be patient. The person I'm with has Alzheimer's" and mouthed, *I'm so sorry.*

The GP they'd had forever checked on her often, and she badgered Vivian about continuing to take care of *herself* while being Jack's caretaker. Vivian's throat closed as she remembered Dr. Prugh appearing at Jack's memorial service. What a dear, dear woman. And she always wore such stylish clothes. Vivian was picturing Dr. Prugh's leopard-skin pumps when a voice called out, "Vivian Laurent?"

Good heavens, this nurse or PA or whatever she was looked to be about twelve years old. All you saw was this tiny body and giant eyes over her pale-pink mask adorned with a darker-pink breast cancer ribbon.

"How are you today?" the twelve-year-old asked, her voice warm and genuine.

"Oh, I'm fine. Well, actually, I'm hoping this little test today *proves* that I'm fine." Vivian put on a brave face. *Let's get this utter nonsense over with.*

The twelve-year-old escorted Vivian to a little changing closet and instructed her to strip to the waist and put on a pink robe. Always with the pink. The twelve-year-old introduced herself as Riley—a name for a pet dog, a peppy dog for sure, perhaps a beagle—and praised Vivian for remembering to wear comfortable clothing. Vivian wore yoga pants and a flannel shirt.

Inside the little mirror-lined closet, Vivian ditched her shirt and bra and looked at her rib cage. She was far too thin. Losing Jack had stolen every appetite she had. Being back home, next to Drew's baking, maybe she'd put some pounds back on. Cooper's baking could help, too, if last night's cookies weren't a fluke but the end of his string of kitchen disasters. He'd made strawberry muffins that were as bland as they were soggy and brownies so salty they were inedible, which was saying a lot coming from her. She *loved* salt. He'd used evaporated milk instead of condensed milk in an attempt at fudge, creating a disgusting yellow liquid that wouldn't harden and that Wren had declared looked like diarrhea. But last night's cookies? Where had *those* come from? They might just put some meat on her bony ribs.

She put on the flimsy robe. Why could no one devise a pattern that allowed the robes to tie properly, to close? You tied this absurd string at your neck and yet the rest of the robe gaped open. Two tiny strips of Velcro could solve this whole ridiculous business. Could no one see how simple this would be to fix? Vivian followed Riley to another room, where her chickpea worry bead would be biopsied.

Dr. Kinnari Patel introduced herself. She looked like an adult, and Vivian could tell she was beautiful even behind her mask. Another assistant of some kind spoke—also an adult woman, but Vivian missed her name. Riley stayed, too. The masks on everyone made this whole thing feel all the more surreal and disturbing. The doctor and assistant wore face shields *and* masks. Vivian knew it was because of COVID, but it made her feel dirty, suspect.

They kept praising how flexible she was as they maneuvered her onto the bed with her left breast hanging through an opening like she was a car up on the rails in a garage. They numbed her up and after that, the only thing that was truly uncomfortable was the way she had to have her arm and head. They stressed how vital it was to lie still, so Vivian concentrated on breathing and looked out the window at the limited view of the hospital roof and bit of sky her head and neck position allowed. The sky was blue, the weather warmer, and as soon as she could leave, she'd be in her garden.

They began to take their samples, which they described as "long slivers, like worms" of material from her worry-bead lump. Their equipment made the strangest, awful clunks, reminding Vivian of the sound of a paper punch, but she didn't feel anything beyond some tugging. That made her think of Ann-Marie, as a baby, and how Vivian had felt lucky to love breastfeeding. How close it made her feel to her tiny daughter.

She shut her eyes tight, and a tear slipped down her cheek.

"Are you all right, Vivian?" Riley asked.

"I'm fine." Why had she let Dr. Prugh harass her into getting a mammogram at all? She hadn't had one in three years. She'd been too busy caring for Jack. Vivian hadn't even told Dr. Prugh about the lump. Silly busybody, doing her damn job. Vivian could have put it off longer and remained in blissful ignorance. If she had cancer, so what? The pills in the bathroom drawer would cancel that out.

The hole punch clunked again. How long was this going to take? Cooper and Wren were both in remote school now, set up in different rooms in the house. Luna was at work. Steven was home next door, as his clinic was temporarily closed except for emergencies. She'd told the kids to call Steven if they needed anything, but she knew those kids were scrappy survivors and would be fine.

Her nose itched under this damn mask. This was torture.

At last, the doctor told her they were done. Vivian moved her arm gingerly and rolled onto her side. They explained that her tiny little dot of an incision was glued shut, no stitch needed. They put a simple Band-Aid over that and handed her a thin, flat ice pack, the kind in plastic. She was told to take Extra-Strength Tylenol, keep some ice on it to avoid bruising, and they'd have results in a couple of days. Vivian tried to discern what they suspected those results would be, but the masks made it too difficult. That, and the fact that no one made eye contact.

And that was that. Riley took her back to the closet, where Vivian put the square of gauze they'd given her between her skin and the ice pack and tucked it all neatly into her bra. With her baggy shirt on, no one could see it. Perfect.

In the car, Vivian took off her mask. There. She'd done it. She'd appeased Dr. Prugh. No matter what the results were, she wasn't going to do more. This had been a waste of time, but here she was, well into seven decades of her life, still being the good girl, following the rules, making people happy. Why did she give a rat's ass about Dr. Prugh's happiness? Just because she wore cute leopard-skin shoes didn't mean Vivian owed her a damn thing.

But she remembered red-eyed, sniffling Dr. Prugh approaching her at Jack's memorial service, giving her a hug. Leaving a whisper of her perfume on Vivian's dress.

And before she knew it, Vivian sat choke-sobbing in her car.

Oh, Jack. The missing him was savage. Gutting. He should be here, beside her, both of them facing this hard thing they would get through together.

Without him, there was no going through it at all. She didn't have it in her.

She stopped by Dorothy Lane Market on her way home. She picked up assorted cookies for the kids and a piece of decadent chocolate cake for herself. She deserved it. As she turned to leave, holding her bakery box, she saw a thin, black-haired woman walking out ahead of her. Something about her slight build, the way her raven hair twisted into a bun above her swan neck, made every nerve ending in Vivian's body screech. She ran after the woman. She didn't think; she just caught up to her. "Excuse me? Miss?"

The woman looked over her shoulder.

Vivian stopped.

The woman kept walking.

It wasn't Ann-Marie. Ann-Marie was dead. Why couldn't Vivian accept this?

In the car, she cried again and ate the cake, the entire piece, with her hands. She used the gauze in her bra to wipe her hands off before driving home.

This entire day could kiss her ass. Then fuck right off.

CHAPTER TWELVE

WREN

Wren had a plan.

Cooper was occupied with a Zoom class in the dining room for now. Mom was at work. Vivian was at some appointment.

So Wren made her way to the library, her very favorite room. That's where the photo albums were. She'd already gone through every one of them, looking for clues on Ann-Marie. She'd already known she looked like Ann-Marie and why Mr. Jack confused them. But with more photos to study, she realized it wasn't just their same shiny black hair and dimples. Wren had the same eyes, the same thick eyebrows as Ann-Marie. Their noses were shaped exactly the same—thin, with a tiny lift at the end, so they looked like elves or sprites.

They had the same small bodies. Only Ann-Marie's body was strong, with lean, long muscles Wren envied. Wren's muscles were bunched and thick, always contracted. Her Popeye muscles were called hypertonia and were part of her CP. Ann-Marie was a dancer. There were a lot of pictures of her in leotards.

Wren had never worn a leotard.

If they looked alike, did they also think alike? Did she and Ann-Marie love the same things? Did Ann-Marie believe in magic? Were *they* magic, the two of them together? It had to mean something, that they looked so much alike, that Wren's wishing had brought them to this house.

Wren had studied these photo albums like a detective. The pictures of Ann-Marie seemed to stop when she graduated from high school. There were pictures of her moving into a dorm, with young Mr. Jack and Vivian looking all sad-happy and proud. After that, there were only some Christmas photos, and in those photos, you could see that everything had changed.

The smiling, dimpled girl looked like a zombie in one of Cooper's movies. Her cheeks sunk hollow, dark shadows smudged her eyes, her hair looked unwashed. She didn't smile in the Christmas-morning pictures, even under the tree with presents. And then . . . she disappeared. There were still photo albums, but after the zombie Christmas, Wren hadn't found a single other photo of Ann-Marie.

Were they connected somehow? Like twins but from different moms? Did Ann-Marie have the key to Wren's body? Could she make Wren strong?

Today, Wren skipped her math class to continue searching for clues. Even before COVID, if she missed a class, no one ever made a big deal out of it, assuming she was at the doctor or using the bathroom. It always took her forever to use the bathroom, even with the help of her aide, Ms. Hannah. Getting from her chair to the toilet was always a dance, and every time she encountered a new bathroom, she had to master a new dance.

Wren wanted to go back to school. She missed her best friends, Dara and Tori, so much. They'd FaceTimed, and they did private chats during Zoom classes, but it wasn't the same.

While her friends and classmates were doing math, she finished looking in the desk drawers. She'd found nothing but folders for utility bills and booklets with directions for things like the stereo system and refrigerator and furnace.

She'd found a few stray photos, but not of Ann-Marie. These were of Vivian and Jack and what looked like a party of people out in the garden, including Drew and cute Steven. Vivian wore a sleeveless blue dress with her white hair up in a twist. Vivian didn't have old-lady flappy arms. Her arms were thin and ropey.

What next? She'd searched everywhere for clues. In junk drawers, in Vivian's bedroom closet, inside books. In the storage unit behind the laundry room, she'd found old tubs of Ann-Marie's childhood things. These would not help Wren find her, but she studied them anyway, for information. Dance recital awards. Artwork that was mostly ballerinas. Or horses. Or people doing gymnastics on horses' backs, like at the circus she'd seen once on TV.

Wren's plan was to find Ann-Marie. To bring her back to Vivian. Then Vivian would be so grateful, she'd let Wren's whole family live here with them forever. Even Wren's dad would live here. Her mom and dad would get back together, and Wren and Ann-Marie would be best friends. They would discover they had secret powers that could be activated only when they were together.

She knew that was weird. She had to remind herself that Ann-Marie was not the age she was frozen in the photos. She was probably as old as Wren's mom. *Old.* But you could be friends with old people. Wren was friends with Vivian.

Vivian had been teaching her to garden, teaching her stuff like deadheading. Wren could deadhead the tall stuff, like butterfly bushes and the limelight hydrangeas. It was hard for Wren to plant, but she could water. And she loved being in the garden, in the sun, with all the smells. Wren had wanted to be here, and she'd made it happen, just like she'd make Ann-Marie return.

Just like she'd gotten her dad out of the hospital.

He'd had COVID, but Wren had used a bunch of wishes, and he'd been in the hospital only two nights. And now he was 100 percent fine.

Wren called him every day. Cooper said, "Don't you care that he never calls *you*?"

If Cooper wasn't such a jerk, maybe Dad would come back to them. She'd loved it when they'd all been together, like how on Saturday mornings they used to go to the 2nd Street Market and Dad's band would play, and they'd look at all the cool displays, and Wren would beg to visit the kittens and puppies at the animal shelter booth. There'd be craft tables for kids, which Wren loved. They were all together.

Okay. Maybe not Cooper, who'd run off with Birdy. Birdy's mom would sometimes braid Wren's hair while they all listened to Dad's band.

Dad would like Vivian's house. Wren told him all about the ramp and the elevator and how nice Vivian was. Wren told her mom that Dad had said, "Sounds like your mother found herself a real sweet gig," and didn't understand why Mom got so mad at that.

Grown-ups were hard to understand. They were complicated and had such stupid rules.

What Wren loved most about Vivian's house, besides the garden, obviously, was all the room. In Wren's "classroom," she had a desk to use for her computer and schoolbooks, but Vivian had also given her a little folding table when she saw Wren working on a collage. Wren had emailed Mr. Buford, her art teacher, that she finally had her own art space. He told her to create great things in it.

Wren loved art. She'd started art in OT, where first she had to do a bunch of dumb things like pick stuff up and move them into little piles. Move pennies. Move M&M's. Move beads. Boring.

But when Wren made a design with the beads she'd moved, her occupational therapist had started art projects. Now, Wren couldn't get enough.

The collages were her specialty. The first one had been an assignment for art class. Mr. Buford had told them to create a collage that represented themselves. Wren included photos of things she loved, even things she couldn't fully explain, that spoke to her for some reason. She included pages she pulled out of her favorite books, *The Secret Garden* and *The Chronicles of Narnia*. She had handwritten the pages and tucked them in the appropriate place in her books so she'd still know what those pages said. She included pictures of birds flying. People dancing. Feet in sand on a beach. She loved hippos and cats, everything about cats. If she came back in another life, she'd want to be a cat. They could jump and leap and run. She was the only student who "incorporated 3D objects," as Mr. Buford said. The lock and key from an old-fashioned diary. Another key she'd found on the sidewalk once. She'd liked the mystery of what it might open. A charm from Grammy's drawer she'd found when they cleaned out her house. A lucky penny. A blue bird feather. A rabbit's foot Cooper had given her long ago. Wren knew all the ways to make wishes and included pictures of those things: the first star you saw at night, birthday candles, a wispy white dandelion, three birds on a telephone wire, a digital clock at 11:11, a fountain full of coins. There was even one of her stray eyelashes in the collage, but no one knew it was there but her.

Wren also loved things that surprised you, that weren't quite "right" and perfect but that were beautiful all the same: flowers that grew in cracks in the sidewalk, a perfect blue teacup with a crack inside that could never hold liquid, old abandoned amusement parks, a one-eyed dog, a three-legged cat.

She loved lists and New Year's resolutions (she made birthday resolutions, too). And so there was a list on the collage of things she loved that she didn't know how to get pictures of: getting an A on a test, laughing so hard you couldn't stop, remembering dreams where she could walk and dance and run, finding surprise stuff inside boxes at yard sales—they felt like clues to mysteries. She ached to have a mystery. She loved stories about people with special powers, especially if they were people who were underestimated by others.

Cooper had told her that her collage was really cool, so she'd made one for him for Christmas. He still had it, now propped up on the dresser in his room here at Vivian's. He wasn't always a jerk.

His was easy, because she knew her brother so well. Cooper loved: movies, movie popcorn, cooking, reading, gaming, chocolate and orange combined, stories about the end of the world. He hated: their dad, most people, talking to strangers, going to school.

Cooper liked to cook and bake. He once decorated a chocolate cake for Wren's birthday and cut it and iced it to look like a minion—the one with one eye. She overheard Dad say to Mom, "You really outdid yourself on that cake, Luna," and Mom didn't correct him. Wren looked up, ready to say, "Cooper made it," but from Mom's look, she knew when to keep her mouth shut and just store information. Mom sometimes talked to her about things like that afterward, times Wren knew something was wrong, but she never talked about the cake.

If you really, really knew a person, you knew the little things they loved, the small things that made them just who they were. Sometimes these were hard to work into the collage, but knowing them, just knowing about them, somehow made the collage more personal, more beautiful. Like, she knew Cooper loved the scent of vanilla, that he liked to bake cookies when he was stressed out, and Mom liked to let him, even though baking supplies were expensive. Once, when Wren was grocery shopping with Mom, Mom put something back so she could buy him flour.

On Cooper's collage, Wren used a lot of 3D things she took from his room, things she knew were trash, like movie ticket stubs (only of movies she knew he loved), a popcorn box, even some pieces of popcorn. She knew one of his favorite books was *The Road*, and his paperback was falling apart, but she took the title page out of it—not a page that would interfere with reading the story. Mr. Buford had tons of magazines, and in some *Entertainment Weekly* magazines, she'd found photos from *The Walking Dead* and other zombies and in cooking magazines, she found cakes and pictures of baking, including one that was vanilla beans. Cooper liked the smell of Band-Aids, which she thought was weird, but it was his collage, not hers, so she put a Band-Aid on the collage. He laughed.

She printed a photo Dad had taken of the three of them once. In it, Mom stood in the middle, with her arms around Wren and Cooper. She chose that picture, one that Dad wasn't in, for Cooper because the collages were about the people you were making them for. She at least knew that Dad had taken the photo, so she could think of him as in the collage, even if Cooper didn't.

She'd been making a collage for her dad, as a get-well present, but then he got well so fast, she thought she'd save it for his birthday. She sorted through the photos she'd gathered for him. Pictures of him playing his bass, pictures of him making the fire when they went camping. Mom, Dad, and Cooper all ice-skating at RiverScape, Wren in a carrier on Dad's chest. Mom and Dad ice-skating, holding hands, smiling at each other, wearing mittens Wren knew Grammy had knitted. Mom, Dad, and Cooper canoeing.

All the things Wren couldn't do. Had *she* ruined things? With her CP?

To avoid thinking about that, she moved on to the next picture. A family Halloween. Cooper was Peter Pan, Wren was Tinker Bell, Dad was Captain Hook, and Mom was Wendy.

There was the year they went as the Addams Family. She'd been Wednesday.

Wren put the photos for Dad away, in a drawer. For now. She'd decided to make one for Steven. Dr. Steven Bae. She thought it was hysterical his last name was Bae. Cooper teased her that she had a crush on him, which was funny because he was the one who hogged every conversation with Steven. She needed more info from him before she could make him a collage. She didn't know him well enough yet.

Vivian's would be easy. Vivian answered questions about what she loved and hated without making a big deal out of it or asking why. They'd be out in the garden, planting seeds or dividing hostas, and Wren could just say: "What are some things you love?" and Vivian would answer. So far, she learned that Vivian loved all flowers but especially peonies, hydrangea, zinnias, and snapdragons, all plants Wren could now identify. Vivian loved the smell of dirt and the sun on her skin. She loved the Rolling Stones and Bob Dylan. Loved ice cream, especially salted caramel, but really anything with chocolate in it, and she loved the combination of salty and sweet, which Wren had never thought about until Vivian shared with her some chocolate-covered potato chips from a chocolate shop right down the street from where her mom worked. Vivian loved all animals, especially cats, which they had in common. Vivian loved her own house and flannel pajamas and really good coffee and doing a crossword puzzle. She loved reading. She loved hosting parties. She loved children. She'd always wanted more children. They only managed to have the one, the mysterious Ann-Marie. She and Mr. Jack had talked about adopting, but never got around to it.

She loved Mr. Jack. Oh, how she loved Jack. Wren could fill a collage just with things Vivian loved about Jack.

"Tell me some things you hate," Wren said.

"I hate Facebook fundraisers," Vivian said without hesitation. "I hate people knocking on my door selling stuff. Especially religion. Oh, but it's okay to sell Girl Scout cookies. I love the Girl Scouts. But what do I hate? I hate political signs and flags. They should have to come down—all of them—the day after the election. And only yard signs. No more of these ridiculous flags and banners. What on earth is wrong with people? We're electing people to govern, not joining a cult." Vivian was weeding thistles, which she called the bane of her existence. "I hate these blasted thistles. I hate the damn rabbits that steal from my garden. I hate people who don't believe in science and people who think their opinions are actually facts. I hate people who won't put their carts back in the grocery store parking lot."

Then Vivian pulled up more thistles, falling silent. She stood up and pointed the roots of a thistle at Wren and said, "I hate Alzheimer's with all my heart and soul."

The way she said it, it was like her voice was empty. Wren's eyes burned. Wren hated Alzheimer's, too, and the way it had stolen Grammy from them.

Wren heard voices and looked out the window. Drew and Steven were in the garden. They were over here all the time on nice days. They ate lunch in Vivian's garden, sometimes with her, sometimes without.

Lunch made her think of lunchtime at school. She loved her aide, Ms. Hannah, but she hated that Ms. Hannah had to sit with her at lunch and cut her food and help her. Usually Dara and Tori would sit with her and Ms. Hannah for a little, but they'd always slip away, and Wren would see them laughing and gossiping with a table of kids with no adult hovering over them. You couldn't talk about your crushes in front of Ms. Hannah. And Wren was insanely jealous she couldn't trade part of her lunch for a Ho Ho or the whole thing for money to see a movie. But she'd happily sit with Ms. Hannah and eat her mom's packed lunch if it meant she could be back at school.

Wren watched the guys, but it didn't look like Vivian was back yet. Wren rolled to the elevator. She had to find a way to get Ann-Marie back here, other than wishing. Even though . . . her wishing had worked. But she couldn't count on it.

She rode to the kitchen, then went out the back door and rolled down the ramp.

"Hey, Wren!" Steven called, smiling. Her heart fluttered. He was *so cute.*

Even Grumpy Drew smiled at her. But then he looked at his watch and raised his eyebrows.

"It's gym," Wren explained. "We're just supposed to go outside. So . . . here I am."

Actually, Wren was missing language arts. It was no big deal. When kids didn't show up to online classes, nobody really called or checked. And she hadn't had to take gym—or "special gym"—since second grade. Her PT and OT counted instead.

They were talking about Steven's dentist office, which had been closed, except for a couple of emergencies. He thought they might be able to open soon, and he and his staff had met yesterday to talk about the new "protocols," a word Wren practiced saying in her head.

Drew's flower shop was closed for walk-ins, but you could still call or go online and order flowers for delivery. "I'm only home for lunch. We're still busy. Flowers make people happy."

Steven smiled at him. "And who couldn't use some happy?"

Wren wished for Drew to go inside so she could talk to Steven alone. She'd decided that Steven would help her, but Drew probably wouldn't. And right after she wished it, Drew said he'd be right back, that he was going to grab his lunch. See? She did have powers!

Knowing her magic worked made her brave, but still, she couldn't just rush right into asking about Ann-Marie, so as soon as Drew started walking away, through their backyard, Wren said, "Tell me some more things you love."

Steven laughed his gentle laugh. "Are you still working on your secret project?"

"You'll get to see it soon, I promise."

"Okay. Well, what haven't I told you? I love smiles. And Drew."

"You already told me Drew."

"Ah, well. He's always going to be the answer."

She wondered what that felt like. He'd already told her he loved decorating for Christmas, baseball, hockey, theme parties, going to plays, helping people, the smell of fresh-cut grass, crunching through leaves on an autumn walk, and the first snow.

He came up with more easily: drawing, waterskiing, Drew's baking, giraffes, laughter.

When he paused, Wren asked, "What about things you hate?"

He laughed again. "Hmm. I hate . . . homophobia. And racism. And raw onion. And cilantro."

"What's that?"

"Cilantro? It's an herb. I think it tastes like soap." He thought a minute. "I really hate that your dad was sick. I hate that your family is dealing with some rough stuff."

The words made Wren feel claustrophobic. What was rough? They were fine. She got nervous about what he'd say next, so she said, "Tell me about Ann-Marie."

He blinked. "Why would you ask that?"

Wren shrugged, but her heart raced. "I'm just curious." She looked into Steven's dreamy eyes and said, "The night you met us, you thought we might be her children. When I said my mom was upstairs, you thought my mom might be Ann-Marie. You thought she was back, and Drew wanted to call the police. That kind of stuff makes you curious. Did she have kids?"

"We have no idea."

"No idea about what?" Drew said, returning. He carried a plate, eating off it while he walked. It looked like green rice and maybe shrimp. A delicious aroma came off the plate.

"She wanted to know if Ann-Marie had kids."

Drew snorted. "Wouldn't surprise me."

"Drew." Steven sounded sad.

Drew sat down on a stone garden bench, eating his green rice.

"Why doesn't anyone ever talk about her?" Wren asked. "I just want to know about her."

"Talking about her makes Vivian sad, and we love Vivian and don't want her to be sad," Drew said. "All you need to know about Ann-Marie is that she was trouble. And a liar."

This felt like a punch to the gut. Poor misunderstood Ann-Marie.

"Was she dangerous?" Wren asked. No one thought Wren was dangerous. She watched the men look at each other. "You wanted to call the police when you thought she was here," she reminded them.

"Yes, she's dangerous," Drew said at the same time Steven said, "It's complicated."

"She's dead. And I say good riddance," Drew said.

Wren glared at him. She hated him right then. "You don't *know* she's dead. Right?"

Drew shrugged and kept eating.

"*Why* was she dangerous? If she's dead, why can't you tell me anything about her?"

They sighed and looked at each other again.

She tried a different tactic. "Okay. Pretend my secret project was about her. Tell me something she loves."

Steven tilted his head. "Ballet. She was a really good dancer. She used to dance with the Dayton Ballet."

She was a *real* dancer. A thrill skipped through Wren's heart.

Drew put down his fork, held his plate on his knees with both hands, and said, in a voice that was not mean but sad, "Heroin. More than anything in the world, she loved heroin."

Steven whispered, "Drew."

Wren frowned. "That's a drug, right?"

Steven was still looking at Drew. "She's *ten*."

"Eleven," Wren corrected him. She wasn't a little baby.

"Yes, it's a drug," Drew said. "It's a very, very bad drug."

"Oh." Wren thought about this information. This—this had to be wrong. "So she's addicted?"

They looked surprised. See? Everyone thought she was stupid. They nodded.

"Okay." What did they think she would do with this information? Cry? Be scared? They didn't know yet that Ann-Marie and Wren were connected. "So what made her dangerous?"

But then Vivian's car came down the driveway.

Drew leaned forward and spoke fast. "Because she was a liar. And she stole. She came to visit her parents and then *robbed* them afterward."

What? That had to be a lie. That couldn't be true. Drew was the liar!

Vivian got out of her car, carrying a bakery box, and walked toward them.

Drew rushed on. "She was a bad person, Wren. Trust us. She stole from her parents and a bunch of other people. She went to jail. She got arrested for *lots* of different bad things."

Steven put a hand on Drew's shoulder to stop him and looked at Wren. He spoke without moving his mouth. "Let's not talk about this in front of Vivian."

Vivian reached them and squinted. "I just love it when everyone stops talking when I show up."

Wren wanted to puke. She thought all three of them looked really guilty and stupid. They weren't good fakers. But then Drew said, "Maybe people with approaching birthdays should not concern themselves with a little bit of secrecy."

"For God's sake, I don't want to celebrate turning ancient." But Vivian smiled. Then she looked right at Wren. "Wren? What's the matter?"

Wren wanted to scream and cry and call Drew a liar. But she smiled. She almost said, "When's your birthday?" but realized that would blow their cover, so she just tried to look fake-innocent. But when she looked at Vivian's face, she could tell Vivian had been crying.

Vivian held out the bakery box but looked at Drew's plate—seriously, the aroma was making Wren's stomach growl—and said, "You made pesto and didn't share with me?"

He laughed. "I'll bring some over. It was the last of last summer's in the freezer. Mine is never as good as yours."

Vivian touched Wren's hair. "Oh, Miss Wren, we're going to make so much pesto together."

Wren loved when she said things like that because it felt like they wouldn't have to leave. Ever. Even if she had no idea what pesto was.

"Everything go okay?" Steven asked.

He asked it in a way that made Wren go alert. What kind of appointment had she gone to?

"Just fine." Vivian changed the subject by opening the box. Inside were big puffy sugar cookies with bright icing. "These won't be as good as the ones Cooper made the other night."

"But they'll be better than the diarrhea fudge!" Wren said.

Everyone laughed, but then Drew circled right back to Cooper's wonder cookies. "He didn't even have a recipe!"

Both men took a cookie from the box. Wren did, too. Vivian was right—Cooper's most recent cookies had been her favorite. Big, fat, and chewy. Oatmeal and chocolate chip and M&M's and Rice Krispies. A bunch of other stuff. He called them Monster Cookies.

"I'm telling you, that boy has a skill," Vivian said. "We just need to encourage him."

Wren felt happy for Cooper. That he had a skill. But she also felt a strange burning heat she didn't like, like she'd made a big mistake. She'd used a lot of wishes to call Ann-Marie to them. And now she wasn't sure she wanted her to come. Maybe if she came, Wren could make her better. Maybe Ann-Marie would be cured once she met her other half. But no . . . someone who robbed her own parents sounded scary.

Wren had never before wished for something and then wanted to change her mind.

But she was *supposed* to find Ann-Marie.

Right?

Wren realized she had no idea how to unwish a wish.

CHAPTER THIRTEEN

VIVIAN

Vivian's left breast ached, the local anesthetic worn off. Extra-Strength Tylenol failed to put a dent in the throb. She'd been attempting to read, but she climbed out of her bed and opened her bathroom drawer to look at the pill bottles. She considered taking one, but opening a bottle frightened her. She didn't trust herself. Better to leave them, like an unexploded bomb in her drawer. She closed her eyes and concentrated on the ache. She decided she welcomed feeling pain that was external for a change. She looked at the clock. Midnight loomed close.

Vivian crept out of her room. Wren's door was closed, the girl likely asleep. In the kitchen, Vivian replaced her ice pack, gasping at the cold but relishing the temporary relief. A glass of wine struck her as a lovely idea and a possible distraction. Sleep felt far away.

She looked at the wine, most of the bottles purchased with Jack years ago. Oh, the fun they had. Why couldn't the man haunt her like he'd promised? Vivian had just pulled a bottle of red they'd selected at a winery on Kelleys Island when the realization stabbed her afresh: Jack was gone. Gone forever. The pills hummed from the bathroom.

"May I join you?"

Luna's voice made Vivian jump but then lifted her, the pills mute again.

"Absolutely."

Luna fetched two wineglasses as Vivian opened the bottle. They took their glasses into the living room. Vivian sat so she had the night view of the garden, the beautiful landscape lighting Jack had installed highlighting the grand trees, the most dramatic plants, and now the Degas ballerina statue up on the wooded hill, the place where Vivian felt closest to Jack.

Vivian braced herself for Luna's daily apology for not having found a new place for her family yet. In the recycling bin, Vivian had seen the circled classified ads, seen Luna's jotted notes in the margins, seen the *X*s marked through all the highlighted posts.

Today, Luna didn't apologize. Instead, she drew her socked feet up under her on the couch and draped herself with one of Vivian's throws. Her hair was still damp from her after-work shower. Since they moved here, Luna came home from work and stripped down in the garage. Each day, she left clothes out there to put on before she came into the house. She didn't greet anyone until she had showered the possible contamination from herself. Just in case. For Wren.

But every day, she still went and faced the virus. COVID had arrived at Sycamore Place. Vivian hated hearing Luna's reports that there were three cases now among the Memory Care residents and two in Assisted Living. Some employees were sick now, too.

Luna's husband was home from the hospital, totally fine. He'd said it "was no big deal," which struck Vivian as ludicrous and irresponsible. He had been *hospitalized* for Pete's sake.

Vivian swallowed the delicious wine and studied Luna. A quiet stillness defined her for Vivian. Although Luna was so sincere and generous, there was also a wariness to her, like a shelter dog afraid to get its hopes up.

Vivian liked that they could sit in silence and enjoy the wine. The throb in her breast irritated her. She took another drink and said, "I used to have a cat named Cooper."

Luna laughed. Her laugh was warm and warming, like the wine. "Oh Lord, I bet that cat was trouble."

Vivian smiled. "Not trouble. Neither one of them. My cat was found on Cooper Street. How'd your Cooper get his name?"

"It was Cal's dad's name." Luna lifted a shoulder, and Vivian saw the regret.

"What was *your* father's name?"

"William. Cooper's middle name is William." Luna set down her wineglass. "He died when I was ten, my dad." Luna combed her damp hair with her fingers. "He had cancer. That's what made me want to be a doctor."

Vivian gasped in delight. "You wanted to be a doctor?"

Luna covered her face, then picked up her wine. "I was ten. I can't believe I just said that. I've never told anyone that!"

"It's nothing to be ashamed of. Why are you reacting like that?"

"It just feels like . . . a fantasy, you know? I mean, I also wanted to be a ballerina, so . . ." She patted her hips and laughed.

Vivian's breath stopped at *ballerina*. Oh, Ann-Marie. Why was the girl haunting her so today?

Into Vivian's silence, Luna said, "My mom was good, loving, but then she was a single mom. She was always gone, working. Just like me." She sighed, a sound that ripped something inside Vivian and set her left breast to aching again. "I want to do better. But I'm just treading water. Always treading water."

Vivian looked at Luna. "Treading water is exhausting."

Luna's eyes shone in the dim light. She sipped her wine. "Now I'm just like my own mom, working all the time, never here for them."

"You are here for them."

"I feel guilty every time I leave. I wish . . . I mean, I have this dream . . ." She shook her head. "If I could be a full-time mom, maybe Cooper wouldn't get in so much trouble."

"Do *not* feel guilty." Vivian leaned forward, which made her flinch a bit. She saw Luna notice. "Do not. Look. I stayed home. I was there for *every* single goddamn thing, and my daughter ended up a crack whore."

"Vivian!"

"I'm serious. Quite literally, at one point, she was a crack whore. She might be again for all I know. If she's even alive."

"Oh," Luna said, pressing a hand to her heart. "I wondered." She whispered, "Does she know? About Jack?"

"I don't know." They both whispered now. "I hired a private investigator when Jack got bad. He found nothing but a police report for shoplifting in Florida from four years ago. He did find seven different Jane Does, in five different states, buried in mass graves, who fit her age and description. But not much else. So she changed her name or she's . . . gone."

Luna made a small sound.

Jack had started to ask about her all the time, only he talked about her like she was a teenager, still the lovely one, fresh and creative and bold, the promising ballerina, before the injury, before the opioid painkillers. After the burglary, Jack had declared Ann-Marie dead to them, which gutted Vivian. She knew he was protecting himself—and her—and that he was grieving, but they fought about it. Oh, how they fought. His decision threatened to drive them apart. Sweet Jesus, that man was stubborn. But when Vivian told him they needed a counselor or she'd leave, they grew closer in their shared heartbreak.

Once he was unable to remember Ann-Marie's transgressions, Vivian loved talking about their daughter, pretending Ann-Marie was still a part of their lives. Vivian displayed their daughter's photos again. Vivian went along with it when Jack said that he'd seen Ann-Marie or that she was thirteen. Vivian loved to ask him, "So how was Ann-Marie today? What did you talk about?" The stories were her own drug, and she hungered for them.

Luna gazed at her with those big brown eyes. "Do you want to find her? To know for sure?"

Vivian held her breath. "I don't know," she lied. Because she *did* want to know. She couldn't help it. But it scared her, the wanting. She was sensible enough to know she wouldn't like what she learned, that Ann-Marie was likely cremated with several other bodies in a grave some random county paid for, or worse, that she was rotting away somewhere in the woods. Vivian was better off not knowing, but . . . "She's my *daughter*."

Luna set down her wineglass, crossed to Vivian, and hugged her. Vivian thought she might burst into tears again, like she had in her car, but then the hug made her flinch.

"What's going on? What's wrong?"

"It's nothing." Vivian tried to wave it away. "So you wanted to be a doctor?"

"What's that?"

Vivian looked down to see the top corner of the ice pack showing. She buttoned her shirt another button.

"Vivian?"

She understood how Cooper and Wren must sometimes feel. Luna may be small, but she had this way. She stood, hands on those ample hips, eyes burning.

"I had a biopsy. It aches a little, but it's no big—"

"Today?"

"Yes."

"Did you go alone?"

"Yes."

Luna sat, near her. "Vivian, *why*? Why didn't you tell me?"

"It's nothing. I didn't want to bother you—you had to work. It's not a big deal."

"But a biopsy is a big deal. Did they see something in a mammogram?"

Vivian sighed. "Yes." She failed to mention she could feel the lump herself. "I was overdue, so they're probably being cautious. I think the biopsy is just a cover-your-ass thing."

"What do you mean you were overdue?"

"I hadn't gotten a mammogram in three years."

Luna shook her head, but Vivian saw in her face that she wasn't judging her. "You were so busy with Jack. I get it."

Those words were like stepping into the sunshine.

"I haven't had a pap smear in three years," Luna admitted. "I even scheduled it once and had to cancel. I've never gotten around to rescheduling. There's always . . ."

"There's always someone else to worry about."

"I know, on an intellectual level, that caretakers *must* take care of themselves," Luna said. "But on an emotional level, I also know how impossible that is."

The women looked at each other, truly seeing each other in a way most others couldn't.

"Survival mode," Vivian said.

"It's *exhausting*."

They raised their glasses to that.

Then they sat in comfortable silence, looking out at the illuminated areas in the garden. After several moments of silence and sipping, Luna said, "When do you expect to hear results?"

"A day or two." She couldn't tell if she liked Luna knowing this. She didn't want to burden this woman with it, especially since the results wouldn't change Vivian's plans. But it had been a relief to share it. She felt better than she had all day. "Did you really want to be a doctor?"

Luna groaned and sank down into the couch. "Why did I tell you that? It's so ridiculous."

"Why is it ridiculous? Were you not a good student?"

"No. I was an excellent student."

"Well, then it wasn't a ridiculous 'fantasy' at all."

Luna looked down at her wineglass, turning it around and around. "No one else in my life has ever dreamed big. Only me. I told my mom I wanted to be a doctor, and she . . . it's not like she squashed the dream or anything, but she didn't nurture it, either. Some of it wasn't her fault. No one in our family has ever gone to college, and she didn't know about financial aid or even scholarships. For her, it all just felt out of reach. After my dad died, her focus was all about scraping by. And I get that—how exhausted she must've been. She didn't have the energy to dream. But then I went and married a man who was the same damn way. I mean, not at first—he was fun and creative. He played in a band." Luna rolled her eyes and laughed at herself. Vivian longed to tell her to give herself a break. "He'd make these elaborate family Halloween costumes, we'd throw theme parties, we had *fun*. But he never wanted more. He was content to just . . . have fun. Just get by . . . and now he's not even doing that. He just . . . he's the king of 'good enough.' He never wants to push, to try, to better himself. He has no ambitions."

A wave of missing Jack hit Vivian so hard, she almost gasped out loud. That man had had ambitions. And dreams. If he said he was going to do something, he did it. She'd loved that about him, although she'd teased him that she had to take him out of town to get him to relax and stop working. "What are your dreams now? Do you still want to be a doctor?"

"Oh, good Lord, no!" Luna laughed. Then she looked Vivian in the eye and said, "But I was going to nursing school about a year ago. I'd saved up, and I was taking classes. I wanted to be a nurse. But then Cal got the airport job, and he wasn't home at nights. Wren can't be left alone. It's not fair to Cooper to ask him to be responsible for her. He helps enough already. And even though he'd be willing, that's just not safe." Luna pursed her lips and cocked her head. "So I gave up my dream, my ambition. For a man who didn't deserve it. But, I mean, we needed him to have a *job*." She halfheartedly punched the couch.

"Is that why you separated?"

Luna was silent so long that Vivian said, "I'm sorry if I'm being nosy."

"No. I was trying to figure out how to word it. It's not that he lost his job. That can happen. But he doesn't *try*. I do everything. It's like he's another child."

Vivian bit her lip to stop from commenting that she and the boys referred to him as Callous Cal or Clueless Cal, since she'd told them about that pansy conversation.

"But . . . no, the real reason?" Luna said. "He doesn't see the kids. He . . . his feelings about Cooper are what made me make him leave."

Her voice was so raw and vulnerable, Vivian's throat closed up. "He doesn't support who Cooper is. Doesn't want him singing in the house, pretending to be Lady Gaga. Doesn't want him cooking." She kept her voice quiet but spoke in a furious, fierce whisper. "And he *ignores* Wren. Disdains Cooper and ignores Wren. No. No way. My kids are visible and worthy of love. Be a better parent or get the hell out!"

Vivian raised her nearly empty glass again. "Hear, hear."

"Whew." Luna's eyes were wide. "That felt good."

Luna poured herself more wine. Just a little.

Vivian thought of Cooper the first night she'd met him, the way he'd spoken of Drew and Steven, said that hateful slur like a defense mechanism, like an armor that would protect him. "When you arrived, Cooper had a black eye. That wasn't . . . Cal didn't . . . ?"

"No. Cal would never do that. And if he did, I would've kicked him out right then and there. No. Cooper has trouble at school with a bunch of bullies. Real assholes. He fights back."

Cooper the boy was coming into focus more and more, like a Polaroid.

Vivian thought, with sudden nostalgia, about the stray cat Cooper. How he'd brought her and Jack to a new level of acknowledgment about their daughter and her place in their lives. Ann-Marie was violently allergic to cats. But they'd brought that stray home without discussion.

Luna said, "Once Wren was diagnosed, Cal acted like she wasn't a little girl anymore. He stopped playing with her, stopped hugging her. It drove me crazy. Rule number one of having a kid with a disability is to always see your child as a *person* first. Not the disability. No matter the degree of that disability! But he just . . . then he goes to the *other* extreme, and I swear he forgets about her needs. It's like he pretends the CP doesn't exist. I want to stab him in the eye sometimes."

"I think you've shown considerable restraint *not* stabbing him."

Luna smiled, but it was wistful. "And all Wren wants is his approval. He can do no wrong in her eyes. And I fight so hard not to trash talk him in front of her."

"She'll see the truth in her own time." After a pause, Vivian added, "What you said about seeing the person first, not the disability. You did that with Jack."

Luna turned to look at Vivian.

"I'm so grateful to you for that. You, more than any other aide in that building, always treated him like the human being he once was." Vivian's mouth tremored. "Thank you. So much. For the way you saw my Jack. For the way you treated him with such dignity."

Luna's face softened. She raised her glass. "To Jack."

Vivian whispered, "To Jack."

CHAPTER FOURTEEN

LUNA

Luna drove to work and focused on her happiness instead of her dread. Work had become a place that scared her. She felt a little guilty, though, about how good she felt at home, after work.

Home. She'd begun to think of Vivian's as home.

Then she felt a lot guilty when she realized yesterday had been the second day in a row she hadn't searched for a new apartment—no classifieds, no phone calls, no drive-bys. Applications cost money, and then if she didn't get approved, that was money she'd just thrown down the toilet. As soon as people discovered her eviction, they refused to rent to her, even if she explained about her husband's job, about COVID, about any of it. Each rejection was another twenty-five or fifty dollars lost and socked her in the gut, chastising her for getting her hopes up, for feeling happy.

But she *did* feel happy.

For once in her life, Luna didn't have to do everything. She didn't do laundry anymore. Cooper did it. She wasn't making meals. Both Cooper and Wren helped with that, with Vivian's supervision. Or Steven and Drew brought something over. She didn't grocery shop, or shop for anything. She had people who willingly did it for her so she didn't have to risk exposure, so that she could protect her residents as well as her kids.

The kids were both doing well academically. Wren hated missing school, but Cooper loved remote classes. He seemed better able to focus, more relaxed, no worries about the bullies or the constant aggression. His midterm grades had been the highest she'd ever seen him earn.

Luna had *time*. A luxury greater than money, she thought. Or were they connected? She had time because, for once, she wasn't constantly hustling for money.

Luna had time to reconnect with her nursing school friends—Jodi, Mandy, and James. They'd gravitated toward each other as nontraditional students, not the nineteen- and twenty-year-olds who made up the majority of the nursing classes. They'd studied together, sometimes over pumpkin pie and coffee at Frisch's. The state of Ohio had updated regulations because of COVID, allowing nursing students nearing graduation to earn temporary licenses, so the three were now working as real nurses. Luna missed and envied them. She'd loved connecting on Zoom lately, hearing their stories.

Luna also had time to be. Just be. That truth had struck her after telling Vivian she'd wanted to be a ballerina. The next morning, as she stood in a hot shower, trying to rid herself of her wine headache, she'd remembered her childhood obsession with ballet. She'd checked out from the library the same giant coffee-table book about the American Ballet Theatre over and over again. She'd pored over the photos of those glorious costumes, the toe shoes. Oh, how she'd wanted *pointe* shoes! She'd also checked out albums of the ballets' classical music: *Swan Lake*, *The Nutcracker*, *The Sleeping Beauty*, *Giselle*, and *Coppélia*. She'd lie on the floor in front of her parents' stereo speakers and listen to ballets from start to finish, imagining herself dancing various roles. She checked out books about ballet technique and practiced the exercises from the books' photos.

Her heart ached, knowing how her mom and dad must've scrimped and saved to allow her to take dance classes. Not at the professional school downtown but at Miss Vicky's School of Dance in a little strip mall. Luna had loved the hollow tinkling of the piano, the whispers of the girls' slippers against the wooden floor, the traffic noises from the parking lot blending with the music. How she always swore the clock was broken and speeding forward.

Her mother had taken her to *The Nutcracker* at the Victoria Theatre as a Christmas gift. The entire performance enthralled her and felt like magic. She remembered her mom describing to her dad later how Luna had danced in the lobby at intermission and after. She hadn't been able to contain herself.

She closed her eyes, the hot shower streaming over her, imagining herself as the Snow Queen, hearing the music, seeing her body capable of those athletic, elegant moves, the stiff white tutu, her hair in a tight bun with a tiara. The snow falling all around her as the Snow King lifted her to his shoulder. Her radiant smile as the audience cheered.

Luna opened her eyes in the shower. She shut off the water, feeling as if she'd lost time. How long had she stood here? She laughed. How long had it been since she'd daydreamed?

There hadn't been time to daydream in decades.

Time.

She'd also had time to walk with Danielle after work like they used to, both of them always trying to lose weight. The sky and sunshine lifted Luna, reminding her of happier days playing outside as a kid. When she used to work in Memory Care at Sycamore Place, before she moved downstairs to Assisted Living, she always volunteered to walk with residents. Watching how they came alive outside brought her joy. Jack had always loved to walk outside. He must've loved being in that garden of theirs.

Luna admitted to Danielle that she felt happier away from Cal. Her children were both blossoming away from him, which made her sad but was the truth. She had spoken to Cal yesterday, and he sounded excited about a new job he'd applied for. He wouldn't tell her what it was. He didn't want to "jinx it." Was that where Wren got her silly superstitions?

Luna turned down a major boulevard in the city, the only car in sight. She didn't miss the previously frantic morning drives. The missing cars were all people fortunate enough to be working from home. Luna was considered essential.

Funny how that worked, that the least-trained, lowest-paid essential workers were doing the most hazardous work.

She shook herself and focused on the beauty in this May morning—the pink-orange sunrise, the blooming dogwoods and pear trees. She hummed the "Waltz of the Flowers" from *The Nutcracker*. She focused on another reason for her happiness: her giddy relief that Vivian's biopsy had come back clean.

"Just something to watch," Vivian said. "Nothing we need to bother with, especially now."

Luna's heart flooded with gratitude. For Vivian being okay. And for Vivian in general.

Luna paid her friend rent. Vivian tried to refuse, but Luna insisted. The amount they'd agreed on was pitiful in Luna's opinion, but she was able to save for the first time since before she had children. Seeing her bank account grow, even by such minuscule amounts, made her feel strong.

That strength fled from her as she pulled into the parking lot at work, looking at the grand old building. She grabbed her mask. They were given only so many in a day. She'd tried to find more online, but everyone was out, people panic-buying them. Luna held hers in her hands and thought, as she did every time she arrived at Sycamore Place: Did these even work? Were they protection enough? Her nose ached. She'd developed a mark, a red band over the bridge of her nose that didn't disappear anymore even when she'd been mask-free for hours. A rash freckled her cheeks, like tiny, miniature acne. Maskne, she and her coworkers called it.

She looked at the redbrick in the barely risen sunlight. COVID was in the building, in nine residents so far. Five had been taken to the hospital, two never to return. One died alone in her room, before even making it to the hospital, fluish one evening, dead less than ten hours later. The other three positive residents, including gentle wandering Dennis, were quarantined, isolated in their rooms, with neon-yellow signs on their doors.

Her head ached.

As she got out of the van, someone called her name. Malik Adofo, another nursing assistant. Tall and broad, always smiling, he could get even grumpy old Louise to laugh with his ridiculous jokes and puns delivered in his musical Ghanaian accent.

Malik wasn't smiling at the moment. "Did you hear about Cachè?" he asked.

"Oh God." Cachè had tested positive for COVID two days ago. *Please don't tell me she died.*

"They took her to the hospital last night. She's on a ventilator."

Luna wanted to burst into tears. Cachè, strong, vibrant Cachè, who followed the Dayton Dragons religiously, who surreptitiously handed Luna Reese's Cups when they passed in the hallways here, making it seem like the candy was contraband. Cachè, who came over and watched Hallmark Christmas movies and true-crime documentaries with her. Cachè was a favorite among the residents for her quick wit and her no-bullshit way of getting things done. Cachè had been tending to Dennis the day he fell ill.

"We do not get paid enough to risk our damn lives," Malik said.

Luna loved the way Malik said *our* with two syllables and overenunciated his words, sounding always as if he were making a joke or were outraged. This time he was outraged.

They *didn't* get paid enough for the current danger. The staff shortages worsened by the week, as Luna's friends and colleagues weren't willing to put their lives on the line for so few dollars an hour. "I worry about taking it home," she whispered. "Wren is vulnerable. And Vivian, too. And I—"

"Vivian Laurent?" His accent made the woman's name glamorous, an expensive perfume brand.

Luna's face flooded hot. She thought for a split second about lying, about saying *my mother* or something, but she said, "Don't. Don't spread it around, okay?"

Malik looked offended. "I would not." And she believed him. "I like Vivian. How is she?"

"She's great. She's doing well." Luna thought of the biopsy result with joy. "She didn't want to be in lockdown here, and she didn't want to live alone. The timing was right. But I know it looks—I know it looks inappropriate."

"Inappropriate *how?*" Malik looked offended again, but this time on her behalf.

She shrugged. "I don't know. You know how people are."

"I do indeed." They walked toward the building. "She was right to get out of here when she did. I am afraid."

"Me, too." Luna now took lunch breaks in the van, afraid to take off her mask inside.

They walked a moment in silence, passing a dropped or discarded face mask on the sidewalk. She and Malik both put on their masks in unison, like a synchronized team, lifting the elastics over their ears. They looked at each other, and Malik reached out and tugged Luna's earring through the elastic. "Vivian left so . . ." He made a gesture like a magician and said, "Poof! Tell her people miss her. That when it's safe, she should visit."

"I will." Who knew when that would be? "She really misses Martin and Vera Jane. Are they doing all right?"

"Memory Care is totally locked down now. Nobody but staff allowed in."

Luna's knees almost crumpled. "Oh, poor Martin." That would be awful. To be so close to your loved one, in the same building, and not be able to see them. Torture. And Vera Jane couldn't use the phone anymore. Vivian had been smart and calculating, moving Jack out of Memory Care as soon as he was no longer a flight risk. She had moved herself to Assisted Living just so she could live with her husband again. Luna remembered thinking that having Jack in Memory Care would help her. The poor woman had looked so sleep-deprived and tortured, so fearful that Jack would leave their apartment and get lost. But Vivian had been miserable without him for the brief five months he had lived upstairs in Memory Care.

Luna also knew enough about Vivian to know that she'd have been busting into Memory Care to retrieve Jack if the COVID lockdown had happened while he was there.

Inside, Luna and Malik waited in the line to sign in, standing six feet apart on the green tape *X*s on the floor. They now had to have their temperatures taken before they could clock in. Luna rubbed her aching temples. The night Luna found out about the biopsy, she'd drunk too much wine and had a killer headache the next day. Last night, she'd had just *one* cocktail with Drew and woke up with a headache just as bad, with dark circles thrown in. Maybe she shouldn't drink at all anymore, if it always made her feel so wretched.

Luna leaned forward to let Sierra at the front desk take her temperature: 98.2.

She said goodbye to Malik and got busy. The work took longer these days because the residents were so lonely. They wanted to talk. Luna worried about the truly lonely ones, the ones like Vivian would've been had she stayed. Most days, residents who lived alone saw or spoke to no one but a nursing assistant like her. The isolation had only been two months. Who knew how long this virus could last? She knew her job was tending to the residents' emotional needs as well as their physical ones.

Throughout the morning, she helped people dress and shower. She combed hair. She changed diapers. She checked skin for rashes. She bagged up soiled bedsheets. She looked at each resident as if she could see the virus itself. She touched for hot or clammy skin; she watched for chills, listened for coughs. The problem was, many of her residents already had chronic coughs. These days, she also helped open windows for fresh air and better circulation. She helped access emails and a FaceTime chat, grateful to her children, knowing she would be unable to do this so handily without them. Before each new room, each new resident, she scrubbed her hands. She changed her gloves, which, fortunately, they still had plenty of, and pinched the metal bar inside her mask tighter over her sore nose.

She felt her watchful guardedness turning paranoid as she touched light switches, doorknobs, lunch trays, and laundry baskets. Her biggest fear was being the one who brought the virus to one of these people.

That's why it filled her with rage to catch Miss Florence, the Chihuahua, letting family members into the building from a side door. "You can't be in here!" Luna said. "No visitors are currently allowed."

Miss Florence looked frightened, but the woman Luna assumed to be Florence's daughter scowled. Neither the woman nor the two teens with her wore masks. Neither did Miss Florence.

The woman said, "Oh, come on. We're only going to her apartment."

Luna wanted to smack her. She pointed to a teenage boy, who had his hands on the railing that lined the hallways. "Her apartment is around the corner, and you'll be breathing all the way there. Look. You're touching the railing, the walls, the doorknobs. This is not okay."

The boy snatched his hands off the railing.

"*We're* not sick!" the woman said, as if Luna had suggested they had lice or scabies.

"People can be asymptomatic." Luna tried to sound patient. "You can have the virus and spread it all over and not know it. We all have to act as if we do have it."

"That's ridiculous!" the woman said.

Miss Florence wouldn't look Luna in the eye. "Maybe we shouldn't," she said to the woman.

"You definitely shouldn't," Luna said. "It's not currently allowed. You know the rules."

"Oh, for God's sake! You're going to keep me from seeing my mother?"

"I know it's hard," Luna said. "We all have to make sacrifices right now."

"C'mon, Mom," the boy said.

"No! I have a right to visit my mother whenever I like. You can't keep me away!"

"You're being an asshole," the boy said to his mother.

The girl, who looked younger, piped up and said, "We'll call you, Grandma." She scurried out the door. Her brother followed her.

"Kara," Miss Florence said. "You should go."

Luna said, "We're trying hard to keep your mother safe. Please help us do that."

Kara's face flushed red. "Oh, for God's sake, this thing isn't even *real!* This is such bullshit!" She didn't even say goodbye to her mother. She just slammed open the door.

Luna wanted to leap on her and drag her to the ground. *Not even real? You wanna tell that to your mother's dead friends?* To Cachè in the hospital fighting to breathe? To Dennis? To poor Martin, who couldn't even see his wife?

Miss Florence apologized when the echo from Kara's slam silenced. "She's just scared."

"She should be scared. And so should you. Don't ever, ever do that again. Any one of them could have the virus and not know it. Do you want to get sick? Or worse, be responsible for someone else getting sick?"

That was the problem: Luna believed that *would* be worse. Knowing she'd had it and had passed it to others. She looked into Florence's face and knew Florence didn't believe the same thing. She was apologetic but only because she'd been caught. Any parent could tell the difference.

"And you cannot leave your apartment without a mask," Luna said. "I know it's hard to remember. We all have to try."

Miss Florence turned her walker around and went back to her apartment without another word. Luna reported the incident at the front desk. Damn it. For all she knew, that awful Kara was the one who'd given COVID to Dennis. Or to Cachè.

On a brief break, she signed a card for Cachè. *Please, please, please be okay.* She texted Cachè herself: I'm rooting for you, friend. You're a warrior. Stay strong. She texted both kids, telling them she hoped their days were going well. Wren sent her emojis of unicorns and hearts. Cooper sent a text: I got an A on my Spanish test.

Luna smiled, but fatigue poured into her limbs, as if someone had pulled a plug in the bottom of her feet and all her energy drained out. She had to stop to sit on a couch in a lounge for a moment. Good thing the days went fast. When she was busy, she didn't notice her stupid headache so much. Damn that Drew and his gay pour. She snorted. She loved those guys.

Movement in the corner of her eye startled her. She turned her head so fast, she felt dizzy a second, white sparkles in the corners of her vision. Ox, the stout black-and-white cat that belonged to Dennis, stood on his hind legs, his front paws on the couch.

"Ox? What are you doing out here?"

The cat, in typical fashion, answered, as if he spoke English. "Mrreoh." He leaped up on the couch and into Luna's lap. He head-butted her arm, yowling, then leaped down and looked back at her. "Raaoh." She laughed at his silliness, but when he repeated it, leaping up and butting her again, then running off, she stopped.

"Oh no," she whispered.

When she stood, the cat took off down the hallway. Luna waited a brief moment to clear the sparkles from her vision and followed him. Good Lord, her head ached. *Please, please let Dennis be all right.*

Ox trotted ahead, then looked back and yowled as if telling her to hurry. Following the cat through the empty, quiet halls felt surreal and dreamlike. She passed Vivian's old apartment, where the sign on the door still read, SYCAMORE PLACE WELCOMES JACK AND VIVIAN LAURENT.

Luna didn't pass another person, resident or staff, the entire way to Dennis's apartment.

At his slightly open door, Luna saw just a flash of the neon-yellow COVID sign before Ox hit the door with both front paws, slamming it open. From the hall, she saw Dennis facedown on the floor, in a crumpled heap, as if he'd spilled out of his recliner.

"Oh, smart kitty, good kitty." She rushed to Dennis. As she knelt, he moved and muttered, and relief coursed through her. *Oh, thank God.* "Hold still. Be careful, Dennis. Let's make sure you're not hurt." Luna radioed for help and said they'd likely need an ambulance.

Dennis rolled himself over, groaning. His forehead was carpet burned from the fall, and one corner of the patch trickled blood. His nose bled as well. He coughed. The coughs shook his entire body, as if he were possessed by a demon. He clawed at his chest, gasping for air, his back arching with his effort to breathe.

"Breathe in through your nose, out through your mouth," Luna crooned. "Calm down. Slow down."

Ox touched Dennis's face with his paw.

Luna stroked Dennis's head. He burned with fever. His legs were in a tangle, and she'd just managed to straighten them when Malik arrived. They examined his limbs for break or injury, but he seemed unscathed except for his forehead.

Malik helped her get Dennis upright, still on the floor but leaning against his recliner. Dennis wheezed, his cough like a seal barking. Ox rubbed himself against his human, pushing his head into Dennis's shoulder.

"Thank . . . you," Dennis gargled out.

"You are okay; we've got you," Malik said in his deep, lyrical voice.

Luna felt certain Dennis had been thanking the cat, not them. The cat had likely saved his life.

Dennis struggled to breathe, panic in his eyes. While they waited for the ambulance, Luna pressed cold, wet cloths to Dennis's forehead. Malik spooned him little sips of water between his coughing fits. Ox curled up on his human's thighs and purred.

Luna worried that Dennis would not want to part from his cat, but when the EMTs arrived, he was not aware or awake enough to notice her hefting Ox out of his lap. Ox tried to follow the gurney down the hall, but Luna caught him before he got on the elevator with the EMTs.

She held the cat on her shoulder. "You be strong, Mr. Dennis," she said. "I'll take good care of Ox for you. You get better now."

The EMTs in their masks, face shields, and full bodysuits seemed like automatons. Luna could see their eyes, though, and they looked at her with pity, as if she were delusional. When the elevator closed on them, Luna turned to see Malik with tears spilling down his cheeks, darkening his mask. "Damn it," he whispered.

She carried Ox back to Dennis's apartment. She made sure he had food and water and his litter box was clean. She hated closing the door on the despondent cat. When she did, she heard him wail. The sound made the breath catch in her throat.

She scurried down the hall, but the tears came. She needed a moment. She could not let residents see her this way. As she passed Vivian and Jack's old apartment, she tried the knob. It was unlocked. She slipped inside just to gather herself.

Standing in the apartment, she was struck by how bleak it seemed. Was it because Vivian was not here to fill it with her light and energy? Vivian had been right to leave. Luna could not imagine her here, watching TV, tending to these tiny flowerpots, their contents now dead and shriveled, not now that she'd seen the garden that was Vivian's passion.

Luna breathed in and out. *Get it together, get it together.* All she heard was Dennis's rasping breath and the heartbroken yowls of that loyal cat. She walked into the tiny galley kitchen. She lowered her mask to splash some cold water on her face.

When she stood, she noticed Vivian's old-school answering machine blinking red. Luna remembered the machine from the days both Jack and Vivian lived here. It still had Jack's cheerful, amiable voice on it. Vivian had five messages.

Luna's heart clutched. Did Vivian even know how to retrieve these from home? Luna would like to say she pressed "Play" without thinking, but the truth was she knew it was a breach of privacy. As soon as she saw those blinking messages, a chill crept into her heart. Before she had time to convince herself it was unethical, Luna hit "Play."

The first call was from a Dr. Prugh, asking Vivian to call her as soon as she could. They needed to discuss her biopsy results.

The second was a repeat from Dr. Prugh saying it was urgent and that she'd try Vivian's cell.

The third was someone calling from a Dr. Wayhall's office saying they'd like Vivian to call them to schedule a consultation appointment to discuss her treatment options.

The fourth was a hang-up.

The fifth was from Dr. Wayhall's office again, only this time it was the doctor herself saying they'd left messages and texts at Vivian's other number as well and needed her to call back to schedule an appointment as soon as possible. "This cancer is aggressive, and it's already spread. You do not want to put this off. Please call, Vivian."

Damn it, Vivian. Luna's hands trembled, and the headache flared to new intensity behind her left eye.

Luna looked up Dr. Wayhall—not sure she was spelling it right—and found a Roxane Weighall, surgical oncologist.

What would make Vivian avoid an appointment and allow her cancer to grow? Denial? Fear? She'd figure out a way to convince Vivian. She would.

But she had three hours of work left first.

The stress and sorrow of Dennis and Cachè made Luna weak and dizzy. She took Tylenol, but it barely lessened the talon grip of her headache.

Vivian had cancer. Aggressive cancer. And she'd lied about it.

Luna's legs were heavy as she trudged up the ramp to the back door. Inside, Steven and Drew were already there. The steamy heat hit her, and she heard pots boiling.

Cooper stirred something, laughing at whatever Steven had said. Vivian perched on the corner of the kitchen island, next to Drew. They looked down, smiling at whatever Wren was doing.

As everyone greeted her, Luna longed to put off this confrontation. To just hang on to the comfort of this lovely scene a bit longer. She was *so* tired.

"Does that not smell divine?" Vivian said, holding up a handful of green twigs. "God, I love the scent of rosemary."

So did Luna.

She breathed deep. *Oh God. Oh no.* She walked to the kitchen island and snatched the rosemary from Vivian, bringing it to her own face. *Damn it.*

She couldn't smell it. She couldn't smell a thing.

CHAPTER FIFTEEN

COOPER

Mom had COVID.

Birds flung themselves against Cooper's ribs. He couldn't sleep. He'd chewed a raw spot inside his cheek. He stood in Vivian's kitchen and waited for Vivian to come down from his mom's room. He tried to calm his breathing.

He'd never seen his mom so sick. It had been four days since Drew had driven her to get a COVID test. They'd both worn masks and left the windows down in the car. Since their return, she'd only been out of her room to use the bathroom. Cooper stayed out of his own room next to hers and slept on the couch. He didn't use the bathroom they shared anymore—he used Wren's. And he hadn't been offended when Wren said she didn't want him helping her in the bathroom. Cooper had coached Vivian, who'd been helping Wren bathe since Mom got sick. Cooper would do the PT, and Vivian could deal with his sister naked.

They'd talked about getting a home health aide, but before they could find someone, Wren and Vivian had the routine down, and Wren said she didn't want a stranger.

Not a stranger. And not her brother. He understood 100 percent.

He talked to Mom through FaceTime, but today, he couldn't call it "talking." She'd muttered gibberish, which had terrified him. Like strip-his-mouth-dry terrified.

He thought of their old apartment with only one bathroom and the windows that wouldn't open. There would've been no way to separate there.

They would have all gotten it.

Wren could not get sick.

Cooper didn't want Vivian to get sick, either.

But he had other things to worry about with Vivian. Vivian had cancer she wasn't going to treat. Mom could die. Vivian could die. And then what happened to them, him and Wren?

Wren was really scared now, so Cooper couldn't tell her he was scared, too. He sure as shit couldn't tell her about Vivian's cancer, even though he needed to talk to somebody.

His mom had to be okay. She had to get well.

He picked at the plate of chicken and noodles over mashed potatoes that Danielle and Birdy had brought them from Bob Evans, Birdy's go-to meal whenever she was sick. Cooper liked more flavor but loved how nice it had been of her to bring it. Even though they'd all stood outside with masks on, it had felt so good to see them, he'd almost cried. Vivian had liked them both, and she'd even complimented Birdy's hair. Birdy's hair had been bright blue when Cooper had seen her last in person, but now she'd also shaved half her head.

Uncle Ricky had texted every day since Mom got sick. Dad and Danielle had both called every day. But Danielle actually showed up.

Vivian came down the stairs into the kitchen, wearing a mask. Actually, he saw she was wearing two masks. She carried a tray of dishes. She put the dishes in the dishwasher, then scrubbed her hands. "Your mom's a fighter," she said, not looking at Cooper. "She ate. She's drinking. She spoke to me. She put all her dishes on a tray outside her room. And she always, always asks about you two."

All of that made him feel a little better. The delirious way she'd mumbled about cats and cows still freaked him out. They'd never had a pet, even though Wren had begged for one pretty much since she could speak.

"Did—did she make sense?" he asked.

Vivian cocked her head. "Well, we didn't have a long conversation, but she seemed to know where she was and answered my questions appropriately. She's very concerned about who's helping Wren. Why?"

"When I FaceTimed her earlier, she was really out of it."

"She has a fever."

"But she wasn't making sense. It . . ." He didn't want to say out loud that it scared him. Saying it out loud would make the fear more real. "She kept saying we should check on a cat."

Vivian whirled around from the fridge. "What cat?"

"That's the thing! We've *never* had a cat."

Vivian zeroed in on him with those wolf eyes. "What did she say exactly?"

Shit. He didn't want to think about how weak her voice had sounded, how she kept her eyes closed as she talked, as if it hurt to open them, even in her dark room. "She kept saying she needed to check on this cat. I said, 'What cat?' and she kept saying, 'Promise me,' and I remember she said, 'It's the least we can do for him.' She wanted me to give her the van keys!"

Vivian put a hand to her mouth over her mask. That gesture scared Cooper more. "Is that bad?" he asked. "Is that common with fevers?"

"Oh, Cooper. I actually think I know what she's talking about."

He watched her pull off her mask, pick up her phone, and dial. "Oh, good, Em, it's you. This is Vivian Laurent. Oh, I'm good. Yes. Yes, healthy. I know, yes, when it's safe, I'd like that. Listen, this is going to sound odd, but is Dennis all right?"

In the long pause, Cooper watched Vivian's face. He watched her absorb news that hurt her.

"Oh. Oh no. Oh, that's awful. I'm sorry to hear that. Is anyone taking care of Ox?"

Cooper stood up straight and whispered to Vivian. "She said *ox!*" Oh, man, thank God, she hadn't lost her mind. She'd been making sense, taking care of others like always.

149

"Good," Vivian said. "Yes. I led him back to that apartment more times than I can count." She sort of swallowed the word *count*, and Cooper saw her blue eyes shimmer with tears. "Does he have family?" She made a small noise. "No. No, he was just on my mind. Oh, please do. Thank you, Em."

When she hung up, Vivian sat at the kitchen island and put her face in her hands.

"Did someone die?" Cooper whispered.

She nodded and wiped her eyes. "Oh, damn it! I'm not supposed to touch my face!"

"Was it COVID?"

She nodded again. She didn't look at him. Shit.

"But he was really old, right?" Cooper hated how babyish his voice sounded.

Vivian narrowed her eyes at him but then seemed to recognize he needed comfort. "Yes. He was old and getting dementia. It's probably a blessing in disguise. But that cat. They were best friends. That poor cat has got to be *bereft*." Vivian drummed her fingers on the kitchen island. He could tell she was mulling something over. She looked up at him. "See? Your mother was together enough to be worried about someone else."

"I thought she was talking about an actual ox, and I was freaking out."

Vivian exhaled a laugh.

Relief swirled through him. "I should make some of her comfort foods. There's stuff she always likes when she's sick."

"That would be lovely. What's her favorite?"

"Chicken adobo. Our grammy made it—Mom's mom." In his mind, Cooper smelled the garlicky tang, heard the bubbling pots, saw the curl of steam from the rice. "And when she gets well, she always wants this peanut butter pie." Could he make that for his mom? Would she want it if she couldn't taste? Mom had to be okay.

"You make a list of what you need, and we'll get it."

He looked over his shoulder to check where Wren was, but she was in her room with the door shut. Still, she spied on people all the time, so he made sure to whisper. "I'm scared."

Vivian studied him, those fierce blue eyes staring into him. "I am, too."

See? That meant something. Honesty. He hated when adults were always saying, "Everything will be all right," or the way Mom always said, "It'll be okay. I have a plan." There was no plan for this. And he was mad at Vivian right now, but this honesty helped.

Vivian also whispered. "But I believe in your mom. What I just said. She's a fighter. But I am scared. I hate this damn virus." She leaned on her elbows. "If this were the apocalypse, poor Dennis would not have been a survivor. But your mother would be."

Cooper believed that.

"And so would you," Vivian said.

He thought a minute. "I bet you would be."

She shrugged. "I'm not sure I'd want to live in a world like that."

"A world like this?"

She snorted.

"I'm scared for Wren. She'd be a goner."

Vivian pursed her lips. "I'm not so sure. She'd be more vulnerable, yes. But she's clever. She's resilient."

This lifted Cooper. "There's never any people with disabilities in the apocalypse stories. I hate that. I think, where are they all? And then I hate it because I know."

"There's Wendell from *Fear the Walking Dead*."

"Really? I never saw him. I stopped watching that show."

"Oh, I know, it started terribly. But if you stick with it, it really gets good. Now I love it every bit as much as *The Walking Dead*."

"There's really someone disabled? I mean, not just deaf but, like, limited in movement? Can't run?" Cooper hated how he said "just" deaf. He knew deafness would be a horrible disability in such a world. But at least they could flee. Wren would be a sitting duck.

"Yes. He's in a wheelchair. They don't really bog down the plot with how he got that way. It wouldn't really matter, after all. But he does well. And he travels with a dear friend, Sarah, who looks out for him. She's pretty badass. That would be you two."

He thought about that. He'd look out for Wren. He'd have to. He wouldn't *want* to survive, knowing he'd left her behind.

"We should watch it," Vivian said. "I like it enough to rewatch it. How far did you get?"

Not far at all. He'd only been watching it during a rare time that both Mom and Dad had jobs and they had good cable. Cable had been the first to go when Dad lost his job.

He followed Vivian into the TV room, where he'd been sleeping since Mom got sick. "I still think it's funny that you like this stuff."

"Oh, Jack and I loved *The Walking Dead*. We used to watch it every Sunday night before he . . . when he was still healthy. Drew and Steven would come over. And Debra and Mike—they used to live down the street, but they've moved now. We'd take turns at each other's houses, providing the snacks. Once, Jack and I did only food they'd eaten on the show. Easy Cheese. And canned food. A big can of chocolate pudding."

Cooper laughed. "That's awesome. You really made people eat that?"

"Oh, we had real food. But we let them believe that's all there'd be at first."

"You didn't cook up a possum?"

"We thought about it." They sat on the couch, and she sighed. "Oh, we had such fun."

She didn't pick up the remote. Cooper could tell she was somewhere else, remembering.

He realized he'd been laughing, and it made him feel guilty. *Let Mom be okay. Please let Mom be okay.* He'd seen images from NYC in the news that morning—refrigerated trucks full of dead bodies because the morgues were full. *She has to get well.*

When Vivian shook herself and he could tell she was back here now, he said, "We should do it. When the show comes back on. We should do a watch party."

Vivian smiled. A real smile. "That is an excellent idea."

But then Cooper felt guilty again. Because the show probably wasn't coming back until next fall because of COVID. And he was implying that they'd live here that long. *No,* he told himself. Wherever they *were* living, they could come over for the watch party. He blinked, realizing: they would be friends.

Vivian picked up the remote but still didn't turn the TV on.

Cooper thought about watching *The Walking Dead* with his dad. Cooper's favorite characters were like Hershel and Glenn, the ones who became the "moral compass" for the group. That was a phrase his English teacher had used.

"And who did you watch it with?" Vivian asked.

Cooper blinked.

"I mean, surely Wren doesn't watch it?"

"Oh, hell no. She doesn't even like to *hear* it. The sounds the walkers make? If she hears it from the other room, she hates it. Just the sounds give her bad dreams."

Vivian chuckled. "How about your mom and dad?"

Cooper shook his head. *Mom. Mom has to be okay. Please let Mom be okay.* "Mom likes 'more hopeful visions of humanity,'" he said, quoting her. "But that's kind of bullshit because she loves to watch true-crime documentaries. And Dad . . ." Shit. Why had he even brought up Dad? He looked at Vivian. "I used to watch it with Dad. Until—" But then his face burned.

"Until they separated?" Vivian's voice was gentle.

Cooper shook his head. "Until Daryl met Aaron. And Aaron's husband."

Vivian pursed her lips. "Ah."

"When those guys kissed, Dad said the show sucked. He said they'd ruined it. He wouldn't let me watch it anymore. I had to watch it at Birdy's house. She had On Demand."

Cooper thought of that kiss. A passionate kiss, quick, but still. It lasted a full five seconds. He'd watched it eight times before Birdy said, "Dude," and made him stop.

Vivian snorted. "As I said before, Clueless Cal sounds like an ignorant ass."

"He's a dick."

"That, too."

See? That made him love Vivian. But . . . but there was that other thing. The thing that made him angry.

And when Vivian pointed the remote at the TV and turned it on, he blurted, "Did you bring us here so Mom could take care of you?"

Vivian looked at his face, her eyes studying him as if trying to read something on his face. "I . . . I don't understand."

"Did you want Mom to live here because she'd know how to take care of you when you had cancer?"

Her blue eyes rounded. She looked genuinely surprised, something he hadn't seen her be yet. Ever. "And who told you I had cancer?"

"I heard you and Mom talking."

"When?"

"That night." That sucky, awful night. "The night we found out she had COVID."

"So you *and* your sister are eavesdroppers. You just happen to be better at it. Well, it's rude, eavesdropping. And for your information, I didn't know I *had* cancer until you all were already here. That had nothing to do with my decision to invite you here. If I had needed something from your mother, I would've asked her outright."

Cooper felt real shame scald inside him. Why was he ruining everything? But he couldn't figure out why she'd brought them here, what she wanted. Nobody did stuff like this for free.

"Why won't you treat your cancer?" he asked, his eyes burning. Shit, he was going to cry.

"Oh, Cooper. It's very slow moving, what they found. It's not going to kill me."

But he'd heard what Mom had said to her. About hearing the answering machine in her old apartment. He sniffed. He wanted to feel angry. Anger was his default, his go-to. But mostly because he didn't know how to tell Vivian he didn't want her to die. And he realized: it wasn't just that he needed her. He *wanted* her to be alive.

"Cooper? What is it?"

"But . . . if Mom dies, then what—what—happens . . ." He shut up before he started to cry.

"Oh, Cooper." She scooted closer and put a hand on his arm. "Cooper. Your mom is strong. She's not going to die."

"You don't know that!" The fury in his voice shocked him, but Vivian didn't flinch.

"You're right. I can't promise that. But she's strong. You know she's strong. Everyone is doing all they can. *She* is doing all she can."

That was the thing, though. She always did all she could. She gave herself away, over and over. She ran on empty. She burned the candles every way she could. She didn't have any reserve left. What other clichés could he use? He was afraid this virus had come for her and she had nothing left to fight it with because she'd had to fight every single damn day. And it had finally caught up to her, just when he thought she was getting a break. *She couldn't die.*

"You're lying about your cancer," he said.

She raised her eyebrows. After a pause, she sighed. "So what if I am?" Her voice sounded different . . . like it was empty. Like it was bruised. "I'm an old woman, Cooper. I lost the love of my life. Nothing feels worth it without my Jack. Why does it matter if I let this thing take me?"

Cooper wanted to throw things. Kick in the TV. Do something to hurt her.

Instead, he took a deep breath. "Fine. If being my friend isn't worth it, fuck you. Let your cancer win. I don't care."

She exhaled. She didn't look angry or even hurt. She looked . . . curious? Intrigued? "Well." She looked at him, into him, with those creepy eyes. "Well then. When you put it like *that*." She sort of smiled but was serious. She wasn't making fun of him. "So we're friends, are we?"

"*I* thought we were. And friends don't leave each other. Especially in an apocalypse."

She pointed at him. "If you are trying to keep me alive just because you need a backup if your mother dies, then fuck *you*."

He almost laughed. But he told the truth. "Maybe I was at first. But not anymore."

Vivian was silent a long time. Like, for real a long time. He looked at the digital clock, and three whole minutes went by while she thought about things. Three whole minutes was a long time for two people not to talk. But it felt okay.

Then, as the digital clock switched into the fourth minute, she said, "I'll make an appointment. I'll go to the appointment. If I do that, will you make popcorn and watch an episode with me?"

"Will you do what the doctor tells you to?"

"I can't promise that until I hear what she says. But I promise to listen and to consider it."

That was a start. And he bet he could keep bugging her. Especially if he had the guys on his side. He stood. "Okay. But while I make popcorn, will you check on my mom again?"

"Excellent idea."

They walked to the kitchen, and Vivian donned her masks. She turned to him, and he surprised himself by hugging her. He had no idea where that came from, but he hugged her like a little baby. But the thing was, she hugged him right back, like she was just as hungry for the hug. She was skinny. She'd always seemed tough to him, but hugging her, her physical body felt frail, her spine like Wren's old pop beads under his hands.

And when she went upstairs to check on his mom, he thought, *Please don't let her die.* Not Vivian *or* his mom. *Please let them live.* Why did the good people always die?

But then Vivian came downstairs right away and said to him, "We need to get her to the hospital."

CHAPTER SIXTEEN

VIVIAN

Vivian pulled up at a red light on the way to her oncologist appointment. The gray pickup truck in front of her had written in black tape across its tailgate: No Masks.

She thought about ramming right into the truck, but then she sighed, her body and energy depleted. "Just you wait, friend," she said aloud, imagining the driver watching someone *he* loved gasping for breath, fear in her eyes, having to be carried by paramedics. Vivian wanted him to experience that terror, but when the light changed and the truck turned left, she made a sound of dismay. What was this pandemic doing to her, making her wish that on anyone?

She drove forward. She didn't want to drive forward, but she would honor her promise to Cooper.

Luna had been in the hospital for three days. She was not on a respirator. Yet. But her blood-oxygen levels were too, too low. She couldn't keep any food in her. And without intervention, her fever would not stay down.

This was bad. Anxiety shot through Vivian's veins night and day. The fear in the house was palpable. She did her best to comfort Wren and Cooper, to keep them busy. She'd called both schools to let them know, so they could take the kids' worry into account in their classes.

She was doing her best to take care of Wren and her bathroom and grooming needs, marveling more and more every day at this girl's resilience and Luna's parenting. It had proven impossible to find good home health care—well, *any* home health care, much less good—during COVID, so Vivian had stepped up. They'd fallen into an easy, no-nonsense grace about it. Vivian earned big points for how she did Wren's hair. As Vivian brushed, braided, and twisted, she remembered styling Ann-Marie's hair for dance recitals.

She pulled into the parking lot of the Cancer Center, not remembering the last miles of the drive. She was early, as she always was. She parked in the back of the lot. "Use it or lose it," she and Jack used to say, of many things but especially their health, their stamina, their fitness. Keep walking. Keep limber.

She parked. Something she couldn't name buzzed around inside her, like a bee trapped in the car. It dawned on her that for the first time since Jack died, she had something to lose. She'd made a promise. She needed to keep her promise.

She *wanted* to keep it.

She walked across the lot, admiring the perfect May day. The breeze was edged with warmth, the air heavy with lilac and promise, and the rains had left the landscape lush and verdant. The hospital lawn was that bright shade of plastic Easter-basket grass. Vivian paused a moment to breathe in. To be aware. "This right here," Jack used to say. "Remember this moment, this beauty, and bring it back on a dark day."

Her eyes flooded with tears. The days were *all* so dark without him.

She donned her mask and entered the front door. Two people in scrubs were the gatekeepers to the lobby. They took her temperature and asked her a series of questions. Vivian had hoped she could delay the appointment because of Luna's COVID, but Dr. Weighall had insisted Vivian get a COVID test, and here she was with her negative result in hand. Both children had tested negative, as well as Drew and Steven.

Vivian rode the elevator up to the second floor, which vexed her. She'd have taken the stairs, but she couldn't find them and didn't want to be late. She had trouble drawing a deep breath, but she knew it wasn't COVID. Panic wrapped its icy fingers around her rib cage, which was ridiculous. *Get ahold of yourself, woman.* The receptionist on the surgical oncology floor took her insurance card and payment and told her to take a seat. The lobby was very posh, but Vivian noticed things like the coffee bar with a red Temporarily Unavailable sign—no one eating or drinking together now—and the tables empty of the glossy magazines that piqued her curiosity at most doctor's appointments. Folded tent tables sat on every other chair saying, Do not use this seat. Maintain social distancing. Only two other patients sat in the lobby.

One woman who waited wore a turban that practically shouted: "I lost my hair to chemo."

Vivian smiled at her but realized the woman couldn't see it under her mask.

She wondered if the other patients were lonely and scared, having to come in alone. She and Jack used to attend all of each other's appointments. She remembered her occasional impatience with predementia Jack, what a grumpy, melodramatic baby he could be when he was sick or injured. Were all men so ridiculous? With the dementia, he hadn't *known* he was sick and so mostly remained his jovial self.

Her missing him was nearly unbearable.

Vivian's reading glasses fogged up with her mask on, so she stared out the window until her name was called. Then she waited in an exam room with no window in another of those absurd little robes that never tied properly. Honestly. How hard *was* it, for the love of God?

When the doctor came in, Vivian was pleased to see that Dr. Weighall was a young woman, but not *too* young. The future was female, as they said. She liked to see women in powerful positions. She trusted women more. Dr. Weighall had an open, pleasant face—at least what Vivian could see of it. An assistant was with her, but Vivian didn't catch her name. And an observing student of some kind. Vivian's thoughts raced, and she couldn't concentrate.

There were pleasantries, of course, and the obligatory talk about the virus and the masks, but then Dr. Weighall got right to it: "Based on the biopsy and images, I recommend a bilateral mastectomy and chemotherapy."

Those words slammed the air from Vivian's lungs. The very first image that popped into her head was having to tell Cooper, "I'm sorry, but I just can't do that."

Dr. Weighall talked on about the urgency, the severity, the spread. Lots of terms Vivian felt she should write down in the notebook she'd brought, but the only thing she wrote was *mastectomy*. As if she'd forget that.

"This is an aggressive cancer that's already spread."

White noise intensified in her brain. The noise was as loud as the Oxycodone pills used to be. Vivian realized, with a start, that she hadn't thought of them today. Or yesterday. How many days had passed without her constant awareness of them?

"Mrs. Laurent?"

Vivian saw that Dr. Weighall was waiting for her to speak. Had she asked her a question?

"I'm sorry," Vivian said. "This is all . . . a lot to take in."

"Of course it is. Do you have any questions?"

Oh, so many. Where did she begin? Why did her husband have to get Alzheimer's? Why did a lively young girl have to be burdened with cerebral palsy? Why did Luna have to be struck down with yet another challenge, another fight? Why couldn't that father see what a gem his son was and lift up and cherish that boy?

"Mrs. Laurent?"

"Couldn't we just remove the tumor?" Vivian asked. "Do a lumpectomy?"

Dr. Weighall said, "The cancer is not confined to the tumor you can feel. It has spread."

Yes, yes, yes. You've told me that already. I need to focus. "And just a mastectomy won't do it? Does there have to be chemo?"

"Some lymph nodes are affected. This is aggressive. We need to stop it everywhere, even places we may not be able to see."

Vivian thought a moment. She respected that the doctor let her, didn't fill the silence. Very few people could do that. Luna could do that. So could her boy.

Vivian cleared her throat. "So. I'm just asking. What . . . what if I do nothing?"

The doctor's brows furrowed. "I'm sorry?"

"What if I choose not to have surgery or chemotherapy?"

Even a mask could not hide the doctor's expression of horror. Vivian had to hand it to her—the shock was brief, just a flash, before she composed herself. "It is the patient's choice, of course. Always. And I know chemotherapy is not pleasant, but there have been vast improvements. If you were, say, ninety, I might be all right with that choice, but you're only seventy-four."

Soon to be seventy-five. Vivian knew the boys were planning a little party, which filled her with ridiculous anticipation.

When Vivian didn't respond, Dr. Weighall went on. "If that is your decision, then I'd like to run tests and imaging every three months. I doubt your insurance would cover that."

Vivian exhaled. "Money's not the issue. I just wondered."

Dr. Weighall leaned forward. "Doing nothing is not an option."

Didn't you just say that it was my choice?

"Unfortunately, the kind of cancer you have, and its spread, makes treatment urgent. I'd encourage you to schedule surgery soon."

"Even with COVID?"

Dr. Weighall nodded. "Is that your concern? Are you worried about the virus?"

Vivian waved her hand, dismissing that. She'd just hoped she could stall longer. She thought of Cooper. Of the way he'd said, "If being my friend isn't worth it." "All right, then. Let's talk. What do I do first?"

Vivian left more than an hour later, laden with brochures, booklets, and information and a pink tote bag full of pink items: a pink-ribbon travel mug, a pink-ribbon blanket, pink-ribbon socks, a pink-ribbon notepad. These were all courtesy of the Pink Ribbon Girls. Vivian knew this group did a great amount of good work for cancer patients, but she found all the pink a bit silly, as if she'd just joined some ladies' club and this was her swag bag from a luncheon. This was not a club she wished to join. She tossed the tote bag into the back seat with more force than necessary.

The armload of information she set in the passenger seat. Was she really going to do this? Dr. Weighall kept saying she didn't want to rush her, but really the doctor *was* rushing her. The rush should scare Vivian, she knew, but instead it made her stubborn.

She'd promised Cooper, but there were considerations. She despised being dependent on others, but she would definitely need help.

Steven and Drew had helped her so many times already.

There were no closer friends, especially in a pandemic, and no other family.

Except Ann-Marie.

"You're ridiculous," Vivian said aloud and opened one of the brochures against the steering wheel. Reconstruction. Would she bother? She read about expanders and fills. Oh, good God, that sounded wretched. No, at her age, there'd be no other men. Why bother when you'd had the best? And it was men who loved breasts. Well, Jack certainly had. He'd loved hers with a fervor. And, actually—she gently touched her left breast—she loved her breasts, too. The idea of amputating a part of her body, of mutilating herself, filled her with a surreal sense of horror. *This is really happening.* She shoved the brochure on reconstruction into the trash pocket of her car door. She'd be fine with prosthetics. That assistant had said something about how hot prosthetics could be. Well, then, in warm weather, she'd go flat-chested. Who cared?

She had a sudden memory of Ann-Marie as a child, grinding a Barbie doll on the driveway to scrape off her breasts. "They just get in the way. I don't want them."

Vivian looked at the bright-blue sky and took time to record this moment. This was a moment that would change her life yet again. Everything would be different. A decade from now, she'd joke with Cooper, "I looked at that perfect periwinkle-blue sky and thought, 'Well, I made a promise to that boy.'"

A decade. Would Cooper still be in her life? Would Luna and Wren? Oh, how she hoped so.

Doing nothing was not an option.

There was more she could do.

As she drove toward home, she passed a yard sign that said, Do SOMETHING—what people had shouted at the Ohio governor after the mass shooting in the Oregon District.

When Vivian saw that sign, she thought: *I haven't done enough.* She hadn't done enough to let Jack know how very, very much she'd loved him. She hadn't done enough to help her daughter. She hadn't used her privilege to help lift other people. She'd stayed in her bubble. She hadn't always done all she could. Could she now? Could everything be different from this point?

At the next intersection, she made an illegal U-turn and headed for Sycamore Place.

When she pulled into the front parking lot, she saw her friend Martin standing on the asphalt, looking up at the front of the majestic redbrick building. She parked and watched him. He was still as a statue, face lifted to the sky. When she got out of her car and shut the door, he didn't even react to the sound. He looked up at the fourth floor, up at Memory Care. Where Vera Jane, his wife, now lived.

Vivian leaned against her car and looked up at the empty windows. Her eyes burned thinking of the brief time Jack had lived on the locked Memory Care floor. Spouses were not allowed to live with the residents who needed memory care. Being separated from him had hurt worse than losing him altogether. She'd gone upstairs every single day, spent most of every day with him, but it broke her heart to see his bewilderment, to see the number of times he'd tried to sign himself out at the elevator, always listing their old address, not their current apartment. He would write that he was leaving to go take care of his wife.

She'd only admitted him there because he kept leaving their apartment. She'd wake and he'd be gone, barefoot, in pajamas, wandering the neighborhood. Because they lived in Independent Living, no code or alarm stopped him from walking right out into the snow or rain or dead of night. Her worry kept her from sleep, starting at every sound, listening for him to leave their bed. She'd been haggard, gray-skinned, with bags under her eyes like purple bruises. Jack had been missing once for three eternal hours, and the terror she felt—of harm coming to him, of someone finding him and being cruel, abusing him in some way—made her finally consent to move him upstairs.

But other than knowing he wasn't crossing into traffic barefooted, she hated it. She hated sleeping without him. She hated being apart from him. She hated not knowing how he felt and what was happening to him every single minute.

"Martin?" she said.

He turned, at first irritated at the distraction, but then did a double-take. "Vivian!" He pulled the face mask up from where it had been bunched at his neck. He returned his gaze to the window. "I called the nurses' station, and someone's going to bring Vera Jane to the window."

Vivian touched her heart, as if to ease the ache. She donned her own mask and approached him but stayed six feet away. It was awkward, strange. They were both huggers.

"You know I can't go up there anymore, right? No visitors at all on the fourth floor."

"Oh, Martin." Vivian's eyes burned. "You haven't seen her? For how long?"

"Fifty-three days."

Sweet Jesus. Vivian knew Vera Jane was much like Jack, unable to use a telephone, much less email. Not seeing them meant zero contact. No way of knowing they were okay at all. Relying on the reports of beleaguered and overworked nurses and aides.

"It would be longer than fifty-three days except I've gone up there twice. Just went in and found her. I *had* to. I had to see her and hug her. I know they're trying to keep them safe. I *know* that. But it's killing me, Vivian. I feel like I've failed her. When I went up there, she said, 'Why did you leave me?'" His voice broke.

Vivian longed to comfort him, to hug him. The space between them yawned wide. "Oh, Martin. I'm so sorry."

"She begged me to take her home. I want to. I do. I want to move her to—Oh, there she is!"

Vivian's neck ached as she looked up, past the grand balcony and rippling flag, to the fourth-floor windows. Vera Jane appeared at the window, an aide behind her. Vivian recognized Malik. Vera Jane put her hands on the glass. Malik pointed. She looked down.

Martin pulled his mask down and waved. "Oh, my love. I miss you." He spoke as if she were right there, not shouting, but as if she were standing as close as Vivian and could hear him. "I love you. I love you so much. I'm so sorry I can't see you."

Oh, wave to him, Vivian begged her. *Please give him something.*

But instead, Vera Jane pounded on the glass with her fists. She looked like she screamed.

"No," Martin whispered. "No, no, no. It's okay, my love. It's okay."

After a moment, Malik took Vera Jane's arms and turned her from the window. They saw him point to something, distracting her. He shot one sympathetic glance over his shoulder.

"No," Martin said. He kept staring up. "No."

Martin sobbed into his hands over his face, and Vivian kept repeating that she was sorry. She waited while he cried. When he stopped, he blew his nose into a handkerchief. He pulled his mask back up and said, "Well. That backfired. I won't do that to her again."

He turned to Vivian and said, "Be grateful Jack passed before this pandemic."

She blinked away the tears hovering in her lashes.

"I just don't want her to get it and have to die alone up there," Martin said.

Vivian knew what *it* was. "I heard poor Dennis died."

Martin moaned. "They were moving his stuff yesterday. Clearing it out."

"Do you know what happened to Ox?"

Martin raised his bushy eyebrows. "I have no idea. I . . . I didn't even think of that cat. I haven't seen it." His face softened. "I hope it's all right."

"If it's still in there, do you want it?"

"Oh, hell no," Martin said. "That's the last thing I need."

Good. She wanted Ox. She could not explain why, but she wanted him.

She said goodbye to Martin and entered the building. All the furniture in what used to be the lobby was gone, and green *X*s were taped to the carpet six feet apart. An unfamiliar woman sat at a desk behind a giant Plexiglas shield, checking people in. Vivian waited behind two employees she'd never seen. From their scrubs, she knew they were hired from agencies and were not Sycamore Place employees. She'd always felt disappointed when Jack was cared for by an agency aide and not a face he knew and trusted.

Vivian stepped up to the desk. The woman asked her name, which she gave, and took her temperature. She told the woman, "I'm going to apartment 232."

"I'm so sorry, but there are no visitors allowed right now. Is there something you'd like us to deliver to a resident?"

"232 is my apartment."

The woman looked confused. "Where were you? Did you go somewhere?"

Vivian tried to explain, but the woman became more confused. "You'll have to quarantine for two weeks, since you left the premises. Let me call—"

"She's all right."

Oh, thank God, Em, her favorite receptionist, came to her aid. Em gave a brief version to the woman: "She moved out right before the pandemic but is here to pick up some stuff."

The woman's eyes blinked rapidly above her mask, but since there were now four other people in line, she shrugged and let Vivian wander away with Em, who was dressed, as usual, like she was attending a cocktail party.

"What are you doing here? You know you can't just come in and out."

"I know. I'm sorry. I need to make arrangements to clear out the apartment. Will you allow movers inside?"

"Nobody's allowed inside. You have to hire the guys from here. Or wait."

"All right, then."

Em leaned close, earrings jangling, and whispered, "Is it true Luna is living with you?"

Vivian's spine stiffened. "She's renting from me, yes."

"Well, that's a little unusual."

"I can rent to whoever I damn well please."

Em raised her hands. "I didn't say you couldn't. But how is she? She's been out awhile."

"She's still in the hospital." Real fear shot through Vivian's belly. "We're worried."

Vivian noticed a flyer on the desk. A photo of that sassy-faced, stout tuxedo cat. *"Ox's owner, Dennis, passed away, and the family is looking to find a home for his beloved companion. Please see the front desk if you're interested."*

Vivian pointed. "The family won't take the cat?"

"The kids don't want him."

"I do," Vivian said.

Em's eyes rounded.

"Has anyone expressed interest?"

Em shook her head.

"I'll take him right now."

"Okay. Good. Good. Just . . . keep your mask on and don't go anywhere else. Oh. Are you going to your own apartment?"

"No, I actually came to see about Ox. That was my mission."

Em tilted her head. "I miss you, Vivian."

"Why, thank you. I miss you, too." Vivian thought about blurting, *I have to have a mastectomy and chemo.* How strange that she made it sound like her only mission today was to pick up this cat.

"Dennis's apartment's unlocked. Have at it."

Two and a half months had passed since Vivian had been in this building. She felt like an intruder. Her pulse raced, and she liked it. She felt alive. She realized she *wanted* to be alive. She took the stairs, as she always did—use it or lose it—and passed no one. This was normally a bustling place. In the past, at times she'd been irritated at always having to smile and chat with people when she only wanted to get her damn mail or some coffee.

When she emerged from the stairwell, she looked up and down each hall. No one. She looked forward to telling Cooper she felt like a character on *The Walking Dead* out on a foraging run. What would you find, searching these apartments? She grinned behind her mask. Lots of stool softener, vitamins, and fiber. Magnifying glasses. Dentures. Hard candy like butterscotch.

She paused outside one door. A neon-yellow sign in the shape of a stop sign said, See nurse before entering. That's all. It didn't say COVID-19. She looked at the name tag. Florence Burkes. Vivian remembered a tiny, sharp-tongued woman with a buzz cut who was an excellent bridge partner. Who was always on the balcony and wanted to chat when Vivian was reading. Poor Florence. Vivian stood outside that door and closed her eyes. *Pull through this, Florence. Pull through.* Florence loved to talk about her grandkids, and Vivian recalled two surly, unattractive teenagers who talked too loudly. *Pull through for them.*

She opened her eyes and kept walking. Outside Dennis's door hung the same yellow sign, even though his name tag was already gone. Vivian opened the door and stepped in. She smelled the litter box even through her mask. "Ox?" she called.

Nothing.

The tiny living room was empty except for some boxes and a recliner. Trash littered the floor—some cat toys, a pen, a ring from a milk top—where the couch had been. The boxes were marked "keep" and "trash." In the "trash" box, she saw framed pictures. She pulled one out of Dennis with Ox standing on his shoulders. Another was a black-and-white photo of Dennis and a smiling, plump woman on their wedding day. He'd been a widower when Vivian had met him.

Who the hell threw away photos? What kind of monsters were these kids? But . . . Vivian realized, maybe Dennis had been a horrible father. Who knew? Maybe the kids had reason to have never been here. Or maybe . . . she thought of their own circumstances. Of how they'd learned never to ask about others' children here unless they volunteered first.

The frame for the Dennis and Ox photo was a hideous glittery thing. Vivian opened the frame and slid the photo out and into her purse. She turned from the box and was about to call the cat again when she saw him.

Ox sat in the hallway, staring at her with dull green eyes. He watched her as if she were someone else here to take more of his person away.

"Oh, Ox. Oh, sweet boy." The cat was as wide as he was tall, a walking footstool, from the food Dennis gave him from the table.

Vivian lowered herself to the floor with a groan and reached out a hand to him. He blinked and kept staring, his expression one of betrayal.

Vivian remembered this ridiculous cat in the dining room. He wasn't supposed to be in there, but everyone knew Ox could open doors and that Dennis never closed them. Ox never arrived right at the beginning of dinner. He'd let Dennis have most of his meal, and then the cat would stroll in and go straight to Dennis's table. Vivian remembered pointing him out to Drew and Steven when they joined her and Jack for dinner, and the next time they came, the boys looked for the cat and anticipated his arrival with glee.

Some prisses, Florence included, had scrunched up their noses, but mostly people loved Dennis and Ox. Dennis would give the cat chicken, fish, mashed potatoes, ice cream, cake. The cat was a walking hardened artery.

Here, in the empty apartment, she crooned to him, made kissing noises, and called his name. He took a step, then sat again. Vivian gazed into those sad eyes. "I lost someone, too," she said. "Maybe we could help each other?" When he stood and came to her, she scratched his forehead, under his chin, his ears, scratching however he turned his head.

In the dining room, Ox would stand, front paws on Dennis's leg, until Dennis invited him to his lap. Dennis fed him from a spoon. Ox never ate off the plate or table, and he never grabbed.

Ox began to purr, louder and louder, and flung himself on the floor, letting Vivian rub his copious belly. He rolled over, and she scratched along his back, trying to feel a spine through his heft, and ran her nails down his tail. He chirruped and purred and writhed. Poor boy had been hungry for some touch.

Vivian took a deep breath, working hard to ignore the ammonia smell of cat pee. Was she really going to do this? Right before a major surgery? She and Jack had always had dogs, just the one cat Cooper. Because Ann-Marie was allergic to cats.

Cooper the cat had come into their lives when they were ready to acknowledge they'd essentially lost their daughter. Oh, Ann-Marie, the asterisk on everything in Vivian's life.

"You want to get out of here?" she asked Ox.

He purred and rolled over again, then back.

"Let's go, big boy." Vivian climbed to her feet, wincing at an ache in her hip. She looked around for a carrier, but everything was gone. She was certainly *not* taking that foul litter box. The food she found on the kitchen counter was cheap crap. "A fresh new start, okay?"

"Mrrrp," he answered.

Ox followed her into the hallway and walked beside her like a dog trained to heel. When she stepped into the stairwell, he plodded down the metal stairs like a champ, and she chuckled at how much noise he made on the steps.

She opened the door to the lobby. The line of people checking in was even longer. No one paid any attention to her as she walked past the line, just as on that fateful night she'd left. At the door, she stooped and hefted the cat into her arms. "Oof. Holy Hannah, you're a chunky one."

She carried him to her car, where he sat upright in the passenger seat, looking out the window as they drove to a pet store. She hauled him inside and put him in a cart, where he sat in the child's seat. The employees oohed and aahed behind their masks and helped her select a collar for him, then engraved a little metal fish tag with his name and her phone number. She got a litter box, litter, and a variety of healthy foods. She let them talk her into some toys and treats; then they helped her load it all into her car. Several times, she thought of telling them, *I have aggressive cancer. I have to have a mastectomy and chemo.*

Vivian talked to Ox as she drove home. "You know what? You are my seventy-fifth birthday gift to myself. And you want to know why?"

He stared at her, waiting for her answer.

"Because this will not be the day I found out I had to have horrible surgery. This will be the day I got a cat. And a very fine cat at that."

Ox was silent. But after a moment, as if he'd thought it all over, he said, "Mrrrp," and lay down, stretching one giant paw to rest on her thigh.

CHAPTER SEVENTEEN

WREN

Wren rolled down the ramp into the garden with fat Ox riding in her lap. She smiled. She had a secret. A big secret. And today, her wish might come true.

Mom was home from the hospital! Mom had finally agreed that they could stay here to the end of the pandemic! School was over for the summer! And Wren had a cat!

Mom still wasn't well. That scared Wren. Mom was tired all the time. She could hardly do anything without having to sit down and rest. She always had a headache. She lay in a dark room a lot and listened to classical music. Sometimes she couldn't find the right words. Wren didn't like that it reminded her of Grammy forgetting to remember. Or Mr. Jack. Mom said it wasn't like that. She called it "COVID brain." Wren wished Mom would get well fast like Dad had. Dad kept telling them that COVID was no big deal.

Wren had wished Mom home from the hospital. Mom was going to get well faster here at home. Wren had wished for this to be their home. "Home," she said out loud.

"Mrrp?" Ox asked.

She had a cat! Wren had wished for a pet! And every single wish had come true. She felt like her magic was stronger here, in this house, where she was more connected to Ann-Marie.

So she'd made the next big wish. And today was the day. It was her secret, and she wasn't telling anyone. She put everything she could into it—she'd wished on the first robin she saw that spring, she'd found a lucky penny and put it in her left shoe, she made the wish as she fell asleep, and . . . She stopped her chair. Ox jumped down, and Wren leaned forward to touch the forget-me-nots in the shade garden. To seal the deal, she closed her eyes and whispered, "Touch blue and your wish will come true."

Ox was allowed outside with someone, but not alone. He never left to go wandering into the woods or into the road. He stayed right by them. Especially Vivian. Or Wren.

He'd been really sad for the first couple of weeks and sat with his face in a corner most of the time. Vivian said he was grieving, and they just needed to give him lots of love. When Wren could get someone to lift him for her, she held him like a baby and wheeled him around in her lap. This morning, he'd jumped up into her lap when she called him. That was a sign.

Today was Vivian's seventy-fifth birthday. That was another reason why this day was so great. It was the perfect day to put her next wish into motion.

Wren and Ox were in the garden to pick bouquets. That had been her mom's idea. Vivian liked to always have fresh flowers in the house. Mom had said how lovely it was that Vivian was always changing the flowers in her room while she was sick. Mom was *still* sick. When would she get well?

It was still "earlyish in the season," as Vivian said, so not everything was blooming yet, but enough were to make some pretty bouquets, and Vivian and Drew both said Wren had an eye for it. When Drew said that, Wren felt light and floaty. She always thought maybe Drew didn't like her. He was harder to know than Steven.

When Vivian thought she was selling the house—before Wren's wish—she'd put little wooden labels next to every plant in the garden so the next owner would know what everything was. Because of those labels, Wren knew the names of what she picked. Some names made perfect sense, like bee balm and red-hot pokers and foxglove. Foxglove had to be the most perfectly named flower ever. Wren pictured a little red fox in a suit—one actually visited this garden early some mornings (not in a suit, of course)—wearing the petals as gloves, like something in the Beatrix Potter books she'd had as a little kid. But some names made no sense at all. Why would a flower so pretty and delicate be called spiderwort?

She selected Stella D'Oro lilies, some purple phlox, and her favorites, Bells-of-Ireland. Vivian had declared it "a damn miracle the rabbits hadn't stolen them. They eat them every summer. Anything I start from seed." Speaking of starting from seed, a couple of zinnias the rabbits had missed had bloomed, and Wren snipped those, too. No one would even notice that Wren cut some of the overflowing snowball or Pinky Winky hydrangea blooms.

She looked around for Ox and saw him hunkered down, butt twitching. She followed his gaze to a rabbit nibbling among faded primrose. Ox was no hunter, but this might be fun. She sat still and watched him. His tail slashed back and forth in his excitement, and she knew the rabbit saw him but wasn't afraid.

Ox pounced, but the rabbit scooted off and hid among some purple salvia. Ox turned in a circle, a very uncool sort of "where'd it go?" She laughed.

He looked at her and meowed.

"C'mon, Mr. Chonk," she said. He trotted after her. She balanced the heap of flowers across her thighs and motored back toward the ramp, but a wonderful smell stopped her. Deep, bright purple blooms shaped like upside-down ice-cream cones. The label said "butterfly bush." The bush stood taller than Wren in her chair. These blooms were new, like they'd opened overnight. The aroma was heaven, soft and perfumy. She clipped some of these as well.

More amazing smells awaited them as the cat followed her back into the kitchen.

Cooper was making the birthday cake. The chocolate smelled a-ma-zing. Wren noticed more and more smells these days because Mom still couldn't smell. Mom had tried to make dinner one night, joking that she needed to contribute around here, and she'd burned the black-bean burgers. She hadn't even realized she'd burned them at first because she couldn't smell the smoke. She'd shrieked when she'd set off Vivian's smoke alarm.

Everyone kept saying it was dangerous not to be able to smell. Wren thought it would be nice not to smell Cooper's farts, or Ox's poop in his litter box, or Drew's armpits when he came back from working at the flower shop. But then she thought about fires and everyone talked about gas leaks, which just gave her another thing to worry about, like she didn't have enough to be afraid of already.

Wren lifted her flowers to the kitchen island.

"Whoa, whoa, whoa," Cooper yelled. "You can't put those there! Don't mess up the cake."

Wren rolled her eyes, but she scooted the pile of flowers to the other end. Ox leaped onto a barstool to watch.

Cooper didn't tell the cat to get down. He'd learned, just like they all had, that Ox was "exceedingly polite." That's what Vivian said. Cooper called the cat Ox the Box.

The cake smelled like the brownies Cooper used to make back in their apartment, but it looked really sad and plain, just two round chocolate cakes on wire thingies.

"They just came out of the oven," Cooper said, like she'd said that out loud. "They have to cool before I do the rest." He had a bunch of printed papers around him and kept looking at his phone. He'd been planning the cake forever, watching videos and TV shows. She knew it was going to be something chocolate and salted caramel. He wore a full apron and had a smudge of some kind of brown powder on his cheek. He looked . . . really happy.

That made Wren happy. Today might turn out to be *perfect*.

She practically shivered with excitement about her secret. She looked at the clock and groaned. They had five whole hours before the party. This day was going to last *forever*.

Six hours later, Wren watched the clock, but this time with anger and dread. The party had started. Everyone was here . . . except for her surprise.

Wren wore a summery dress with sunflowers on it. Vivian had curled Wren's hair, and Wren had put on lip gloss. Mom had showered and washed her own hair, which made Wren glad, then had rested all day for this. Mom had told them all earlier, "I'm determined to be at this party."

Wren had tried to get Mom to wear a dress, too, but Mom wore yoga pants and a soft pink sweatshirt that fell off one shoulder. That shoulder looked bony. She'd put on a little makeup, though, and looked really pretty even if she looked fragile and tired.

Balloons and flowers filled the kitchen. Even though there was a formal dining room, they always ate around the kitchen island. The kitchen was Wren's favorite room in the house, all white and bright and full of life. It's where things were always happening.

Cooper had worked on the cake all afternoon and had rushed away to shower and dress right before the party was starting. He always did everything last minute! She didn't want him to miss the surprise. But he made it.

The guest of honor looked like a queen. Vivian wore makeup for maybe the first time Wren had ever seen her wear it. The eyeliner made her eyes even bluer. With her white hair pulled up in a twist, her neck looked like a swan's, and she even wore a necklace. She wore a blue dress that matched her eyes. She'd been in the garden a lot lately, and her skin glowed with sun. She looked so happy, even though she had cancer and she had to have a major surgery next week. Wren had had plenty of surgeries herself and knew how scary they were. She'd had surgery on her Achilles tendons to keep her from walking on her tippy-toes, way back in second grade when she still walked. The most recent surgery was to have her abductor muscles released.

Wren's heart sank as they all decided it was time to eat. *No! Not yet!* She looked at the clock, not knowing where to direct her frustration. The grown-ups had all been drinking their grown-up drinks, something Drew had shaken in a weird container with ice and basil from the garden. Why couldn't they keep drinking and laughing for longer?

But no, they were sitting down, and pretty soon they'd notice that Wren had set an extra place. Sure enough, Cooper said, "Doofus, can't you count?"

Wren laughed and said, "Oops!" but she knew she sounded really fake.

Mom took the extra place setting and moved it over to the counter. *No, no!* At least it was all close by and would be easy to grab. Wren saw Cooper squint at her.

Ox sat on a barstool, upright and formal, watching everyone.

Cooper served the salad first. Drew and Steven helped him put one in front of everyone. The greens and the cherry tomatoes were from the garden. Little slivers of some really good cheese looked super fancy on top of each salad.

"This dressing is lovely," Vivian said. "What is it?"

Why was Cooper blushing? He said, "It's a cilantro lime vinaigrette. The cilantro's from the garden."

"He even made the croutons," Steven said.

"Seriously?" Mom said. "Hon, these look so good."

Everyone fussed over Cooper. Cooper never got attention except for getting in trouble, so that was okay. But just wait. Wait until they saw what she had planned.

The doorbell rang, and a crazy mix of emotions twisted inside Wren. *Finally!* She rolled back fast, hitting Steven's chair, jostling his water glass. "I'll get it!"

"Who on earth?" Vivian asked.

Wren saw Cooper shaking his head, looking at her with disappointment.

Wren rolled to the back door and flung it open.

Then . . . she blinked. This—this wasn't who she'd expected.

A woman stood there. Wearing a black face mask. She held a small wrapped gift in front of her.

"Who is it?" Vivian called.

"I—I don't know." But she looked oddly familiar.

The woman looked down at Wren and said, in a warm and friendly voice, "Who are you?"

"I'm Wren."

"My name's Ann-Marie."

The whole house tilted sideways. Wren couldn't breathe. She couldn't speak.

Ann-Marie was alive.

And she was here.

Wren felt as if she were rising above the people in the room, hovering in the air, looking down at herself, looking at the woman in the doorway.

"What the hell did you do?" Cooper hissed at Wren.

But Wren could not make any words work in her mouth. She stared at Ann-Marie, but Ann-Marie didn't look at Wren at all. She looked only at her mother, Vivian, standing by her chair at the kitchen island.

Ann-Marie walked past Wren, toward Vivian. Wren saw in everyone's eyes that they thought she'd somehow brought Ann-Marie here.

Had she?

Ann-Marie said, "Happy birthday, Mama," and handed the box to Vivian.

Vivian looked like Wren felt—her mouth open and eyes wide. She blinked at the gift like she'd never seen a box before. She set it on the table and continued staring at Ann-Marie.

Ann-Marie lifted her gaze but noticed Ox, sitting on his stool. Even with the mask on, you could tell the cat surprised her.

Wren's head swirled. She actually felt dizzy. She wanted Ann-Marie to take her mask off so she could see what she really looked like, but Wren could tell she was pretty. Did they still look alike? Ann-Marie's black hair shone in really pretty curls. She wore a simple black dress with a sunflower border on the bottom and one sunflower off-center at the neck. Wren remembered she was wearing sunflowers, too, and her face flushed hot.

Ann-Marie looked at the boys and said, "Drew. Steven."

Steven nodded. Drew did not. Everyone was standing. Mom sat first. Cooper sat beside her, and Wren heard him ask, "You okay?" Mom looked really tired again, like she'd deflated.

Vivian said, "Ann-Marie, these are my friends Luna, Cooper, and Wren. This is my daughter, Ann-Marie."

Drew and Steven whispered something, and both dug around and pulled masks from their pockets. When they put on face masks, Wren saw Ann-Marie's neck turn bright red.

"Oh, yes," Vivian said. "We've been a pod together. That's probably a good idea." From the basket on the kitchen counter, she selected a blue-and-white mask that complemented her dress. She set the basket on the island next to Mom.

Cooper handed one to Mom, then to Wren. As he brought it to Wren, he whispered, "What the hell, Wren?"

Wren still struggled to find words. She couldn't defend herself. She still couldn't breathe right. Her pulse raced.

"So," Vivian said. "How did my little friend Wren manage to rustle you up when even my private investigator couldn't?"

Ann-Marie shook her head. She looked at Wren. "I've never seen her before in my life. She didn't—I—it's your birthday."

"Oh. I believe I have a birthday every year."

Ann-Marie's shoulders slumped. "Yes. You do." She took a deep breath. "I saw Dad's obituary."

Vivian turned around and sat back at her place at the island.

Ox jumped down and went to Vivian. The cat stood with his front paws on her leg.

Drew said, "You should go," to Ann-Marie.

Wren almost gasped. Drew was so *mean*.

Ann-Marie's eyes were hard and icy as she stared back at Drew. "I will if she wants me to."

Wren held her breath. She'd wished for this moment so hard and so many times. But not right now, not right here. This was messing up Wren's secret plan. *Go. Please go.*

"Fine. Stay. I can get my once-a-decade report on how you've been," Vivian said, petting Ox's head, not looking at her daughter.

Ann-Marie raised her head, and the look she gave Drew scared Wren. It was like she'd won something.

Ann-Marie's voice softened, and she looked at the rest of the guests. "There's some things I really need to talk to my mom about."

"Oh, hell no," Drew said.

Steven shook his head. "We're not leaving."

Vivian looked at Ann-Marie and said, "I'm having a birthday party. And you will not ruin it. If you'd like to stay, you may. But you don't get to sweep in here and change my plans or dictate what happens next."

"Okay," Ann-Marie said. "Thank you. For letting me stay."

Vivian pointed to the counter. "There's an extra place setting right there, if you'd like to eat."

No, no, no. That isn't for her. Wren looked at the clock again, frantic. She couldn't believe her luck when the doorbell rang again. *Finally.*

"Oh shit," Drew said. "You brought backup already?"

"I'll get it!" Wren said. This was really happening. Why was it all happening at once?

"No," Drew said, blocking Wren.

Vivian looked at Ann-Marie. "If you brought anyone with you, I'm not comfortable with them coming in. They're not welcome."

"I didn't. I'm here alone."

"Oh, no one's outside, casing the place?" Drew said. Wren had never seen Drew be so nasty. His eyes shone with hatred.

"I deserve that. But no. Things are different this time."

The doorbell rang again.

Steven looked. "It's some guy. I've never seen him before."

Drew looked, too. "Some loser. Sure that's not some friend of yours?"

"No!" Wren cried. "Let him in. That's my dad!"

CHAPTER EIGHTEEN

LUNA

Wren's announcement kicked Luna in the gut. *Oh no. Oh, honey. No. No.*

Into the stunned silence, Cooper said, "No, you didn't."

Wren looked at Luna, her eyes wide, her face so earnest, so hopeful . . . so misguided.

Vivian laughed. Really laughed. Like church giggles, and once she got going, she didn't stop. She laughed so hard, she cried. Luna *loved* Vivian for seeing the absurdity, even though the others were staring at her in alarm.

The doorbell rang again.

"Ohhhh," Vivian said, catching her breath and wiping under her eyes. "Well, let him in. Don't leave him standing out there forever."

"Vivian," Luna said. "He doesn't have to come in."

But Vivian waved her hand at Luna as if dismissing her worry.

"*Who* is this?" Ann-Marie asked.

Everyone ignored her.

When Drew opened the door, Cal looked pissed. Luna braced herself to feel some emotional response, some little crumb of the love she'd once felt for him. He looked good. Luna could objectively register that he was handsome. But . . . that's all. What was he thinking, coming here like this? Especially after divorce proceedings had officially begun and he'd told her he didn't "need" any custody. He wouldn't even get it together to make sure he had any claim to his own children.

Wren yelled, "Dad!" and he bent to hug her. The hug was awkward because he carried things. Oh God. He had *presents*. Wren had invited him specifically to the party. She'd coached him.

"Hey, everybody, this is my dad," Wren said, hanging on to his elbow.

"I'm Cal." He wore tattered jeans but a nice button-up shirt he'd probably borrowed from his brother. He'd tried. But, damn it, he always put his rare effort into the wrong things.

Wren rushed into introductions, talking too fast and too manically. *Oh, baby girl.* Luna alternated between wanting to shake her and wanting to hug her.

Vivian stood and shook Cal's hand. She then squeezed Wren's shoulder, as if to tell her to *calm down*. Vivian's eyes told Wren it was all right. She wasn't mad. Thank God. Luna wondered what her own eyes showed.

"So this is who you invited?" Vivian asked.

Wren nodded.

Luna wished Wren *had* invited Ann-Marie. "Cal," Luna said. "Why are you here?"

"Because my daughter invited me."

Rage flashed through her, but she swallowed it. "I mean, why didn't you call?"

"I figured I didn't need permission to come see my daughter when she asked me to."

Luna caught a glimpse of Cooper. He sat frozen and looked miserable. This had been his night every bit as much as Vivian's. What a mess.

"You need to put on a mask," Luna said. "And maybe we should go outside? With all these extra . . ." Damn it, she didn't want to call Ann-Marie an extra person.

"Nah. I already had it," Cal said.

"Cal." Luna made her voice a warning.

"If you're going to stay," Vivian said, "I ask you to wear a mask like everyone else."

Thank God for Vivian. In so many ways.

"I don't have one."

"Oh, I have several," Vivian said. "These are freshly laundered." She picked up a stack of masks and pulled one out to hand to Cal.

It was pink.

Luna knew she was safe smiling behind her mask. She couldn't make eye contact with Cooper or she'd get the church giggles herself.

Cal hesitated. But he took it. He put it on.

Wren exhaled when he did. *Oh, my poor girl.* She'd obviously wanted this so badly, and it was a disaster. Her daughter's sorrow depleted the last dregs of Luna's energy.

Luna's head throbbed while Vivian took gracious control of the situation. "What do you think, gentlemen, should we go outside?"

"No!" Cooper sounded desperate, gesturing to the kitchen, to everything for the meal spread out on the counters.

"It's ungodly hot out there," Cal said.

Shut up, Luna wanted to beg him. *We're debating going outside because of you. You don't get a say in this.*

They discussed options. The only table outside was inaccessible to Wren. Cooper looked like he might weep at the idea of people holding their plates in their laps. Luna could see: his dad was ruining everything he'd planned.

Steven and Drew opened all the windows, even though the AC was on. They cranked the ceiling fan and brought up a box fan from the basement.

Steven got out another place setting. Wren whispered to Cooper to move, but he wouldn't, and Luna saw that Wren wanted Cal and Luna to sit next to each other, like she was setting her parents up on a date. What would Wren say if she knew Luna had filed for divorce? The only empty seat was between Wren and Steven. Before Cal sat down, though, he approached Luna's chair. *No, no, no.* She wanted to disappear. He hugged her, but she didn't stand. He kissed her cheek. He and Cooper only lifted chins at each other.

Ox returned to Vivian's side, standing, the size of a toddler, his front arms on her thighs.

"Well," Vivian said, rubbing the cat's ears. "This is my birthday party, and we're just going to keep calm and carry on, aren't we? I, for one, am so excited about my birthday meal."

"Oh! Happy birthday!" Cal handed two unwrapped packages to Vivian. A rose in a plastic tube and what looked like a necklace that was a flower. "Wren told me you like flowers."

These were gifts you'd get in a gas station. Luna recognized the necklace. He'd given Wren that same one two years ago. She'd worn it every day until it broke. He hadn't wrapped Vivian's gifts or brought a card. He'd obviously bought them on the way over, probably why he was late.

"Why, thank you," Vivian said. "We'll have dinner first, then presents."

Steven set the gifts with the others on the kitchen counter. He brought Cal a salad.

Everyone ate their salads in profoundly painful silence. The sticky heat crawled through the open windows.

Luna tried to eat, but the salad tasted like aluminum foil and felt like sawdust. Lifting her fork felt like moving through water. Today had been a good day . . . until now.

She forced herself to chew and swallow. The daily panic tightened in her chest: *What if this never goes away? What if I'm never normal again?* She had trouble remembering the thirteen days in the hospital other than her constant, overwhelming concern about Wren left without her. Only fragments came to her: her determination not to be vented; begging a nurse to "please don't let me die"; gasping for breath after every word; never knowing if it was day or night; hearing someone say her temp was 106; the vivid, horrific nightmares (she'd dreamed the doctors cut her apart and stitched her back together); every muscle cramping like someone had twisted them; every joint filled with lava; each cough a sharp-edged rock smashing into her ribs.

Her constant mantra: "I'm going home; I'm going home." The way Danielle repeated it to her the many times a day she called: "You'll pull through. You're going home."

Jodi and James, her former nursing-school friends, checked on her, having been promoted by that point. James worked at the same hospital where Luna was staying and called Vivian daily with detailed reports. Mandy had quit by that point, burned out from the stress of nursing in a pandemic. Luna understood. None of them judged her.

Cal's voice startled her. "I didn't catch all your names."

"These are the neighbors," Wren rushed out, her face panicked.

"I'm Drew, and this is my husband, Steven. We live next door."

Cal didn't react, thank God. He said, "Nice to meet you. And you?"

Ann-Marie looked startled. She sneezed. Then she said her name. Only her name. Vivian didn't claim her. No one did. Luna's heart went out to her in spite of herself.

"And I know the rest of you." Cal ruffled Wren's hair, not noticing that she bristled. Vivian had spent considerable time curling Wren's hair. Here he was, messing it up.

Everyone put their masks on again, while Cooper cleared the salad plates. Cal commented on the marble kitchen island top. He kept looking around, commenting on everything, how big and nice it was, which made Luna's face burn. He was such a clueless child. She needed to get him out of here as soon as she could. Steven and Drew helped Cooper serve up bowls of the pesto risotto. They'd been talking about this meal for days. Cal looked skeptical. But, to be fair, so did Wren.

Drew scooped the risotto into a bowl; then Cooper garnished each bowl with Parmesan cheese, toasted pine nuts, and little ribbons of basil. Steven served Vivian first.

Cal pulled his mask down and started eating as soon as he had his bowl, but everyone else waited until the three cooks sat down to dig in. Cal didn't even seem to notice.

Ann-Marie sneezed again. When she removed her mask, her cheeks were blotched pink. "I'm not sick," she said. "It's the cat. I'm allergic."

No one reacted. Luna thought it would be easy enough to put Ox in another room, but she took her cue from Vivian.

Vivian took a bite of the pesto and closed her eyes. She made a little moan. "Gentlemen. This is divine. Absolutely divine."

"Oh my God," Ann-Marie said. "So good."

Luna took a bite, and her heart broke at the metallic taste. Damn it. "I still can't taste, but this looks every bit as good as anything you'd order in a restaurant. Cooper, I'm so proud of you."

"Cooper, you made this?" Cal asked.

Luna froze, on alert.

Cooper shrugged and nodded.

"What is it?" Cal asked.

Cooper didn't say anything, so Wren piped up. "Pesto risotto. With shrimp."

"It's very good, son."

Luna's heart lifted. *Thank you, Cal.*

Cooper shrugged again.

Steven talked about how Cooper was a quick study. He said Cooper had made the pesto himself, and it was Cooper's idea to put the cherry tomatoes and braised zucchini in the pasta. Steven said Cooper wanted them to supervise the risotto today, but they didn't really do anything; he had it down.

Cooper didn't say a word. Cal had rendered him silent.

"This is amazing," Ann-Marie said, sounding as if she held her nose plugged. "Seriously."

"Wait until you taste the birthday cake," Steven said.

Luna smiled at Cooper. She touched his cheek, then tucked his hair behind his ear. She tried to convey to him that it was all okay. He smiled back, releasing that grin he saved like he only had so many to use. But he gave one to her. She cherished it.

Cal asked Drew and Steven what they did for a living. Thank God he seemed interested. Then he asked Ann-Marie.

She looked at her plate. "I wait tables. And you?" Nice diversion, moving the spotlight as fast as she could.

Cal sat up straight. Oh. He'd *wanted* someone to ask him this. "I just got a job at Amazon."

Cooper snapped his head up and then looked at Luna, as if to gauge her reaction. "That's good," she said, as much to Cooper as to Cal. "I'm glad you found a good job." She was, truly. Cal wasn't an asshole. He was just a thoughtless mess.

"I used to have a job in TSA," Cal told the others, "but lost it during this COVID BS. The airport was dead, everyone afraid to fly."

Amazon was a pretty secure thing with everyone stuck at home.

Luna caught Wren's expression, saw the bright, unabashed *hope* in that face.

Luna hated this trapped limbo. The courts had been closed because of the pandemic. Then, once they'd reopened on a limited basis, she'd gotten so ill. Then her lawyer had been sick. Delay after delay. Even trying to get a document notarized took exhausting effort these days.

Ox returned to his spot on the barstool.

Cal turned to Luna. "Hey, babe, are you back to work yet?"

The question filled her with shame. She should be back. What was wrong with her that she couldn't shake these headaches or this fatigue? That she still had chest pain and trouble breathing? Cachè, who'd been *vented*, was back and seemed almost normal. They'd gotten coffee together on Luna's first—and last—day back.

"No. I was, briefly. I went back for a day . . . but I'm not strong enough yet."

Cooper found his voice. "They kept pressuring her to go back, but when she tried, she passed out at work. She's still sick. She had to get stitches in her chin from where she fell."

Luna lifted her chin to show the scar. She knew the green bruise was still visible but so much better than the original mass of dark color. Her tender jaw reminded her of the fall every time she spoke or chewed.

Cal said, "You must have something else. That can't still be COVID."

Luna bit her tongue.

"It most certainly *is* COVID," Vivian said.

Cal shook his head. "Nah. I had it. I was over it in, like, a week and a half."

So clueless. She didn't have the energy to protest.

Ann-Marie turned to Cal, and Luna recognized Vivian in the woman's expression. "You do know the virus affects individuals very differently, right?" Her voice was so stuffy it was comical, her eyes now pink and watery. "Some people have hardly any symptoms and others are very, very sick. You were lucky."

Dad leaned back and said, "Well. I don't know about that. If I had a sweet gig like this, I might have milked it a lot longer, too, that's for damn sure."

His words hit like a slap. *How dare you?*

Cooper slammed his spoon down into his bowl and glared at his dad.

Luna shook her head. Vivian looked at her across the table again. Her blue eyes sent comfort. They'd be rid of him soon.

Ann-Marie tilted her head, trying to keep up. She sneezed twice, then asked Luna, "Where do you work?"

"Sycamore Place." Although it felt like another lifetime since she'd been there. Except for that fateful day the room had spun, her vision sparkled, and she split her chin open on Ms. Louise's dresser. "I'm a nursing assistant."

"Wait." Ann-Marie looked at Vivian. "That's where you and Dad were living. I was just there. I went there first. When they told me you didn't live there anymore, I hoped it meant you'd be here. So. I mean." She turned back to Luna. "Did you take care of my dad?"

"I did."

"She was amazing," Vivian said. "She's an angel. She's very, very good at what she does."

Luna smiled at Vivian. "Mr. Jack made it easy." Luna looked at Ann-Marie's pink, rashy face. "I loved your dad. He was a very special man. But I'm sure you know that."

"I do," Ann-Marie whispered. "Did he get COVID?"

Both Vivian and Luna shook their heads.

Drew snorted. His meaning was clear: *She doesn't even know how her own dad died.*

Ann-Marie dug in a pocket, produced a tissue, and blew her nose. Then she turned to Drew and spoke with such patience and kindness, Luna had no idea how she did it. "I get it, your anger. I know I deserve it."

Then she turned to Luna. "I don't know what you know about me already, if anything, but I'm an addict. I've treated my parents horribly in the past. I've been sober now for sixteen months." She looked at Vivian and said, "And five days."

Luna saw Vivian soften toward Ann-Marie for the first time. Vivian touched her daughter's arm. "That's good. Congratulations."

"I know it's not enough. I just wanted to see you on your birthday. And tell you I'm sorry."

And Luna knew: she and the kids needed to leave. She wanted Vivian and her daughter to be able to have each other. Vivian would need that support as she headed into her mastectomy and ruthless chemotherapy.

Luna looked around the room, at all the faces, at the love on Vivian's face as she gazed at Ann-Marie. Luna needed to memorize this. Then she needed to find a new home for herself and her children.

CHAPTER NINETEEN

COOPER

Cooper had to hand it to the woman, owning her shit like that. He kinda liked her. He liked her a hell of a lot better than he liked his dad. As mad as he was at Wren, he also saw how badly she wanted Dad's approval, how clueless she was about Mom and Dad getting back together.

He also felt bad for Vivian, because this was supposed to be her birthday party and now it was this awkward shit show. He made eye contact with her across the table, and when she smiled at him, her eyes twinkled. She was making the best of it. He could do that, too.

He looked over at his dad, but his dad was looking around the kitchen, just so blatantly assessing everything, it was mortifying. Something had dissolved in Cooper when his dad walked in. He'd felt it, like he'd shrunk or something. And now, after those fierce eyes from Vivian, he realized: before then, he'd been proud. And honest-to-God *happy* making this birthday meal. Being really good at something.

Good at something his dad did not approve of.

He thought of all the times he'd cooked with Grammy. How he'd *loved* those times. How he wished he'd paid attention to the recipes, the spices. Grammy never wrote any of it down or looked at a book. She'd just known what to do.

Grammy once made tomato sauce in a kettle over a fire in her yard. He wished he could've learned all that canning from her. Mean Grandma Rainie might have a RAPTURE READY sign in her yard, but Grammy was the one who'd been 100 percent apocalypse ready.

"This is *so* good," Ann-Marie said, snapping him back into the present.

The woman's nose and eyes were now red and puffy.

Cooper didn't look at his dad. He said, "Thanks. I'm glad you like it. I know Vivian loves pesto, so I wanted to make her something she loved."

"It's the best I've ever had," Vivian said. "Thank you. That's a perfect birthday gift."

"Oh, don't worry, there are other gifts, too," Cooper said.

"Is it time for presents?" Wren asked.

Man, Wren, shut up. Could she not tell the train wreck she'd caused?

"Cake first," Drew said.

Again, the three guys cleared the plates. Ann-Marie offered to help, but Drew just said, "No."

Of course, his dad didn't lift a finger.

Wren couldn't. Mom shouldn't. And Vivian was the guest of honor. He liked that Ann-Marie at least offered.

He'd hidden the cake in another room so Vivian couldn't see it until it was ready. Steven brought in the two candles, a seven and a five, and lit them. They carried it in, already lit, and began singing.

Everyone in the kitchen joined in.

While they sang, Cooper felt such lightness, such joy. He hated that his dad was there, but it made him realize that in these months, he'd already begun to think of these people—this old lady and these gay guys—as his family. Mom and Wren, of course. But this, this was the apocalypse pack. Danielle and Birdy, too. Dad would just be deadweight.

When Vivian leaned forward to blow out the candles, Wren shrieked, "Wait! Did you make a wish? You *have* to make a wish."

Why was she such a freak?

"Oh, I made a wish all right," Vivian said, smiling at Wren. "But you know what? I don't think we thought this through. Should I really blow on the cake?"

"Oh shit," Drew said. "We're idiots."

"Here," Steven said. The candles were big enough that he could lift them off the cake still lit. "Follow me."

Vivian stood.

"Why can't she blow them out?" Dad asked.

No one answered him.

Steven held the candles in front of the open window, and Vivian blew out, toward the garden. Everyone clapped.

"Oh. Look at this," Vivian said, blue eyes alight, turning back around to the cake. "Just look at this. Cooper, what have you done?"

"And this is *all* Cooper," Steven said. "He made us a test one earlier this week, just one layer."

Cooper blushed, the heat in his cheeks more to do with Steven's smile than the compliment. Birdy had agreed with Cooper that Steven was "stupidly beautiful," and he'd admitted to her that sometimes it was hard to hear what Steven was saying because his teeth were so white. She'd snorted and punched his shoulder.

Steven took over the serving, thank God, because Cooper didn't really know how to do that. Vivian, of course, got the first piece. She waited, smiling, while Steven served up the others.

"Is there ice cream?" his dad asked.

Seriously? Cooper didn't answer, but Drew said, "You won't need it."

Dad muttered, "You gotta have ice cream with birthday cake."

Everyone waited. Dad got the second-to-last piece, before Steven's own, and once again he started eating the minute it was in front of him.

Cooper couldn't eat until Vivian had tasted it. He watched her fork up a bite that included the chocolate fudge-y cake, as well as the salted-caramel filling. Double filling, just for her. She put it in her mouth and chewed. She closed her eyes. "Oh, holy Hannah, Cooper."

He smiled. Good. He took a bite of his own piece. Oh yeah. Hell yeah.

Mom touched his arm again. "God, I wish I could taste this. Good job. It's beautiful."

"Eat your piece anyway," Cooper said. "Please?" She was too skinny. She'd lost so much weight.

"That filling," Ann-Marie said. "That's divine. Wow. Holy wow."

"This is good, son," Dad said. "What mix did you use?"

Cooper cocked his head. "Mix?"

Drew laughed. "No way. No cake *mix*. This kid is a master. He made this from scratch."

"I mean, I used some recipes," Cooper said. He felt himself blushing. *Cake mix? Are you kidding me?*

"Recipes, plural?" Vivian asked.

Cooper nodded. "I knew you love rich chocolate cake, but you love salted caramel, too. Most of the salted-caramel-filling recipes I found went with caramel cakes or pound cakes or spice cakes. There weren't any for chocolate cakes, so I mixed and matched. And the first filling wasn't salty *enough*."

"This is *the* perfect cake," Vivian said. "My ideal cake. You have to promise me you'll make this again once I—" She stopped. Her face flushed red. Oh shit. She didn't want Ann-Marie to know. "*Later*. Promise me you'll make it for me long before my next birthday."

"I promise." They held eye contact a minute. Her mastectomy was next week. He was kinda scared about it.

"Where'd you get the recipes?" Ann-Marie asked.

"Different places. The actual cake was from *The Great British Baking Show*." Oh shit. Did he actually say that in front of his dad?

Vivian laughed. "That's our palate cleanser after we watch zombie movies. I need something like that before I go to sleep." She pointed her fork at him. "You have an amazing memory, young man. This is the cake I said, 'I'd do just about anything for someone to deliver that here right now.'"

He grinned. "Then I just dug around on the internet for recipes. And these guys have some cookbooks they let me borrow."

"Well, it's amazing," Ann-Marie said. She turned away and sneezed into her elbow. "You've got a gift."

"Yes, gifts! Let's open gifts!" Wren said.

Cooper saw the hard light in his sister's eyes. Shit, she was *mad* that he was getting attention that she'd hoped to get with her secret guest. Cooper wanted to grab her shoulders and scream, "Can't you see we're better off without him? That Mom is better off without him?" but he felt sorry for her.

For a second, just the tiniest fraction of a second, he missed that image in his mind, of all four of them together on Christmas morning, laughing and opening presents.

"That's a great idea, Wren," Cooper said. "I think it's time for presents."

CHAPTER TWENTY

Wren

Nobody was helping her. Nobody. Everybody suddenly wanted to just interview Cooper. Cooper, Cooper, Cooper. She wanted to get her *dad* talking. She wanted him to talk to her mom. She was so close to getting them back together.

Nobody was talking to Dad. Everyone pretty much ignored him. Mom hardly even looked at him. If only Ann-Marie hadn't shown up right at the same time. Wren couldn't even believe she was thinking that after wishing for Ann-Marie to return so hard and for so long. But her plan was getting ruined. She had to get Mom and Dad to talk to each other. Mom looked really tired, and she knew Mom was mad at her. Cooper was pissed.

Okay, Cooper's cake was pretty good. Probably the best one she'd ever tasted.

And that was dumb of Dad to ask about a cake mix. Whoever saw a cake-mix cake look like this? So tall and pretty and sparkling with those salt crystals.

Wren had an idea to get Mom and Dad closer to each other. "Should we go into another room to open presents?"

"Oh, I think we're comfortable here," Vivian said. "Everyone is cozy."

"Or we could go out to the garden," Wren pleaded.

"It's too humid and gross," Cooper said.

"Exactly why we should close the windows," Dad said.

Everyone shot him a look. *C'mon, Dad, stop being a jerk.*

"We are absolutely fine just as we are," Vivian announced. She used That Tone that meant the matter was settled, and nobody better touch the windows, either.

They brought the gifts over to Vivian. "You all didn't have to do this," she said. "This is so special. Especially this year." Wren didn't know if she meant Mr. Jack dying, or COVID, or maybe her surgery coming up. Maybe all of it.

The boys gave her a seventy-five-dollar gift certificate to her favorite garden center, but when she opened their other boxes, there turned out to be *three* seventy-five-dollar gift certificates. Plus, they offered delivery service with the Bloom van and watering and labor during her recovery.

"Recovery?" Ann-Marie asked.

Vivian laughed, too fast and fake.

Ann-Marie frowned.

"It's a joke," Vivian said. "It's . . . it's a long story." She looked at Drew and Steven, who laughed, too. They were horrible fakers.

Wren saw that Ann-Marie didn't believe it was a joke, but Vivian reached for Wren's gift. Wren went hot all over. She was proud of her collage. But she'd never had so many people *see* one. It felt like being onstage.

Wren's stomach did a somersault as Vivian pulled the wrapping off and stared at the collage. The way she was sitting, no one else could see it but her. She stared at it for so long, Wren felt the walls closing in on her.

Then Vivian started crying.

"What it is?" Dad asked. He sounded worried. "What did you give her?"

Vivian said, in a choked-up voice, "This is the most original, the most beautiful . . . oh, Wren. I love it."

Wren felt made of air, floaty, like a helium balloon.

Everyone jumped up to look at it. Wren liked watching their faces as they looked. She knew it was her best one yet. The focal point was at the bottom left of the canvas—a carry-out coffee cup from Vivian's favorite coffee shop, with her name and order (a salted-caramel latte, always) penned by the barista. The cup was cut down the middle vertically so it looked like it was embedded in the canvas. Strawflowers from the garden filled the cup—the wispy flowers that looked like tiny daisies but with stiff, papery petals that wouldn't fade when you cut them. A gardening glove with the fingertips worn off and a hummingbird Christmas tree ornament were the best of the big 3D pieces. She'd collected pictures of bees, hummingbirds, Jane Goodall, coffee, latte art, and chocolate desserts. Wren had used real photos, too, taken from the photo albums she'd studied. She'd asked Steven to copy them for her, and he'd brought her glossy color copies that looked better than the originals.

Wren had selected an old photo of a very young Vivian and Jack with the Eiffel Tower behind them. She'd also featured a more recent picture of them at a garden party here, holding hands.

And one photo of Ann-Marie, as a little girl in a green leotard and tutu. It reminded her of a photo of her own mom as a little girl in a dance recital, wearing a yellow-and-pink tutu with a big yellow flower behind her ear. Mom had been so excited to see that photo and kept it on her mirror in her bedroom now.

But the coolest thing on Vivian's collage, in Wren's own humble opinion, was the coffee beans. She'd painted twenty-three coffee beans to look like little bumblebees with wings made from strawflower petals. She could only do three at a time before her hands and wrists hurt and cramped, so it had taken forever. The coffee-bean bees and plain coffee beans swirled through the entire collage.

"Oh, Wren. Oh, Wren," Vivian kept repeating. "I love it. Oh, I love it." She walked over to Wren and hugged her. Wren couldn't stop grinning.

"Well, damn," Cooper said. "I wish you'd opened mine before hers. Nobody can top that."

Everyone laughed. Wren felt like she'd grown taller. She loved that feeling, but she was also relieved for the focus to shift.

"Yours?" Vivian teased Cooper. "Your gift was the meal. And that cake."

Cooper made a face and handed her three books. More of those apocalypse stories they liked to talk about so much. "These are new. I've never read any of them. We could maybe read them while you . . . you know."

Ann-Marie focused in. Wren sensed her curiosity. Wren knew Cooper meant while Vivian recovered.

"One of those books is narrated by a *crow*," Cooper said.

"Well, I think that's the one we start with." Vivian hugged him as well.

Mom gave Vivian a framed photo of Vivian and Mr. Jack taken at Sycamore Place. It was when Mr. Jack still walked and talked, and they were outside and dressed nice. They both looked at each other, smiling.

"I've never seen this picture," Vivian said.

"Someone took it at work," Mom said. "It's actually on the Sycamore website now."

Vivian stared at the photo. She touched Mr. Jack's face with her fingertips.

Ann-Marie leaned in to look at it. Wren thought she was crying, but it was hard to tell because her eyes were all bloodshot and puffy and she sounded like she'd plugged her nose.

Ox came up to Vivian's thigh and asked, "Mrrph?" Vivian scooted her chair back and let him hop into her lap. He sat, facing her, rubbing his head on her chin.

Ann-Marie sneezed, three times in a row.

Wren noticed that Ann-Marie took the box she'd brought for her mom and moved it back toward her own cake plate. When Vivian gestured to it, Ann-Marie shook her head and said, "Not yet."

Wren also noticed that Ann-Marie didn't even look at Wren. Not really even one time once she was inside the house. All of her focus was on her mom. What a weird feeling to know you'd thought about a person every day for months, but that person hadn't even known you existed. And here, in the same room, that person didn't even *care* you existed.

After the presents, the boys poured more cocktails—a drink they called "Vivian's Garden." Ann-Marie said, "No, thank you," to the cocktail, and Wren's dad asked if there was any beer.

After more chatting, Mom said, "I'm so sorry, you all, but I've been up as long as I can be. I need to excuse myself."

No, no, no, no. Mom! Come on!

As Vivian said, "Of course, dear," Dad stood up and said, "I was hoping I could talk to you in private."

"Cal." Mom sighed. Wren saw the exhaustion, the way Mom's skin looked gray, the way the lines in her face deepened when she was tired these days. "I can't. Not now. I didn't know you were coming."

"It'll just be a second."

She shook her head. "I'm sorry. I need to lie down."

She gave Vivian a hug. "Happy birthday." She put a hand on Ann-Marie's shoulder and said, "It was nice to meet you." She turned to the boys and touched her heart. "Thank you. Thanks, everybody. I'll see you tomorrow."

And she turned and left. Just like that. Nothing to Dad. This was awful. Nothing had worked. Dad's face was red.

He stood. "Welp. I'll hit the road, then."

"No!" Wren said. No one else said anything.

Ann-Marie said, "She lives here? You all live here?"

After a tense pause, Drew said, "Yep. So there's no room at the inn. You're shit out of luck."

He was so *mean*. It made Wren wince.

Dad's eyes widened at Drew, but he kissed Wren on the head. "Good to see you, sweetie. Good to see you, Cooper."

"See ya, Dad," Cooper said.

"Let's walk Dad out," Wren said.

Cooper shook his head once, a "no thanks."

Wren felt so bad for Dad, but she acted like this was all no big deal and said, "I'll go outside with you."

She followed him down the ramp. "Before you go, you wanna see the garden? I've been working in the garden. There's a section that's mine."

Dad hesitated, then said, "Sure, sweetie."

He followed her as she pointed out this and that. She knew she was talking too much. Once, back when they all lived together, he'd told her, "You chatter just like a damn bird." But she was nervous. They were losing their chance. And she didn't know how to stop.

When she realized he was looking up at the house and not at anything she was pointing out, she stopped talking and just watched him, feeling deflated. After a minute, he seemed to notice she wasn't talking. He shoved his hands in his pockets. "You told me your mom knew I was coming."

Her eyes prickled with tears. "I wanted to surprise her."

He rubbed a hand over his face. "This is a real sweet setup you all have here."

Wren frowned. That didn't sound right, but she didn't know why.

"You know how much money this broad must have?"

Wren shrugged. "She's really nice."

"She's seventy-five? She seems younger than that. I thought she'd be, like, you know, handicapped or something."

Wren flinched.

"Like, I thought she brought your mom here to take care of her? But she seems fine."

"She's just a nice person. She's our friend."

Dad laughed. Wren didn't like his laugh. He laughed like she was stupid. "Okay, sure." He patted her head, and she jerked her chair away from his reach. Dad looked both directions in the garden. "Which house belongs to the guys inside?"

She pointed.

He looked at their house, only a little of it visible through the trees, especially now that it was just starting to get dark. "They're a bad influence on Cooper. Your mother is playing with fire."

"What? Those guys are great, Dad. They're not a bad influence!" What did her dad even mean? Cooper was better than she'd ever seen him. "He got all As this semester."

"That's not what I'm talking about. I don't want you hanging out with them."

"Dad. These guys *saved* Mom. A bunch of times." She wanted to say, "When you should have." The thought surprised her and made her face burn.

Dad looked skeptical.

"They helped us move all our furniture. Drew took Mom to get her COVID test. She was too sick to drive, and she couldn't get time off unless she had a positive test. He took her and waited *three hours*. She slept in the car the whole time, and he kept the windows down and it was freezing. They're awesome. They've helped us. A bunch of times."

"You're too young, Wren. You don't understand."

"But they took Mom to the ER the night her—"

"I *said* I don't want you spending time with them. Do you hear me?"

She nodded. But she thought, *How will you even know? You're never around.*

But she wanted him around.

Didn't she?

A flash of fear shot through her, and she thought of her early PT days and the way they taught her over and over again to practice *falling*. She felt terror every single time.

The garden landscape lights popped on. They were on timers, and Wren usually felt like it was magic if she was looking right when they came on, but it didn't feel magical tonight. A mosquito buzzed around her ear, and she was suddenly too hot and sticky out here. She had slid down in her seat, straining against her seat belt. She struggled to scoot herself back upright. "Are you and Mom getting back together?"

"I think that ship has sailed."

"What's that mean?"

"Your mother wants to divorce me, Wren. She doesn't want me back."

Sweat dripped between Wren's chair and her back. "But *I* want you back."

"Oh, sweetie." He sat on a concrete bench across from her. "I messed up. I let your mother down. She was right to ask me to leave."

Wren's heart fluttered like the white moth on the butterfly bush. "*She* made you leave?"

He froze, and Wren saw that he hadn't meant to tell her that. "*Why?*"

"It's . . . complicated, sweetie. I needed to grow up. I'm sorry. I let you and Cooper down, too."

Her mother had lied to her. Hadn't she? Mom had never said why Dad had left, but that was a kind of lying, wasn't it? "I want to come live with you," Wren blurted.

He shook his head. "That's not a good idea."

"Did *she* say that?"

"Whoa. Sweetie, don't."

"She won't let me live with you?"

"Your mother knows what's best for you. Don't you worry about it. I'll visit you when I can."

Wren wanted to smash something.

"You keep being friends with this nice lady, little girl." Dad reached out to pat her head again. She didn't bother pulling away this time. The humidity had already made her hair droop. She could tell the curls were gone. She couldn't wait to have it back in a ponytail.

"She's got that junkie daughter," Dad whispered, looking up the hill at the still-open windows. Wren hated that he said that. Ann-Marie was more than that. "You all be the family she lost out on. And then she'll repay you."

"What do you mean, repay us?"

"Just . . . keep doing what you're doing."

He tousled Wren's hair *again*, like all the stupid people who patted her head in crowds. She was not a stupid *puppy*.

"I gotta go, hon. You be good. And keep me posted."

He kissed her head and walked to the car, whistling under the driveway lights like he was onstage in a play.

Wren stayed put and watched him drive away in some black car she'd never seen before.

Her stomach felt icky, and she knew it had nothing to do with the food.

CHAPTER TWENTY-ONE

VIVIAN

Vivian glanced out the window for the fifth time, checking on Wren and Callous Cal. She did not trust that man. He seemed reckless in his ignorance. Like a dangerously big, clumsy puppy. Cooper kept watch, too.

"You want me to go out there?" Drew asked.

"Nah, I think he's leaving," Cooper said.

The boy's face was tortured as he turned to Vivian and said, "Look, I'm really sorry Wren did that. I had no idea. Mom had no idea."

"Please don't worry." Vivian realized he'd always looked this worried back when he arrived. What a difference a few months made. "Tonight was just full of surprises." Drew snorted, and she felt her daughter stiffen beside her. "But everything worked out."

She turned from the window to regard her daughter. Ann-Marie looked healthy. Well, aside from the allergy harassing her. But Vivian had been fooled before. Ann-Marie's lovely skin was clear (again, at least before the cat), she wore some makeup, but not too much. She looked younger, fresh. And Vivian couldn't admit it to anyone out loud, but her heart sang to see her. How could it not? This was her only child. A young woman who'd been so, so lost, who'd possibly found herself again? Dared she hope?

Ann-Marie had said she needed to talk about some things with Vivian, and she was stalling, clearly wanting some privacy. Vivian couldn't really blame her, not with Drew here. Both Drew and Steven, really, but Drew was the imposing one. Vivian knew he loved her and wanted to protect her from the crushing heartbreak he'd seen her experience before . . . but a tiny, tiny part of her wished he'd leave. She knew he shouldn't, that Ann-Marie was her blind spot, and that he wouldn't, but a tiny part of her wanted to just embrace Ann-Marie and love on her. Invite her in, do all her laundry, make all her favorite foods.

That part of her existed, but Vivian also recognized another, shaky, unstable-with-rage part of her that wanted to scream at her: "Your father's dead! Dead! You missed it. He asked about you, and you were never there. I'll never forgive you. You broke his heart. And mine." She'd rehearsed that every day in the shower, or when she was driving alone, for the past four months.

"Dad left," Cooper announced. "But Wren's just sitting there. I'm gonna go make sure she's okay."

"Good man." Steven patted Cooper's shoulder as he walked past and out the door. Then he looked at Drew and said, "Let's clean up." The two men began collecting plates and wrapping paper. Vivian knew they'd load the dishwasher, wash the martini glasses by hand, and leave things spotless. She also knew they would make this task last for hours if need be. They would not leave her while Ann-Marie was here.

They're protecting me. Remember that.

Ann-Marie watched them a moment, then turned to Vivian. Oh, how Vivian adored those dimples, those bright eyes that had arrived at her door. Ann-Marie blew her nose. "Want to go to another room? Outside, maybe?"

Yes, yes, yes! "No, dear," Vivian said, her tone as gentle as she could make it. "I don't."

"It's just so hot," Ann-Marie said. "And the cat." She blew her nose again. Ox purred in Vivian's lap. "If we went outside, you could close the windows and get the AC going again."

Vivian shook her head and patted Ann-Marie's arm, recognizing her need to touch her daughter as often as she could, to drink her in, to save the sensation and the memory for the inevitable years of drought without it. "It's best we stay here."

"Okay," Ann-Marie said, no judgment, no reaction. Oh, she was being so careful. Vivian saw that Ann-Marie recognized she had no right to ask for anything.

And that mattered to Vivian, that her daughter recognized this.

"So," Ann-Marie said. "They live here, that family?"

Vivian nodded.

"That's very generous of you."

"I'm getting plenty out of it as well."

"Are you sure? It seems . . ."

Drew turned around from the sink. He was itching for a fight, Vivian could tell.

She saw Steven touch Drew's arm, a "lighten up."

"It seems what?" Vivian asked.

"I just don't want anyone taking advantage of you."

"Oh, that's rich," Drew said.

Vivian chuckled at how predictable he was.

Ann-Marie held up her hands, as if in surrender. "Hey, I would recognize that more than most, don't you think? It just seems kind of . . . sudden."

Vivian hugged Ox to her as she leaned forward with a fork to take more of Cooper's amazing salted-caramel frosting from the cake.

"I mean. So soon after losing Dad."

Vivian put her fork down and said, her voice raw and urgent, "They saved me."

She saw Steven and Drew notice this.

"They saved me. I would literally not be here today without them. It made sense for them to come here during the pandemic. I couldn't stand to be in this house alone. And I love this house, this garden. I *want* to be here. They made it possible."

Ann-Marie sniffed. Vivian watched her fidget with the present she'd brought and wondered if she'd completely changed her mind about giving it.

"How well do you know them?" Ann-Marie asked.

Vivian looked into her beautiful daughter's splotchy face and said, "It pains me to say this, but I know them far, far better than I know you."

Ann-Marie nodded, not offended. "That's not saying much, right? Can you trust them?"

"Yes."

"That dad seemed pretty sketchy."

Drew laughed out loud. "And you'd recognize that more than most, don't you think?"

Steven shook his head and sent an apology to Vivian in his eyes.

Vivian chuckled again, and to her relief, Ann-Marie did, as well. "So, Drew," Ann-Marie said. "Do *you* trust them?"

He turned and leaned against the sink. He crossed his arms. "I do. Completely. But not that dad. At all."

"Which is fine," Vivian said, "because *he* doesn't live here."

Ox pressed his face into her chin, his purring comically loud. Vivian hugged him, wishing she could hug her daughter.

"Okay," Ann-Marie said. "These guys are looking out for you, and that's what matters."

Oh, she was trying so hard. So hard.

Steven sat back down at the kitchen island and said, his voice low, "So are they divorced or what?"

"She wants to be," Vivian said, taking another forkful of icing. "The courts are backed up after being closed so long. And then she was *so* sick. He hasn't signed. He wants them back together."

"No doubt so he can cash in on this 'sweet gig,' too," Ann-Marie said.

"That's what I thought, too," Drew said. "Vivian, for God's sake, cut yourself another piece instead of desecrating the entire cake."

Everyone laughed.

"That boy is gifted," Vivian said. "Split a piece with me, Steven?"

Vivian sliced a piece from the spot she'd been mauling for icing. Steven grabbed a fork, and they ate off the same plate. *This is my family.*

Could Ann-Marie ever be family again?

"So did you get it? COVID?" Ann-Marie asked her.

"No. None of us have except for Luna. She was bad. And she's still not well, no matter what that idiot husband says."

"Did you?" Drew asked Ann-Marie.

She nodded. "I was being as careful as I could, but where . . . the population I was living in, it spread like wildfire."

A loud silence permeated the kitchen. Vivian wondered what Cooper and Wren were doing, rather than contemplate what her daughter had just said. Drew, though, asked the question Vivian was avoiding.

"Were you in prison?" His tone was neutral. His meanness had softened.

Ann-Marie shook her head. "Not this time." She gave a rueful grin. "No, I was briefly in a shelter. Three nights. That's it. Just long enough to get COVID."

"A homeless shelter?" Vivian's pulse stuttered.

Ann-Marie looked down at the present she'd brought. Did she realize she was shredding the wrapping paper? "Yes. But I'm not homeless now. It wasn't very long, I swear. I lost a really good job when the restaurants had to close. Before I could find another one, I was behind on rent. I couldn't stay with the people I was living with anymore."

Vivian couldn't meet Steven's or Drew's eyes. It could happen to anyone. It's why Luna was here now.

"I have a job. I have a home. Things are good right now."

"Where do you live?" Vivian asked.

Ann-Marie turned around and reached into her bag. She pulled out a card she'd obviously prepared in advance. "I'm in Indy."

That wasn't far. She was two hours away. That was a normal distance. Could they ever be normal? Perhaps see each other on holidays? Be in each other's lives?

"Here's my address. And my phone number. I want you to have this."

"Thank you." Vivian worried she might cry. "What on earth are those children doing out there?"

Drew went to the window. "Looks like they're just sitting. Talking."

"Maybe they're trying to give us some privacy," Ann-Marie said, looking at Drew.

"Not a chance. I'm not leaving until you do."

Ann-Marie leaned toward Vivian. Vivian inhaled her shampoo—something tropical, a hint of coconut. "I was afraid to call, in case you told me not to come. Which I would've deserved. I needed to see you, even if it was for two seconds before you slammed a door on me."

Vivian had never, ever slammed a door on Ann-Marie. She had never, ever told her not to come. She never would.

"I'm so sorry about Dad." Ann-Marie's voice choked off. "I hate that I wasn't here. I should've been here."

Vivian did not, could not reassure her otherwise.

"I'm just in town until tomorrow. I wondered if maybe we could go to his . . . to his grave together?"

You don't know anything about us, do you? "Oh, hon, your father doesn't have a grave."

Ann-Marie's eyes widened.

"We've donated our bodies to the medical school."

Ann-Marie winced.

"Your father always wanted to help people, to be useful. This way, he still is. Once they're done with . . . with his body, they'll cremate the remains, and he'll be put into a stone wall out at the university cemetery. Someday, I'll be there with him."

She might have already been on her way to joining him, if it weren't for Luna and the kids.

Ann-Marie wiped a tear. "That's so like him."

Vivian felt her heart harden a bit. *You didn't know him. Not anymore. You don't get to say what's like him or what's not.*

She thought about telling Ann-Marie about the spot in the garden she'd begun to think of as Jack's Hill. But she kept it for herself during the long silence.

She and Steven finished their cake. Drew snatched the plate from them the minute they were done, then covered the remaining cake and moved it—pointedly—to the kitchen counter.

Ann-Marie said, "Well, maybe, could we go to that stone wall together anyway? Just us? Or someplace like Glen Helen that he liked?"

"No," Drew said. "You're not going anywhere alone with her."

Ann-Marie's eyes flashed, and she turned to her mother, appeal in her eyes.

Drew went on. "Vivian, if you want to do this, then I'll go with you guys."

Oh, dear, protective Drew. Oh, beautiful, broken Ann-Marie. Oh, sweet, complicated life.

"Doing nothing is not an option," her surgeon had said.

Vivian was exhausted. When she was tired, she was vulnerable. She knew this. She was grateful for Drew and Steven being here. She wanted Ann-Marie to go now.

"Hon, you said you needed to talk with me about something, so you should get to that. I know you'd rather talk alone, but that's not going to happen. Just ask me what you need to now."

Ann-Marie fidgeted with the box some more, digging her fingernail into the wrapping paper. Her nails were pretty, painted pink. Not bitten to the bloody quicks like before. She blew her nose again, stalling. "I wanted to ask you about going to Dad's grave. I just . . . I just wanted a place, a way to say goodbye to him. That's all."

"Okay," Vivian said. "We can do that. When are you free, boys?"

"Tomorrow's Sunday," Steven said at the same time Drew said, "Bloom's closed tomorrow."

Vivian turned back to Ann-Marie. "We can leave from here. Name the time. You know I get up early. We'll want to beat the heat."

And Vivian saw in Ann-Marie's eyes that she'd called her daughter's bluff. That Ann-Marie had no interest in visiting her father's grave. *Just go now. Please go.*

"Early's good," Ann-Marie said. "Like, say, ten?"

Well. That's hardly early. Vivian wanted to roll her eyes, but she said, "Sure." She felt a wall forming between them. The wall made her sad, even as she knew it protected her.

Ann-Marie opened her mouth to say something but then closed it.

She held the wrapped box out to Vivian, then pulled it back to her own belly.

She inhaled and blurted, "I need a place to stay, Mom."

Silence bruised the kitchen. She heard the children's voices. They were almost back.

"I can't find work during the pandemic. I've tried. I'm not going to be able to stay where I am without money. I want to stay sober. I need to come home."

Silence. Drew and Steven had both frozen, their hands in the dishwater, their backs to Ann-Marie and Vivian.

Vivian felt so many things at once. Anger. Betrayal. That her daughter had come here of course wanting something. Hope that maybe she could help mend what was broken in Ann-Marie. Sorrow that any mending couldn't come from her and could only come from Ann-Marie herself.

But mostly: exhaustion. She was so tired of this game. Of this repeated, boring, merciless game.

"You can't stay here, hon. I'm sorry." And she was.

"I could sleep on a couch."

"It's not good for either of us for you to stay here."

"Please, Mom. I need you."

Vivian paused long enough that Drew turned around. She shook her head at him. She was only pausing to find the kindness she needed. "No," she said.

"I won't stay sober if I have to stay with friends."

Vivian exhaled and rubbed her temples. She shook her head.

"I will always, always love you, my darling, but you can't stay here. I'm sorry that it has to be that way. But it does. I love you."

Ann-Marie sat silent, tears streaming down her cheeks. Vivian wanted to scream. She wanted to break things. And she wanted to grab Ann-Marie, hug her fiercely, and never let go.

Ann-Marie wiped her eyes on the back of her hand. She grabbed one of the happy birthday napkins and blew her nose in it.

Cooper's laughter sounded, closer. She heard Wren say, "Shut up!"

Ann-Marie stood. "Here." She thrust the box at last into Vivian's hands. "Happy birthday." She grabbed her purse and headed for the door. "I'll be back at ten tomorrow, okay?"

Oh, hon, don't lie to me.

She turned to go just as the kids opened the back door. There was awkward maneuvering as they came in and Ann-Marie left, and Vivian had to fight the urge to run after her daughter screaming, "Wait! Come back! Stay here forever!"

But then Cooper said, "Mom? You okay? I thought you went to bed."

Luna stood in the entryway to the kitchen, at the bottom of the stairs.

Shit. Vivian wondered what all she'd heard.

CHAPTER TWENTY-TWO

LUNA

Luna stepped into the kitchen. "I was just coming to check on the kids. I . . . Vivian . . ." Luna couldn't believe what she'd just heard. "Vivian, you can't keep us here and send her away. She's your *family*."

"Luna, don't start," Drew said. "Vivian knows what she's doing."

"We can't stay. Not in good conscience." Luna's heart was shredding. She looked in the faces of her children and felt it wrench apart even more. Wren looked horrified. Cooper looked pissed. At her. "It's a *pandemic*. What's she supposed to do?"

Luna studied her friend's face. Vivian looked . . . defeated. And yet, when she spoke, she was resolute. "Even if you weren't here, staying with me, I wouldn't let her stay. I can't let her. It feels horrible, but it's the right thing."

The floor tilted under Luna. "That's your daughter."

"Oh, Luna. It's so complicated."

"Vivian," Luna pleaded. "I can't stand in the way of—of—"

"You're not!" Vivian shouted. Ox, still in her lap, pinned his ears.

Luna took a literal step back. Vivian had never shouted at her.

"I am not a monster," Vivian whispered. "I'm not. This is not the first time. You don't . . . you don't . . ."

To Luna's horror, Vivian began to sob. Luna had only seen Vivian cry this way once—the day Vivian moved Jack up to Memory Care. Luna had found her in a stairwell, hunched over, clutching her belly and wailing that she'd failed him.

Oh, this poor woman. Why did the universe do this? Throw so many tragedies at one person? Hadn't she already had her fair share?

The children remained frozen by the back door.

"Kids," Luna said. "Can you please give us some time?"

Cooper's face flushed. He opened his mouth, but she held up a hand. "You need to give us some time."

He glared at her a moment. *Oh, God, honey, no, don't test me. I don't have the strength.*

"C'mon," he said to Wren, leading her away.

Luna hated how worried they both looked. "And none of your eavesdropping," she called.

Steven moved toward Vivian first, sitting in the chair beside her and pulling her into a hug. Ox stubbornly clung to his spot in her lap. Vivian cried and cried. Luna sat on the other side and stroked Vivian's back.

When Vivian's crying ran down, she pulled from Steven and sat up. She looked around the room and said, "Oh, for fuck's sake. I'm a mess."

Ox swiped his head on her chin over and over.

"Hey," Luna said. She wanted more than anything to comfort her friend. "Do you remember the day Jack went to Memory Care?"

Vivian's shoulders slumped. "That was the worst day of my life. The very worst."

Luna knew she meant it. That told her so much, since Luna now knew some of Vivian's other tragedies.

"This is like that, isn't it?" Luna asked.

Vivian frowned. She picked up a napkin from the table and wiped under her eyes.

"That day I found you in the stairwell, you felt you were abandoning him, but I tried so hard to convince you that it was the right thing. I *knew* it was the right thing. That even though it felt horrific and wrong, it was the safest thing for him. Right?"

Vivian moaned. She still clutched the box Ann-Marie had given her.

"Well, this is like that. I'm sorry I questioned it. I didn't know. I didn't mean to judge you. I didn't. I'm sorry. I don't understand it, but I know you. And I know if you think this is best, then it is."

"Oh God," Vivian said. "It *hurts*. It literally *hurts* me." She pressed a hand against her bony sternum. Ox purred and rubbed his head under that hand.

Drew walked behind them and put his hands on Vivian's shoulders.

Vivian took a shaky breath. "I want, more than anything, for her to be healthy. For her to be sober and able to stay here with me. That would be a dream come true. But . . . it's happened too many times. I can't save her. I had to stop trying. *She* has to save herself. If she . . . if she . . . disappointed me one more time, it would kill me. I can't do it again. I just . . . can't."

Luna hurt inside. That woman, Ann-Marie, was suffering because of the pandemic, just as she had. Ann-Marie needed a lifeline, someone to cut her a break. Luna didn't understand. She didn't. But she would trust Vivian.

Luna thought of her kids. Her heart ached, knowing they had to leave sometime.

"Do you really think she'll come back tomorrow?" Steven asked.

Drew snorted.

Vivian shook her head. She sighed, a sound that seemed to scour her from the inside. "No. She won't be back." Vivian picked up the box Ann-Marie had brought her as if it were a bomb. "I'm afraid to look."

Luna had been coming downstairs to talk to Wren, to make sure Cal had left. She longed to be in bed, but she took a seat, along with the boys.

She held her breath as Vivian opened the box, hoping it was something that would heal her and give her comfort.

Vivian gasped. She turned the box so they could see a beautiful pair of sapphire earrings. Even just holding the earrings near her face, you could see that they matched her eyes exactly. "Oh my God," Vivian said. "Jack had these made for me. For our forty-fifth wedding anniversary."

"I remember," Drew said. "I thought . . ."

"I thought, too," Vivian said. "Did she have them this whole time?"

"I don't understand," Luna said.

Vivian sighed and said, "She stole them. She stole a great many things. That was the last time she robbed us."

Luna sucked in a breath. Oh God.

"This was before Jack's diagnosis," Vivian said. "She turned up at Christmas. She was sober; she looked great. She apologized. She said she had a place to stay. She didn't stay with us, said she couldn't impose. She came the next day for dinner. And she left. That was it. But a month or so later, we were robbed. We went away for a weekend and came home to everything of value gone. Televisions. Jewelry. Stereo. Computers. Art. God, so much art. Pieces we'd collected on our travels. Years' worth of collecting. Ann-Marie was arrested, with two other friends, after pawning some of that stuff in Cleveland. She sold us out for money. To buy drugs."

Luna wanted to vomit. How would you ever forgive that?

Vivian lifted the earrings. "These were missing all that time."

"Are you sure they're the same ones?" Steven asked.

Vivian smiled. "I'd know them anywhere."

"I thought for a while she wasn't going to give that box to you," Drew said.

Vivian nodded. "I'm sure she didn't want the story told in front of everyone. Plus . . . I hate to say it, but I wonder if she thought she might need them, for money, once I said she couldn't stay?"

That stabbed Luna. She'd thought that very thing, too, but it was chilling to know Vivian had gone there, too, was aware that her own child might be making those calculations. "I'm so sorry, Vivian."

"I am, too," Vivian said. "I learned. And it was a hard, painful lesson. Let's . . . let's get the kids back in here."

Drew called for them, and they emerged from Wren's room.

"Are we leaving?" The old Cooper was back, the angry Cooper.

"Not right away," Luna said.

"What's that mean?" Cooper demanded.

"Is Ann-Marie moving in?" Wren asked. Luna's daughter looked miserable. Her eyes were red, like Ann-Marie's had been with the allergy, and her lip quivered.

"No. She's not," Vivian said. "We're going back to the way we were. Before tonight, but . . ." Vivian sat up straight and took a deep breath. "I learned the hard way. When people show you who they are, *believe them*. Well, because of who Ann-Marie has shown herself to be, we should be extra careful for a while. Any of your valuables"—she gestured to Luna and the kids—"hide them well or lock them up. I've got a safe you can use. Your laptops, stuff like that."

"I hate this feeling," Drew said. "Like now we're going to be waiting for the other shoe to drop."

"Life is never boring, is it?" Vivian chuckled. "That was certainly a dramatic evening. You all planned such a nice party, and it kind of got tipped over, didn't it?"

Luna groaned. "I'm so sorry about Cal. That was . . ."

"Painful?" Cooper said. He mock-slapped the back of Wren's head. "You're not the one who should be apologizing, Mom."

Wren burst into tears.

"Oh, for heaven's sake," Vivian said. "What is it, Wren?"

Cooper rolled his eyes behind his sister's back.

"I'm sorry!" Wren cried. "I'm sorry! I'm sorry! I don't know why you're all so mean to him."

Oh. Luna sighed. This. *Damn it, Cal.*

Luna rose from her chair, every muscle aching, and went to Wren. She kissed the top of Wren's head. "No one was mean," she said. "I know you didn't mean any harm, but you shouldn't have invited him without asking Vivian or me. That's just bad manners."

Wren sniffed. "I knew you would tell me no."

"You're right. I would have said he couldn't come to Vivian's party, but he could have met you some other time. Think about it, Wren. He doesn't even know Vivian. Tonight was supposed to be a celebration for her." Luna wanted to say: "Your father had ample opportunity to come here before tonight." Danielle had come numerous times. So had Cachè.

Wren sniffed. She glared at her mom. Luna wondered where this anger was coming from. She recognized fury. Wren was working through something big.

"Why'd you make him leave us? Why won't you let us live with him?"

The words punched Luna in the gut.

"Whoa," Cooper said. "I don't *want* to live with him, and you're crazy if you think he wants either one of us."

"Shut up! You hate him. *I* want to live with him. Mom won't let us."

Luna couldn't find words.

Cooper had no trouble finding some. "That's bullshit. Did he tell you that?"

Wren trembled with rage, sliding down in her chair, her legs out straight.

Oh, Cal, Cal. Luna got ahold of herself. "Wren. You are out of line. You know you can't speak to me this way. If you want to talk about this, you need to calm down."

Luna watched her daughter struggle with herself, but it was as if the fury could not be stuffed back in its box.

"Why won't you let him come back? I want him back! I hate you!"

Luna's world flashed white-hot before her eyes. Rather than smack her daughter, she wanted to scoop her up and pour on the love she was so hungry for.

But Wren zoomed out of the room and slammed her door.

Cooper's eyes were wide. He looked . . . afraid. "Mom, I think Dad really messed with her mind out there. She doesn't mean it. That's not, that's not her. I think—"

"Shh, hon, it's all right." He was always protecting his sister. And her.

She crossed to him and hugged him. With her arm around Cooper's shoulder, she turned to the others. "I guess the party needed a *little* more drama."

Everyone laughed, but she could see their worry, the concern on their faces.

"I'll go talk to her," Luna said. She was so tired. She only wanted to go lie down, but her daughter needed her.

Cooper repeated what Vivian had just said. "When people show you who they are, believe them. Dad shows her and shows her, and she just won't see it."

Luna brushed her boy's hair back behind his ear. "I think she does see. And that's where that anger's coming from. She sees, but she's not ready to believe."

Luna walked to her daughter's room and tapped on the door. She knew that believing who he was came at a price. To see that truth, Wren would have to see a whole lot of other ugly truths in addition.

When Wren didn't answer, Luna let herself in.

CHAPTER TWENTY-THREE

COOPER

Nobody had slept well. And Mom needed to sleep. This morning, Cooper's heart stopped when he peeked in her room and didn't see her, but he found her in bed with Wren. He stood in the doorway, watching them sleep, all tangled up with each other, still in their clothes. Ox slept between their pillows, looking like a pillow himself. Cooper swallowed. Poor Wren.

Poor Mom, having to deal with this shit.

Why couldn't Wren see the truth about Dad?

Cooper hadn't slept well, either, mostly jazzed on too much sugar from the cake. That cake. He was pretty damn proud of it. And proud of himself for still talking about it, for claiming it—the cake *and* himself—in front of Dad. But when Cooper had drifted off to restless sleep, he'd dreamed about robbers in the house. He'd startled awake a couple of times, convinced he'd heard something. Once, he'd even tiptoed downstairs, certain he'd find Ann-Marie stealing things.

In the light of the morning, he didn't feel so jumpy. But he couldn't shake his wary disgust, the disappointment. The way disappointment should be *expected*. He'd let his guard down, and he needed to be ready. Just in case.

Vivian had left a pot of coffee and a note in her fancy cursive that reminded him of Grammy's writing in the birthday cards she'd give him—always with one dollar tucked inside. Vivian had gone to the garden center, to use the gift certificates "the boys" had given her. He smiled. That lady and her plants. He hoped she'd be okay. He'd been reading about her surgery, and it sounded crazy brutal.

He poured himself some coffee, added milk and sugar, then cut himself a hefty piece of the birthday cake. Damn, this shit was good, if he did say so himself.

The boys. What had his dad thought of the boys? Anger simmered inside him, imagining his dad thinking badly of them. Those guys were awesome. Cooper looked at them now as a model of what could be. His dad had made it seem like being gay meant you'd be a loser, lesser somehow, but those guys had everything. They owned their own businesses. They took care of people they loved. That's what mattered more than the money: the fact that they took care of their pack. Cooper wanted to be that way. He could picture a future now, because of them.

He wondered if they'd gone with Vivian this morning.

Cooper took another bite of cake. Oh man, with coffee, this was heaven. He closed his eyes, savoring the crunch of the salt crystals.

A tap on the door made him jump.

He opened his eyes to see Ann-Marie staring in at him. His stomach dropped. Holy shit.

She smiled and waved.

He looked at the clock. It was 9:55 a.m. She'd *said* she was coming back. Shit.

What should he do? She looked so normal. In the middle of the night, he'd pictured her in a car, just up on the road, watching the house, but she looked showered and clean, and she'd changed her clothes. She was actually a pretty lady. Her face and eyes were clear again.

She waved again. "Can I come in?"

He got up and opened the door. "Your mom's not here." He felt bad for her.

She made a face and shrugged. "She didn't believe me." She did that thing, like she'd been doing last night, where she just owned her shit. "She has good reason not to believe me. I'm not surprised." She shoved her hands down in the pockets of the dress she wore and pulled out a mask, which she put on. "Will she be back soon?"

"I don't know. She went to the garden center."

Ann-Marie laughed. Her laugh was warm, friendly. "Of course she did."

They stood there, awkward.

"Can I come in?"

"Um . . . I don't know if I should . . ." He felt like an asshole, but no way was he letting her in.

"It's okay. I get it. But—" She stopped and pointed to the island behind him. "Oh my God, can I have a piece of that cake?"

"Sure." He offered her coffee. She accepted, saying she drank it black. He didn't know how people did that.

"I'll wait out here."

Thank God she was cool about it. He carried cake and a coffee out to her at the bottom of the ramp. She sat in a chair in the shade. Next to her was a new hanging basket of some draping plant with pink-orange puffs. "I brought this for my dad."

He sat across from her. He hadn't brought his coffee, so he could keep his mask on. He didn't want to be the one who got Vivian sick. Not right before her surgery.

Within minutes, he felt okay, though. Ann-Marie was nice, real. She asked him a lot of questions about himself, about his cooking. "Do you want to cook for a living? Be a chef?"

He thought about that and felt his skull actually expanding to make room for that idea. "Maybe. I never thought about it before."

"What do you want out of life?" she asked.

He laughed. "No one ever asked me that until I met your mom."

She smiled. Her mask was off so she could eat. She had the same dimples Wren did. "She's pretty great, isn't she?"

"She really is."

"Did you meet my dad, too?"

He shook his head. "My sister did."

"Your dad. He doesn't approve of your cooking, does he?"

Cooper's face burned.

"Does he know you're gay?"

He almost choked. But Ann-Marie's face was open, soft. And before he gave the words permission, out marched: "I don't know."

He'd never said it out loud to anyone except for Birdy and the counselor Mrs. Gross. "I don't know if he knows for sure or if he's just afraid I might be."

She pointed her fork at him, the gesture so much like Vivian. "Don't let him hold you back."

He felt so weird. Like he wanted to hug her. Or cry. Or laugh and spin around. He was glad he wore a mask because he didn't know what to do with his face, and he desperately wished he had coffee or cake so he'd have something to *do*.

"So what's wrong with her? My mom?"

He felt like he'd lost his balance. "What do you mean?"

"She's sick, right? What's going on?"

He knew he shouldn't tell her this without Vivian's permission. "Why would you think that?"

"Because I saw her go into the Cancer Care Hospital."

Shit. "That's . . . creepy. What were you doing? Following her?"

"Look, I just want to know. Is she okay?"

"I think you have to ask her that."

"Does she have cancer?"

"You gotta ask her."

Ann-Marie sighed. "Fair enough. So I'll ask you this, and be honest: *If* she's sick, *if* she has cancer, are you guys going to take care of her?"

Cooper's heart pounded. Was this a trick question? "Of course."

"You swear?" She leaned forward, and her eyes looked crazy serious but mostly crazy, like she might whip out a knife and cut him if he said no.

"Yes."

She held out a hand. "Pinkie swear it."

Was she for real? This woman was nuts. He linked his pinkie with hers. "Pinkie swear."

She jumped out of her seat and said, "I need to use the restroom, okay?"

She took off up the ramp without waiting for him to answer. He followed, wanting to say no, feeling like an idiot. What was he supposed to do? Tell her to pee outside?

Inside the kitchen, she started opening cupboards. Oh, hell no. Was she going to steal stuff right in front of him? But she just opened and closed doors, like she was looking for something.

"Hey! What are you doing? Cut it out." The cupboards banging was going to wake Mom and Wren, though he kind of wanted that to happen.

"There it is!" She pulled out a bottle of Jameson. "Now, where are the shot glasses?" Again with the cupboards.

"Look," Cooper said, "I don't think you should take anything without Vivian's permission."

"Oh, no, I'm not taking them," she said, searching in a cupboard and bringing out two shot glasses. "I really do want to do something for my dad. This was his favorite. I thought Mom could do a shot and we could leave one for him. At that stone wall she talked about."

"She's got a place in the garden where she says she goes to talk to Jack," Cooper said. "She goes there at least once a day."

Ann-Marie sucked in a breath. "That would be perfect. Will you show it to me?"

"Sure." Thank God he had a reason to lead her back outside, out of the house.

"Excellent. Will you pour me more coffee? I'm gonna pee."

She moved through the hall, knowing exactly where she was going, before he could stop her. He poured her coffee. He examined the Jameson bottle. Just as he was getting antsy about her taking so long, she came back. She grabbed the bottle and the two shot glasses and breezed through the back door.

He guessed he was carrying her coffee.

He followed her and was relieved to see the Bloom van pull into Vivian's driveway. They'd taken the damn van. That's how serious she was about buying plants.

Ann-Marie watched the van and smiled. "Of course," she said. She shifted the bottle into the crook of one arm and picked up the handle of the hanging basket she'd brought.

Cooper watched Vivian get out of the van and look at Ann-Marie. He wasn't sure what to make of the emotions that crossed Vivian's face.

CHAPTER
TWENTY-FOUR

VIVIAN

Vivian sat on the stone bench up on Jack's Hill and had to admit it felt nice to sit with her daughter up there. Well, that is, once her initial flash of horror had passed at seeing Ann-Marie standing there with a liquor bottle. Ann-Marie had immediately held it up and said, "It's not for me. It's for Dad."

Cooper followed them up the hill at first, but Vivian assured him and the boys that they'd be fine for a conversation up there. She could tell Drew was skeptical, but they'd had such a lovely morning, and Ann-Marie had come back. She'd returned, just like she'd said she would.

All three boys worked in the garden below them. The day was already too hot, but this spot was shaded.

Vivian still felt the shot of Jameson in her throat and chest. The ritual had moved her. The other shot sat at the statue ballerina's feet. Ann-Marie, as promised, had not partaken herself.

"You're wearing the earrings," she said. "They're beautiful. They make your eyes really stand out."

Vivian reached up to touch them. "Did you have them all this time?" She didn't think it could be true. Ann-Marie had been in jail, after all.

She shook her head. "No. I put in some effort to find them. Get them back for you."

Well. Vivian didn't want to know details. "Thank you. That means a lot to me."

"It meant a lot to me to see you listed me in the obituary."

Vivian startled, a jolt of electricity buzzing through her. "Ann-Marie. You're our daughter. No matter what happens, you're our daughter. I . . ." She paused, remembering. "I didn't know, honestly, as I wrote it, whether he was survived by you or not."

"I know. I'm sorry."

They were silent, listening to the insects and the birdsong.

"Was it awful?" Ann-Marie asked her, and Vivian knew she meant Jack's dementia.

"Yes. Awful. And unfair. He deserved better."

Vivian looked at the basket of fuchsia Ann-Marie had brought. It was perfect, really. Suitable for the shade up here, and Jack would love the way it attracted the hummingbirds.

"Did he know you?" Ann-Marie whispered.

"He did. I think he always knew who I was. Toward the end, he may not have remembered my name or that I was his wife, but he knew I was someone who loved him, someone he could trust. I know he knew *that* until the end."

The men below them carried plants and watered. She didn't want to leave them outside working too long in the heat, but she needed this. She was gearing up for something.

"That last time"—Vivian touched her earrings and saw Ann-Marie recognize that she meant the burglary—"your dad was adamant that you were dead to us." She didn't let the pain that crossed her daughter's face deter her. "I knew he was grieving, but that's how he needed to process it. It nearly broke us; it nearly tore us apart. How we fought over it."

"You two fought?" Ann-Marie looked shocked.

"Oh, holy Hannah, how we fought. Don't look so surprised. It didn't mean we didn't love each other. The whole thing with you, it ultimately pulled us closer. Shared grief can do that . . . if it doesn't destroy a couple. We went to counseling."

"Yeah?"

Vivian nodded.

"I'll go now," Ann-Marie said.

"Good," Vivian said, genuinely glad of this. "But I want you to know something. Something happened, with your father's dementia, and I think he forgot all that had happened with you. He remembered you, but not how things had gotten . . . broken." Should Vivian do this? Could she do this? Would it be a gift for Ann-Marie or would it be too painful? She worried that some dark part of her wanted to hurt the girl. "And that girl, Wren, when he met her—"

"Ah," Ann-Marie said. "She looks like me. It's a little eerie."

"He called her your name. And even when she wasn't around, he thought you were a girl again. And"—her throat closed, and her nose burned—"it was a gift, a gift of his awful, obscene dementia, that we could talk about you again. I felt awful, like I was lying to him, but he'd talk about you as if everything was okay, that you were still in our lives and everything was happy." She sucked in a breath. "I *loved* those conversations. I looked forward to those talks, those memories, every day. I was even able to put out photos of you. He'd . . . he'd taken them all down at the house and packed them away. He didn't throw them away. He could never bring himself to do that. But he couldn't look at them."

Ann-Marie wept. She cried, quietly but back shaking. Vivian remembered that from when she was a child, how good she'd been at hiding her pain.

Ann-Marie wiped her eyes and pulled her knees up to her chest on the bench. Still flexible, still graceful and lithe. Oh, what could've been.

"Thank you," Ann-Marie gasped out. "Thank you for telling me that. I—I don't deserve to know that. That means so much to me."

Vivian stroked her daughter's hair.

She looked down the terraced garden beds. The boys sat in the shade. She saw Luna walking down the ramp, barefoot, to talk to them.

Ann-Marie watched her, too. "She's my age."

Vivian nodded. *Just think, I could have grandchildren.*

"Is she like the daughter you wished you had?"

Vivian didn't take the bait. "She's not my daughter. She's my friend." *A true friend.*

Silence blanketed them again. A hummingbird came to the fuchsia basket and drank.

"Dad was a wakeup call," Ann-Marie whispered when the bird zoomed away. "Seeing that obituary. Knowing how much I'd screwed up. How much I'd missed and lost out on. I want to get my life together, Mama."

Mama. "Good. I hope you do."

Ann-Marie looked up at the sky, then down at the garden, all around. "This is the happiest, healthiest place I've ever known. I wish I could start over."

Vivian had thought all night about a plan. She'd run it by the boys this morning, and even Drew had grudgingly approved. "I have a proposition for you."

Ann-Marie held up a hand. "Stop. I need to know: Are you okay? You're sick, aren't you?"

Oh, Cooper. "What did that boy say to you?"

"That's the thing. He didn't. He wouldn't. And I tried. He said it was something I needed to ask you. So I'm asking."

Well. Thank you, Cooper. "I have breast cancer. It's invasive."

Real pain crossed her daughter's face. "Oh, Mama. I'm sorry."

"I'm having a mastectomy. And then lots of chemo. They think it can be treated."

"They *think*?"

Vivian hated this. "It's bad. But . . . my surgical oncologist *does* think it can be handled. I'm going to try, and I'm going to fight like hell."

Vivian thought about how, just months ago, she'd been ready to end her life. And now so much had changed. So, so much. She was ready to fight for it. She'd fight dirty for it if she had to.

"So here's my proposition. This surgery, the chemo, it's not going to be pretty. And I'm going to need help."

Ann-Marie sat up. "I owe you."

No, no, no. Wrong answer. "I don't want you here because you feel you owe me. That would be awful. I'd *hate* that, do you hear me?"

Ann-Marie nodded.

"I meant what I said last night. You can't stay here. But you could stay nearby. I could help pay for an apartment. If you want to stay and help me. But listen to me: You *can't* leave me again. Or steal from me. Or fall off the wagon. Not now. If you stay, it has to be at least until I'm gone. Do you understand? Can you sign on for that? Are you strong enough?"

Ann-Marie swallowed. Vivian watched her slender white throat move. And she smelled it, the fear. Fear sparkled in Ann-Marie's eyes.

"I don't expect you to decide right this minute. I want you to think about it. *Really* think about it. Search your soul, Sweet Pea; will you do that?"

Ann-Marie stared down at the garden. "What if I'm not strong enough?"

Vivian sighed. "Then you tell me the truth."

"I'm not . . . a very strong person."

"But you are. You actually are. The fact that you're still alive is a testament to your strength. The fact that you keep trying. The fact that you're sixteen months sober. Sixteen months and *six days* now." *Oh shit, was that all a lie, too? Am I being gullible?* "Is that even true?" she asked.

"It is true."

"That shows strength. You are remarkable, my love. You said you had to leave tonight?"

Ann-Marie shook her head. "Maybe not. Maybe . . . I don't know."

"You *are* strong. Surprise me."

Ann-Marie's smile was sad.

"Surprise *yourself*," Vivian said.

Vivian stroked her daughter's hair again, somehow knowing she needed to fill up and store the memory. *Surprise me,* she wanted to plead. *Surprise me.*

That evening came and went with no word. Vivian's disappointment was sharper than she'd imagined it would be. No one asked her about it. Only the boys had known anyway, and they were too kind. The answer was clear.

By the second day, she began to feel a bit of relief. This was better. She needed only the strongest pack around her for the fight ahead. No distractions. Eyes on the prize.

And on the third day, the day before her mastectomy, with moths fluttering in her stomach and her heart racing, Vivian wanted to do something useful. Luna had one of the pernicious headaches that COVID had left her. Nothing would put a dent in it. Vivian couldn't stand to watch the woman sweat and move through life in that cramped, pained fashion. She said to Luna, "I have Oxycodone. Would you like one?"

Luna's eyes lit, but she hesitated. "I can't take your painkillers. Wait. They didn't give you a prescription already, did they? For the surgery? They can't do that."

Vivian shook her head. "No. These are left over from a surgery years ago."

"Then yes, please. *Something* has to work."

Vivian went to her bathroom and opened the drawer.

The bottles weren't there.

She stared a moment. She opened the other two drawers. Silence. These bottles hadn't sung to her for ages. When had she last seen them? It didn't matter. They were gone. She knew they were gone.

Ann-Marie had stolen them. She had stolen from her again.

She strode from the bathroom into the kitchen, feeling her rage crash ahead of her.

Luna's face registered alarm.

Cooper, who was making their lunch at the kitchen island, lifted his head, eyes wide.

Vivian announced, "She stole them. She fucking stole from me again!"

Ox, sitting on his barstool, flattened his ears.

"Oh, Vivian," Luna said. "I'm so sorry."

She moved toward Vivian as if to hug her, but Vivian would not be comforted. This rage felt necessary, and she wasn't done with it. "She's an addict. A *junkie*. She'll *always* be a junkie. I don't even know when she took them. Cooper, when she was here Sunday morning, did she go in the restroom?"

Cooper looked frozen. He opened his mouth. He started to speak, but Vivian needed to keep cutting, to keep punching, with her words, her voice. "She stole from me! Why did I think it would be different? I will *never*, ever fucking learn!"

Cooper whispered, "What did she steal?"

"My Oxycodone! I wanted to give one to your mother. And now I can't."

He set down the knife he was holding and left the room. Vivian realized she was perhaps scaring the boy. That perhaps she needed to calm down. But she couldn't. "God *damn* it!" she screamed. She really screamed, savoring the scraping rasp in her throat.

Ox hopped from his barstool and fled the room.

"Vivian," Luna said. "Oh, Vivian, I'm sorry."

Vivian flushed with shame. This poor woman before her felt terrible, was practically debilitated with pain. She didn't need Vivian's temper tantrum. And really, why was Vivian so surprised and angry? She should have known. She should have known.

"I'm sorry," she said to Luna. "I'm . . . I'm not myself today."

This time, she let Luna hug her. She was looking over Luna's shoulder as she saw Wren wheel into the room, looking nervous, checking on them. For heaven's sake, the poor girl had heard Vivian shrieking and carrying on—of course she was alarmed.

Then, behind Wren, Cooper came back to the kitchen. He set a gallon Ziploc on the kitchen island. The Ziploc contained five amber pill bottles.

"She didn't steal from you," Cooper said. "I did."

CHAPTER TWENTY-FIVE

COOPER

Cooper hated the shame he felt. But not for one second had he considered letting Ann-Marie take this blame. That woman had done some hideous things in her life. She'd betrayed Vivian over and over again.

But not this time.

Vivian stared at the bottles. No one spoke.

Cooper's mom clutched one hand to her forehead, digging her thumb into her temple. He knew she was in pain. He hated that he'd just made it worse. Story of his life.

"Cooper?" Mom whispered. "Why?"

The fact that she sounded sad, not angry, twisted a knife in his chest.

He thought about lying. He thought about making it no big deal. He could say he wanted to try one, or he wanted to keep them from Ann-Marie, or something like that. But when he opened his mouth, the truth walked out. "I thought we were leaving."

Vivian lifted her head. She, Mom, and Wren all stared at him.

His mom shook her head. "I don't understand."

"You said we had to leave. I just wanted something to help . . . to help us."

Mom blinked. He might as well be speaking Chinese or something. "Help us . . . do *what*?"

He stood up straight. He tried to channel Ann-Marie and the way she owned her shit. "I could sell these. For money. *Lots* of money. I wanted to help us."

Mom's expression killed him. She looked like he'd just told her he'd murdered someone and chopped them up in the basement.

Vivian sat at the kitchen island, her face in her hands. Cooper hated himself.

Wren had wheeled out of sight, but Cooper knew she was still listening.

Vivian's back shook, and a muffled sound came from behind her hands. Cooper went to her. "Vivian. I'm so sorry. I messed up. Bad. I know I must've—"

But when he touched her shoulder, she moved her hands. She was crying . . . but smiling. Her tears were happy tears. "This is wonderful!" she said, laugh-sobbing. "She didn't steal from me. This time, she didn't steal from me." She stood up and hugged Cooper.

He blinked at his mother's shocked face over Vivian's shoulders. He kept his arms at his sides while the old lady embraced him and kissed his cheek.

"But Cooper *did*!" his mother said, her words hard and cutting.

Vivian released the hug and held him at arm's length. She scowled, but he could tell her heart wasn't in it. "And why were you snooping in my bathroom, young man?"

"I wasn't!" He held up his hands and stepped back from her grasp. "I swear. I saw them, like, a month ago. When Mom was really sick and I was staying down here. I saw all these and, to be honest, at first they scared me. I mean, why do you *have* all this Oxycodone? This . . . this is a lot."

Vivian sat back down.

Mom paced the kitchen, her hands on her head, clutching her hair.

"I kept checking, to see if any pills were gone, but they never were. But then. When Ann-Marie came back and Mom said we had to leave, I thought of them."

"Oh my God, oh my God," his mom said, still pacing. "I'm just the goddamn Mother of the Year, aren't I? My son feels the need to *steal* to take care of me! To steal from someone who has been so, so good to us! What have I done? What kind of life have I given my children?"

No, no, no. His mom's anguish tore Cooper's chest open. This . . . this wasn't what he'd wanted her to feel. Not at all. He was only trying to help.

"Luna." Vivian's voice was sharp. "Stop that nonsense. You are an amazing mother and human being."

"But I—my son—"

"You are resourceful and resilient and a fighter. Cooper was misguided, but his intention is good. You have to see that."

"Resourceful and resilient? How? I've stayed here for months, living on your charity! What kind of lesson is that for my kids? Vivian, without you, what would have happened to us? And for my son to repay you by stealing because . . . because he thought that's what I needed!"

Cooper wanted to disappear. His eyes burned.

"Charity?" Vivian said, her eyes hard and bright. "You think you're living on charity?"

"What else can you call it?" his mother cried. She kept clutching her head. Tears streaked her cheeks.

"I could call it saving my life," Vivian said.

Something in her tone made the hair on Cooper's arms raise. His mom held still.

"I don't mean that figuratively. You saved my life, Luna. All of you did."

The silence was weird. Cooper felt like he couldn't move or breathe.

"You want to know why I have all that Oxycodone? Because I'd been stockpiling it. The day you all came here? That morning, right before you and Wren came to my door, I was standing in my kitchen with a glass of water, ready to swallow them all. I'd already taken one;

I'd actually started. I didn't want to . . . be here without Jack. I didn't want to be anywhere without him. I didn't want to . . . *be*."

Cooper couldn't breathe. He hated that Vivian had ever felt that way. He'd felt that before. The not wanting to be. He wouldn't wish it on anyone.

His mom put her hands over her mouth. Tears slipped over her fingers.

"I couldn't tell you that because I—what kind of bullshit emotional blackmail would that have been? I couldn't tell you that *you* were my reason for living. I couldn't hold you hostage with that manipulation. I knew you wanted to leave."

"*I* didn't!" Wren said, out of view in the hallway.

Nosy little shit. But she made everyone—even Mom—exhale. A little.

Cooper opened his mouth. "That's why you didn't want to treat your cancer."

She turned those laser eyes on him. "Yes."

"Do . . . do you still want to . . ." He gestured to the Oxycodone bottles.

Vivian shot him a look that said he was a moron. "Do you think I'd be letting them amputate part of my body tomorrow if I did? *No!* No, I do not still want to kill myself." She shook her head at him, but her eyes softened. "And that's because of *you*." Damn it, the burning in his eyes spilled over, and a sob hiccupped out of him.

Vivian turned to his mom. "And you. And even you, you sneaky little spy," she called to Wren. "You may as well come in here where we can see you."

Wren rolled into view, Ox sitting in her lap.

Vivian turned to face his mom. "I don't know how to get it through your thick, stubborn skull, woman, that this is *not* charity. That you've helped me every bit as much as I've helped you."

His mom still cried. "You—you *saved* us."

Vivian rolled her eyes. "We helped *each other*. I didn't save you, Luna. I've never known another human in so little need of saving. You are the scrappiest, smartest, strongest survivor I've ever known."

His mom crumpled down to the floor, her head in her hands, crying. Wren looked scared. And Cooper had to admit it was kind of scary to see your mom crying on the floor. He moved to sit beside her, his hand on her back.

Vivian sat down on the floor right in front of his mom. He heard her knees pop. He saw her grab her right hip and wince, but then she took his mom's hands. Wren rolled over beside them.

Vivian leaned in and spoke to his mother. "All I did, Luna, was give you a rest. Give you some breathing room. You are strong. You are an amazing mother. But after years of living in survival mode, you were exhausted. That's all. All I did was let you rest."

Mom went into a whole other level of sobbing, her back bucking under his hand. And Vivian cried, too, she and Mom leaning their heads together, clasping hands. Then something broke loose within him, too, and he let another sob escape. Then another. He didn't hold back, he didn't worry about *crying like a girl*, he just let that shit fly.

It felt good. So good.

Wren's hand touched his head, so he reached up to hold her hand. They all cried together, Ox watching them with his unreadable owl face, and eventually, the crying turned into giggles. And Vivian gave his mom an Oxycodone. Then Vivian hugged everyone.

She hugged him last, and while she held him, she said, "Turns out being your friend *was* enough. Thank you."

And damn it if he didn't start crying all over again.

Fortunately, the Oxycodone worked on his mom's headache. She didn't say anything else about him stealing. He hoped that would never come up again.

He made Vivian a nice dinner of caprese salad with tomatoes and basil from the garden, of course, and honey-garlic salmon. The guys came over to join them. She wouldn't be allowed to eat after midnight. Fortunately, the surgery was crazy early, so she joked she wouldn't have to be hungry long. Steven and Drew were going to take her to the hospital. She would have to stay one night, maybe two, and the guys would take turns staying overnight there with her. The hospital was allowing one guest again because COVID cases were down. Mom had wanted to stay with Vivian, but the guys convinced her she should rest and get real sleep—which they probably wouldn't, on a hospital cot—so that she could take care of Vivian when they brought her home.

Mom said people needed to have advocates with them while they were hospitalized. It made his insides twist to picture his mom all alone in the hospital for those thirteen days she had been.

But it was good that Vivian would have someone. And it was good that cases were down. For now. Everyone was talking about a variant spreading in Europe and Brazil that would be worse.

Maybe the apocalypse really would come.

As long as he was with these people, that was all right by him.

CHAPTER TWENTY-SIX

VIVIAN

Vivian weeded in the garden after dinner, the fat cat lounging nearby as if supervising. The weeding calmed her, even though the mosquitos were a nuisance. She'd been told that after surgery, she wouldn't be allowed to push or pull, to lift more than five pounds—sorry, Ox—or lift her arms above her head for several weeks. She was enjoying a little dirt therapy while she could.

As she weeded, lightness sparkled through her, and she caught herself smiling.

Ann-Marie had not stolen from her.

And Vivian no longer heard the pills singing. Had not heard them at all, in fact, for months. Had, frankly, forgotten them. The sparkles poured out of her as laughter.

Cooper, the dear boy, came down from Jack's Hill. He squinted at her laughing in the twilight by herself. She must look batty, but she didn't care.

"Hey," Cooper said. "I found this." He held an envelope in his hand. "This was on the ballerina statue."

Vivian recognized the childish scrawl, as if Ann-Marie's handwriting had stayed frozen from when she was untroubled and sober. For a split second, it disturbed her to think that Ann-Marie had been here, had snuck on to the property undetected. But mostly, she felt a bit of sorrow, because she knew what the note would say before she even opened it.

You deserve strength, Mama, and I'm not strong. I'm glad you have a strong pack to protect you. Be fierce in the fight. Know that I'll be rooting for you every step of the way. But from a safe distance so I can't harm or hurt you anymore.

Vivian didn't cry.

She'd already known. Because when her daughter told her she wasn't strong, Vivian believed her. But this note, this decision, it was strength of a sort. And for that, Vivian was grateful.

CHAPTER TWENTY-SEVEN

VIVIAN

June 2021

Vivian sat on Jack's Hill in the early-morning breeze, in the sacred silence before the Brood X cicadas began their screaming. She was in a wheelchair, had been for about three weeks now. At first, she and Wren had raced. Wren had taught her many things. Vivian had all the more admiration for the girl after being burdened with this cumbersome contraption herself.

It was nearly time.

She watched the sun rise, a neon pink. Cooper had helped her get up this morning, and she knew he was lurking somewhere nearby. She'd wanted to beat the heat of the day. She was cold, always cold, but the humidity depleted her. She felt more alive outside, close to nature, even the deafening chorus of these strange, frantic cicadas. She felt more alive in her garden, close to Jack.

She was certain today was the day. She pulled her note from the sweatshirt pocket with trembling fingers and placed it at the ballerina statue's feet. A note to her daughter.

A hummingbird whizzed by her ear. She felt the breeze it created on her scalp, covered now in white chick fluff. Cooper had told her she looked punk rock. She had to admit, her bald look was striking: her giant eyes, her prominent cheekbones, her sapphire earrings, which she never took off.

"You okay?"

Cooper's voice.

But she felt dizzy, a bit disoriented. Where was he? "I'm fine. I'm happy. Thank you."

He dropped into her view, in his "100% Vaccinated" T-shirt, his own head shorn, his dark hair coming in straight and shiny. He'd been the first to shave his head in solidarity. Then Drew, then Steven. Two days later, even Luna. Wren had been last. They now looked like odd cult members.

"You sure?" Cooper asked.

She reached a hand out to his cheek. She didn't tell him she was finding it difficult to draw a deep breath. Or think clearly. She was on a lot of morphine. But not too much. She'd told the Hospice worker that she wanted to stay present.

"I'm sure," she whispered. "Look how beautiful."

He sat near her, on the end of the bench. He stared up at the pink-and-orange parfait of a sky. He took her hand. It hurt, the way he squeezed it; everything hurt her now, but she didn't tell him. She exhaled through her nose and focused on the warmth of his hand.

Jack holding Ann-Marie, so tiny in his hands, for the very first time. Grinning. "She looks like a football."

"Are you scared?" Cooper asked.

"No." That was not a lie. "I'm just sorry I didn't hold up my end of the bargain."

"What are you talking about?"

"I was supposed to stick around to be your friend."

"Shut up." His voice was angry. She turned her head to regard him. "Stop making me cry."

She wanted to poke him in the shoulder, but it felt like too much effort. Yes, she was glad she'd put the card on the statue.

He laughed and wiped his eyes. "What do you feel? Like, not physically. Emotionally."

She thought a moment. "It's all bittersweet." The word made her think of the bright-orange berries that would bloom later, closer to the back door. *Jack kisses her at last. Outside the high school gym. Snow falling, gathering in their hair, their eyebrows, their lashes.* "I'm sad to leave you. All of you."

He sniffed.

"But I'm happy to join Jack."

"What do you think happens? You'll see him in heaven?"

Jack hugs her after his diagnosis, his eyes haunted, horrified. "Will you take care of me?" he asks. She promises.

"I don't know." She really didn't. "But he went before me, so it feels . . . closer to him. Like I'll join him. Somehow. That . . . that's happy."

She thought of the plans she'd set in motion. Was she doing the right thing? She'd longed for a sign. She was still pissed that Jack had not haunted her, had not visited her and guided her.

Ann-Marie onstage. A snowflake in The Nutcracker. *Those arms of hers. Vivian can always find her in an ensemble onstage by her arms. That graceful back and neck.*

Cooper's voice felt farther away, even though he was close. He was urgent, his mouth moving. She concentrated hard to hear him.

". . . because of you. I swear. I promise you. I will be here now and make it matter."

She felt like she might be lifting away. Or being pulled under. Or both at once, which she didn't know a word for.

Toddler Ann-Marie rubs her eyes with chubby fists when she wakes.

Cooper was saying her name. ". . . get you back to the house." He started to move her chair.

She mustered every bit of strength she had remaining and said, "No!" loud enough for him to hear.

He knelt before her. "I think we need to get someone."

She held his arm. "You live like a motherf . . ." She didn't have the strength to finish, but he half laughed, half sobbed, and nodded.

Luna, gentle Luna, holds Vivian's pain ball and lymphatic drain tubes, cradles them outside the shower door while Vivian showers post-surgery. Luna pats her dry with soft towels. Luna kisses her forehead.

"Bring . . . the others . . . up."

He nodded. Tears streaked his face, so gaunt-looking under the shorn hair.

When he left, she closed her eyes. But then she made herself open them. She didn't want to miss anything, not one second.

She holds Jack's hand as Drew and Steven face each other, reciting vows in husky, trying-not-to-cry voices. Jack whispers, "I hope they have as great a time as we've had."

She watched the hummingbird at the fuchsia basket, a new basket that Ann-Marie had brought two weeks ago. The breeze caressed Vivian's face. She heard a cicada nearby start its electronic chatter. So much noise, so much fuss, from such a small creature. All that drama they produced for being here such a short time. She breathed in the lily of the valley, the viburnum.

Another cicada started up somewhere behind her. Soon, their sound would be overwhelming.

In her line of vision, a cicada lifted into clumsy flight, but a cardinal swooped in and snatched it from the air, the insect shrieking.

The hummingbird drinking from the fuchsia was unfazed.

Another hummingbird appeared.

Vivian watched the two, drinking together.

CHAPTER
TWENTY-EIGHT

WREN

Wren snuck back into the house, hoping none of the gathered guests noticed. Once inside, she rolled quickly through the kitchen, where guests might wander in, and to the privacy of Vivian's room. The effort of "sharing" Vivian with all these other people today at the "celebration of life" made her feel sick.

When Grammy died, Wren had been too young to really understand or feel it. She'd been sad but in a strange, faraway kind of way.

Losing Vivian was specific and *close*, inside her. Vivian's absence hurt her, ached in her joints. Wren rolled up to Vivian's dresser and looked at the collage she'd given Vivian on her birthday last year.

Wren remembered that weird, awful night. The night she'd first "seen" who Dad really was. Even that didn't hurt like missing Vivian—it only made her tired.

Dad was here now, outside, with all those other people. People from Sycamore Place, people who used to work for Jack, Danielle and Birdy, people Vivian and Jack had been friends with in another life. Dad's showing up had surprised her. In a good way. Everyone seemed to think it was good that he had come. And he'd gotten to know Vivian, so it made sense. When Wren had come inside, he'd been talking to

Drew and Steven, the three of them in a tight circle near the fountain. Whatever happened to "stay away from those guys"? Now Dad acted like they were his new BFFs.

Mom, and Steven and Drew, and Ann-Marie—and, really, Vivian herself—had put together a really nice celebration. They'd rented all these white chairs and spread them out on every level of the garden, like one of the fancy outdoor theaters she'd seen in books. Vivian had insisted that people gather in her garden after she died. Wren remembered the first time Vivian had said that—"After I die . . ."—and how it had punched the breath out of her. The way Vivian had said it so matter-of-factly. Vivian loved her garden, and with the stupid Delta variant of the Coronavirus spreading all through their area, it seemed safest to be outside, but those gross, awful cicadas ruined everything.

Wren hated those disgusting bugs and their nasty red eyes and stupid life cycle. Early this morning, Cooper was out there sweeping up all their smelly dead bodies and crunchy shells. Wren couldn't stand it, even though the boys were all laughing at how ridiculous it was.

"But it's what she wanted," Steven said, laughing. "So we'll do it."

They'd rented a podium and put it by the back door, near the foot of the ramp, and a microphone, and different people had talked about Vivian. They had to use the microphone because the cicadas were so loud, it was crazy. Occasionally, someone talking got dive-bombed by one. While Drew talked, a cicada landed on his shirt. First it just sat there, and he didn't notice it as he told the story of how Jack and Vivian stood in for his parents at his wedding to Steven, because his own parents wouldn't come. Then the cicada started to screech, and he said, "Shit! Holy shit!" right into the microphone. Everyone laughed. Vivian would have loved it.

But listening to people Wren didn't know talk about Vivian made her feel weird. She didn't believe that other people missed Vivian the way *she* did. She felt like a baby, thinking like that, even though she was twelve now, but she couldn't help it. That's why she'd snuck into the house. So she could think about Vivian by herself.

The door popped open, fast and pushy, and Wren turned, ready to be snotty to whoever was intruding on her, but she smiled when she saw Ox.

"Mrrp?"

"I'm okay. I just wanted to be alone. But you can be here. You can always be with me."

Ox was her cat now. Wren had promised Vivian she'd always take good care of him.

Ox crossed the room to jump in her lap. He was thinner now. Still taller and wider than any cat she'd ever known, but a year's worth of healthier eating had slimmed him down. She curved forward to kiss his forehead, and he rubbed his face against hers again and again. That crowded, awful, smothering feeling she'd had outside with everyone else slipped away from her, replaced by the calm of his purr.

Wren looked at herself in Vivian's mirror. Her hair looked stupid, so short. It was maybe an inch long now, it was taking forever to grow back, but she was glad she'd done it. When she'd shaved her head, she'd felt something else falling away from her along with her long black hair. She knew her dad wouldn't like it, and she hadn't cared.

Only Cooper looked good this way. No one else did. Well, maybe Mom.

Wren stared into her own face, Ox still rubbing his cheeks along her jaw, and knew she looked older. Wiser. Next year, she'd be a teenager.

Next year, maybe this pandemic would be over. Maybe she'd be back in school. She and Cooper had both stayed remote this year. Wren had done it solely to protect Vivian, missing in-person school desperately, but she knew Cooper had loved not going to school.

Vivian is gone.

Wren sucked in a breath so sharply that Ox stopped his headbutting and looked up at her. "Mrrp?"

That happened four or five times a day—at least—that sudden realization that her friend was gone. Did not exist anymore. And every time, it felt like the floor gave way underneath Wren's wheelchair and she was plunging into space below.

She looked up at that collage. She knew that it should be hers now. With great effort, she managed to reach it. She propped it against her chest, and Ox seemed to understand it was fragile and gave her the space for it. Wren listened at the door and heard people in the kitchen. She wheeled herself into her own bedroom without anyone calling to her.

She shut the door behind her and propped Vivian's collage on her own desk. She sat still and stared at it until Ox got bored and jumped down from her lap.

Wren didn't know what would happen now. All the adults kept telling her that she didn't need to worry, that they would stay here, for now anyway, and there was no hurry to leave.

Wren knew a secret.

She'd asked Vivian once what would happen to them, and Vivian had asked her, "What do you want to happen?"

Wren had said, "I want to live in this house forever."

And Vivian had taken Wren's hand and said, "Then that's what you'll do."

They'd never talked about it again, but Wren knew it would all be okay. She didn't know how, but if Vivian said so, it would be. Wren was just waiting for everyone else to know it, too.

Vivian is gone.

Wren jerked to life and rolled to her desk. She opened the big box her father had given her on her twelfth birthday. It was the first gift he'd ever given her that was actually *for* her and not just some dumb thing he'd picked up at a gas station. Inside the box were art supplies—glues and paints and markers and special scissors for her awkward hands and glass beads and wire.

He and Mom were officially divorced now.

Mom had sole custody.

And Wren had learned, before her birthday, that Dad hadn't even asked for any custody.

She'd asked Cooper about that, whispering in the middle of the night, and Cooper had said, "I don't really know. I think, if he doesn't have any custody, he doesn't have to give Mom any money? Or maybe he was just too lazy to bother?"

She thought about that. She'd stopped calling him. She'd stopped texting him every day.

And then the weirdest thing happened. After about five days of no contact, *he* called *her*. Then he brought her this real gift when she turned twelve. She decided she could keep both of those things—his letting her down and the gift—at the same time. One thing didn't have to win out over the other. She'd told this to Vivian, who'd said, "That's very wise, young lady."

Wren wanted to go to her art table, but there were too many people in the house now, and she didn't want to talk to anyone, so she used her bed as her table. It wasn't great, and she had to lean too much, since she couldn't get her legs under the bed like she could a table, but it worked.

Ox batted something around under the bed.

She put a piece of foam board down and started cutting photos of Vivian and her family. She and Cooper had gone through all the photos to display today for the celebration, and Wren had copied several for herself. She selected a picture of Mom and Vivian, side by side, on the couch, both with knees drawn up and wrapped in quilts. One of Vivian lying on the couch while Cooper read to her. Vivian and Wren in the garden, Wren holding an armload of gladiolas that Vivian had cut. Vivian wearing a hot-pink wig and posing like a model. She found one photo of Dad and tucked it underneath all the other pictures, so she'd know it was there.

Ox batted his toy out from under the bed. Wren looked down and saw it was a cicada shell. She leaned down, flailing her arms, and managed to take it. "Mowwff," Ox protested.

Wren pushed herself back into position in her wheelchair and examined the light-brown hollow shell, light as paper, brittle as straw. "I need this," she said to Ox. "You have lots of other toys. Okay?"

He sighed. He flopped onto his side, as if defeated.

Wren placed the cicada shell on the collage. She planned to glue it into place next to a picture of Ann-Marie with Vivian, the two of them up on Jack's Hill, holding hands. Wren stared at that photo a long time.

Ann-Marie wasn't magic. She wasn't the other half of Wren. She didn't activate Wren's powers.

She was just a lady. Wren liked her. A lot. But she was just a regular person living her own life.

And Wren's powers?

They belonged to Wren alone.

CHAPTER TWENTY-NINE

LUNA

Luna hung up the phone after an emotional conversation with Vivian's attorney, then laughed out loud.

She was alone in the house. The kids were helping with a party at Drew and Steven's for Steven's clinic staff. Wren had done all the flower arrangements, and Cooper was doing the cooking. The boys were paying them. Later, Danielle and Birdy were coming for dinner.

Luna ran her hands over her short, soft hair, a new habit she couldn't stop. Her hair felt like velvet. "Oh, Vivian, you sneaky, sly . . ."

Ox strolled into the kitchen. "Mrff?"

Luna scooped him up, then spun in a circle, the cat purring. Still holding him, she did a little *pas de bourrée* and a *pas de chat*, moves she'd brought back to life after long dormancy in her body. "Guess what, Ox? Ms. Vivian is still giving us tricky little gifts."

Well, *little* was the wrong word.

Oh, that woman.

Luna panted, winded from her dance. She was getting stronger and stronger but still wasn't herself. She missed her friend. Missed her spunk and sass, her foul mouth, her generous spirit, her no-nonsense approach to . . . well, everything.

Luna remembered Vivian's reaction to the oncologist telling her the cancer had metastasized and that there was no point in continuing treatment. "Well, shit," Vivian had said. "Shit." Then she'd sat up straight, slapped her thighs, and said, "You don't have to ask me twice. I'll be thrilled to stop chemo."

Once they were alone in the car, Vivian grabbed Luna's hand and said, "I don't want to go yet."

She'd never shown a single scrap of self-pity or fear.

When Luna had cared for Vivian toward the end, helping her bathe and go to the bathroom, Vivian apologized and said, "This is not how I wanted it to be."

Luna told her, "If this had to happen, then this is exactly how I wanted it to be."

She considered it a privilege to care for her friend.

Luna knew she'd been a good nursing assistant, but she couldn't stop thinking about the nurse who'd saved her when she had COVID. Lisa had given her sponge baths in her hospital bed, helping her feel human. Lisa had washed Luna's hair. Lisa had wheeled Luna outside to breathe in fresh air. Lisa had held Luna's phone—Luna was too weak to hold it up herself—so that she could FaceTime Cooper and Wren. Lisa had told her every day, "You're gonna get through this. You're gonna get home to those beautiful kids."

Luna wanted to be like Lisa.

When Luna told Vivian she wanted to go back to nursing school, Vivian said, "You will be an excellent nurse."

Luna had met up with her former nursing-school friends, the four of them laughing that making plans during a pandemic was so much easier than in the Before Times. Jodi and James were full-time nurses now, their graduations accelerated due to the shortage. Mandy didn't miss nursing, saying, "People are too stupid. It's not worth it," but Luna had sensed that for Jodi and James, it was everything. They were exhausted but felt their days had real purpose and passion.

Luna tried to get back to work, to save money, but she didn't have the stamina. She knew the Sycamore Place administrators' patience was wearing thin. At first, she got paid through workers' comp, but they dropped her because COVID was considered only a two-week disease. She should be getting unemployment, but the errors in the overloaded system meant she hadn't seen a single check in the many months since she'd qualified.

She heard from Cachè that the facility was woefully understaffed. Luna knew she wasn't strong enough to return to that chaotic situation and shouldering so much work.

Luna sat at the kitchen island, holding Ox in her lap. "Thank you, Vivian," she said aloud. Luna knew the only reason she had recovered at all was that being here in this house had given her the privilege to sleep fourteen hours every night and take a two-hour nap every day.

Every single day, including this one right now, she pictured what would have happened if she hadn't known Vivian.

"What if someone can't get tested?" she'd asked Vivian. "What if they can't get medical care, can't get a diagnosis, or they can't take paid time off work?"

"That's a huge problem," Vivian said, her eyes so big and round in her skeletal face.

"We got through this simply because I *happened* to know you. I am so grateful, but I also feel so guilty."

Vivian shook her shorn head. "You didn't just happen to know me. You treated my husband with dignity and grace. You helped me through my darkest days. Twice."

Luna hadn't pressed it but sat there, frustrated. It didn't sit right.

And into that silence, Vivian had said, "You're right. It's like those stories of a school donating money to a teacher with cancer or buying a custodian a car. People's survival shouldn't depend on the off chance they know someone."

"Yes!" Luna said.

Vivian had fixed those giant anime eyes on her. "Maybe you could change that."

Huh. No pressure, lady.

Luna didn't know how to change it. Yet. But she wasn't going to let it go. And in the meantime, she'd quit her job and enrolled in nursing school—all online for now. She'd just learned from Vivian's attorney that her tuition was paid for. And that she had a grocery and utilities stipend for the next seven years, and the name of Vivian's financial adviser, who could help that stipend last even longer.

When she'd told Cal about nursing school, he said he was proud of her. They were done. For real, done. She knew, from Ricky, that he was even dating someone he'd met at work. But he was trying with the kids, he really was. He was still such a kid himself, but she was proud of the changes he was making. He told her he'd argued with his mother about Cooper, defending his son against his mother's beliefs. Luna had thought he was exaggerating to make himself look good, but Ricky verified the story.

Luna stood, craving coffee, even though it was late in the afternoon. Coffee had been the last flavor that had returned to her and the one she savored the most. Chocolate and, oddly, salmon had been among the first. (She'd begun to believe that Vivian was haunting her.)

Vivian. Her friend had tricked her in the best possible way. She wanted to be angry, but when she thought about what Vivian had done, Luna laughed again.

She started the coffee maker, shaking her head at the memory of their fight over this house. "Do *not* leave this house to me," Luna demanded. "Because I will give it to your daughter."

Luna dried her hands on the dish towel Ann-Marie had brought her mother, in honor of the Brood X cicadas. Instead of the LIVE, LAUGH, LOVE that Vivian disdained, it had a picture of the red-eyed insect and said SCREAM, FUCK, DIE. Vivian had laughed and laughed.

Ann-Marie was very much Vivian's daughter.

Luna had worried Vivian would be angry with her for finding that card with Ann-Marie's info on it and calling her, telling her about the cancer's spread to Vivian's hip and bones. But Vivian had been bolstered by the still-sober Ann-Marie's consistent visits. Luna had met Ann-Marie for coffee, just the two of them, three separate times. She liked the woman. She hoped they could be friends. This dish towel, the woman's irreverence, and her brutal honesty were why.

It was because of Ann-Marie that Luna was dancing again. Luna had started with some videos on YouTube, but then she'd asked Ann-Marie about her ballet career and worked up the courage to ask her for lessons. At first, Ann-Marie made the same dismissive hand gesture her mother did, but Luna had pressed. "I've been looking online for adult classes, but no one is open yet. I really want to do this, just for me. I'll pay you."

Luna'd taken money from her savings to buy a portable ballet barre. Cooper called it the "handrails," which made her and Ann-Marie laugh. Luna had ordered herself pink leather ballet shoes—just the soft slippers, not pointe shoes, of course. Ann-Marie claimed pointe shoes were instruments of torture. Luna had ordered two leotards, some tights, and a short wrap-around tulle skirt. She couldn't remember the last time she'd used her money to buy anything for herself. Especially something *not necessary*. Not practical.

Ann-Marie was a surprisingly good teacher. She pushed Luna and treated the lessons seriously. Their classes were short, since Luna didn't have great stamina yet, but she knew ballet was helping her get stronger and more limber.

More happy.

When dance schools were able to open up again, she planned to screw up her courage to take an adult ballet class downtown, in the school attached to the theater.

Ann-Marie got an odd look on her face when Luna said, "You ought to teach for them. You used to be in the company, right?"

Luna smiled, here in the kitchen.

She listened to the symphony of the doomed bugs screaming outside. Plague. Locusts. What was next? Frogs falling from the sky?

She heard Wren's voice calling, "Mom? Mom!" and her heart shot full of adrenaline. She rushed to the back door to see Cooper and Wren coming up the ramp. She opened the door but saw them smiling, their faces eager, like Christmas mornings long ago.

"Ann-Marie just texted!" Wren said. "She wanted to know if we knew the news yet! She said we had to hear it from you. But she put in a ton of smiley faces, so we know it's good news!"

Luna laughed. She couldn't help it; it spilled from her, buoyant and light.

Cooper watched her laugh, his eyes laughing, too. "Did she leave you the house?" he asked.

Luna shut her mouth. She shook her head. "No. She did not."

She couldn't stand the confusion that clouded her children's faces. Even though she knew it was temporary, she had to rush on and tell them Vivian's punch line.

"She left it to Wren."

CHAPTER THIRTY

COOPER

Cooper rose early on Vivian's birthday. He remembered last year and the cake. She hadn't made it to seventy-six. That sucked. He missed her.

God, he *missed* her.

Like, every day, he missed his best friend.

She'd truly been his friend. He'd *hated* her the night they met, this rich, snobby woman acting like their savior. But he knew now he loved her.

He could say that and not feel like a creep or a dork because of their Valentine's dinner. Her husband, Jack, had died on February 15 the year before. Vivian had said that was perfect because he was her valentine, her love forever. On Valentine's Day this year, their pandemic pack had dinner. Cooper had made the meal, of course (a honey-garlic salmon with coconut rice and sugar-snap-pea salad and another tender, luscious chocolate cake cut into a heart shape with raspberry whipping cream filling and a chocolate ganache).

Vivian had talked about love.

Not just romantic love but the love of human family. She'd been teary-eyed and sentimental, and they'd all thought at first it was just from remembering Jack. She'd gone on about how on this "Hallmark holiday," as she called it, the messages could be tough if you weren't in a romantic relationship. She got so weepy, going on so long about how she loved all her friends and Ox and people she saw at the grocery store and the hospital that Cooper thought she was a little bit drunk. She rambled on about how there were "countless kinds of love out there, including random acts of kindness for and from strangers," and raised her glass to make them all toast to "Love. Just love. Let's celebrate love, human family. And know that you all have mine."

They clinked their glasses together, and he knew he loved her, too, as much as he loved his mom and sister, and Birdy, and these guys who'd changed his life.

But right after the toast, she'd told them what she'd just learned from her oncologist. That the cancer had spread and there was nothing more they could do. Cooper had been filled with rage for any oncologist telling a patient such news on Valentine's Day.

On the anniversary of her husband's death, she knew she was going to die too soon, too.

Life sometimes sucked.

He used to think life always sucked.

But Vivian had changed that for him.

Although it completely sucked that she was gone.

He wanted to honor her birthday. He knew he'd make her cake again, but he wanted something private, too. He thought of the way Ann-Marie had poured the shots of Jameson for her dad.

Vivian had loved her cocktails, but Cooper didn't know how to make them.

So he made a pot of coffee. Strong. He poured it into her favorite red cup and flavored it with caramel syrup. He sprinkled thick, coarse salt on top. He carried this up to Jack's Hill and set the cup at the ballerina statue's feet.

This was where she'd come to feel close to Jack, and it's where Cooper came to feel close to Vivian.

"I miss you," he said aloud.

A cicada upside down on the ground screeched to life, as if in answer.

God, he was sick of these cicadas.

Vivian had delighted in them, calling them a phenomenon.

Cooper knew they were dying out, these poor Brood X suckers. Every day, their screaming was quieter; every day there were fewer of them in the trees, hitting the house, flying into him. The one on the ground was the only one making sound at the moment. Cooper couldn't stand to watch it trapped on its back, so he crouched and flipped it over with a flick of his fingernail. The cicada took flight into a tree and screamed at him from there.

He hoped it was thanking him.

Tons of the empty, abandoned husks of the cicadas lined the trees and the bushes, and the dead bodies of the emerged still littered the ground, but not like when he'd had to sweep them up on a daily basis.

Ox ate them, sometimes alive, so the cat wasn't allowed outside anymore until the cicadas were gone, disappeared for another seventeen years.

The cicada he'd flipped continued to shriek at him.

What if it wanted to die? Like Vivian had once? The hair on his arms raised, thinking of it, as he often did, imagining that she'd swallowed the pills, and when his mom and sister had gone to her apartment, they'd found her dead. What if they'd never come to this house; what if Cooper had never met her?

He sat on the bench and picked up a hollow cicada shell. He held it up to the light, the morning sun shining through it.

He put the shell back in the same spot and ran his hands over his cropped hair, aching at the memory of Vivian's long white hair falling out.

The day she'd shaved her head, saying, "Let's get this over with," was the day Cooper had come out to his dad. He'd told Vivian he was going to, and she had squeezed his hand and wished him luck. She told him, "However he reacts, that's about him, not about you."

But Dad cried. Like, not sobbing or anything, but honest to God sniffling and tears in his eyes. Cooper had not expected that. At all. Dad said, "I'm just scared your life will be harder."

"Nothing is harder than pretending," Cooper said.

Dad nodded, and when he rose to go, Dad hugged him. *Hugged* him. It was awkward and brief. But still.

When Cooper told Drew and Steven about it the next day, Steven said, "He's trying. He means well." Then he laughed and said, "Even if he did call COVID the Kung Flu right in front of me last time he was here."

Cooper put his hands over his eyes. "Jesus, he's such an asshole."

Drew surprised Cooper by getting stern. "Hey. You know how my folks wouldn't come to our wedding? Your dad may be a clueless idiot, but he wouldn't do that. I guarantee you. If you were marrying a man and your dad was invited, he would come. He might show up wearing something that embarrasses you, and he might eat a piece of wedding cake before you cut it, for fuck's sake, but he'd *be* there."

Cooper picked up the cicada shell again.

He couldn't believe his family lived here now. Vivian was so smart, giving the house to Wren. Wren had to let him and his mom stay, if they wanted, until she was eighteen, and then it was up to her. The house was perfect for her. Wren would always be okay.

Mom was going to nursing school. He was taking online cooking classes with the money Vivian had left him. And he was already looking into culinary schools for after graduation. He had Vivian's car.

Cooper and Wren would both be going to a new school system. The assholes at his old school were behind him. He'd get a clean slate, a new start.

All because of Vivian.

That is, unless some new variant came along and wiped everyone out. Humans were fucking up right and left, leaving a shit show for him and his sister to deal with, literally protesting against new discoveries and tools that could save them, refusing to stop the things that would destroy them; the West Coast was on fire, the East Coast was flooding, the hate was escalating.

Everything was so damn bleak. But Vivian had said that thing, that thing she said her Jack always told her: "Remember this moment. Be aware of the good. Keep it for the dark days."

So he did. He breathed in and focused on this summer air. The warmth of the sun on his skin. The hummingbirds flitting in and out of the feeders he now changed weekly. His mother getting stronger, more energetic. The sound of her laughter. The sight of her taking her ballet lessons. The security of knowing his family had a break, a chance to get its footing, to stop the exhausting hustle of solely surviving.

He watched two hummingbirds, a male and a female, sipping from the feeder and the basket of trailing fuchsia. He wondered if Vivian had found Jack. He wondered what happened after they died. He tried to be glad her suffering and pain were over, but shit, how he missed her.

This one person had changed him, changed his whole family.

He remembered sitting up here with her toward the end. He told her, "You know how there are those people in the apocalypse who do good? Who help people? You're one of them."

She reached out and took his hand.

"You built a new community," he said.

She squeezed his hand and said, "You can build a new *world*."

He laughed then. But now, he thought, as he had every day since she'd said it: How exactly was he going to do that?

ACKNOWLEDGMENTS

This book would not have been possible without the following people:

For being the very first eyes on the rough draft of this book, even during a pandemic while they dealt with children remote-learning at home and with limited writing time of their own: Elly Lonon and Kristina McBride.

For sharing with me the particular details of being a nursing assistant, for inspiring me daily, and for lovingly caring for my dear, sweet mother: J. R. Kelly.

For generously sharing her gorgeous poem "This Is How a Pandemic Ends, Not with a Bang but with Cicadas": Kathleen McCleary. That poem, posted on Facebook when I was about three-quarters through my first draft, unlocked the end of the novel for me and helped me see what my story was really about.

For endless inspiration and my title: the beautiful poet Mary Oliver. The title is a phrase from her poem "Invitation," which I invite everyone to look up and read. You'll be glad you did.

For brainstorming, and for convincing me that yes, I needed to kill someone: Helena Kaler.

For sharing with me details and stories of living with cerebral palsy: the amazing, shining light of a human Dara Cosby.

For being such a staunch champion of my work: Jill Miner of Saturn Booksellers. I am so grateful for all you've done for me. I will miss the store greatly, but I have no plans to stop seeing you.

For being kindred spirits on the same rocky, perilous path, my dearest fellow writers I'm lucky to call friends: Meredith Doench, Christina Consolino, Erin Flanagan, Kristina McBride, Rachel Moulton, Sharon Short, and Jessica Strawser. We've huddled around a fire in freezing temps just to meet during the worst COVID days. We've laminated our goals. We've had writing retreats. I cannot imagine this journey without you.

For the endless moral support, expertise, and inspiration: the Fiction Writers Co-op. Every one of you has helped me.

For support, inspiration, and community: my past and present Word's Worth students and colleagues, and my University of Dayton family.

For keeping me sane and entertained during two of the strangest, sometimes darkest, years: our Pandemic Pack, the Fancies, Horror Salon, the Pervs, the For Realz women, and our EFF group. I love you dearly.

For jump-starting my "comeback": my amazing agent, Maria Whelan at InkWell Management. Thank you for your guidance, your belief in me, and the three-hour lunch on the Hottest Day Ever.

For seeing the heart of the story and wanting to bring it to an audience: Erin Adair-Hodges, my dream editor. Thank you for guiding this story into shape and for making me think of you every time I hear Falco (or "die Beastie Boys!"). Huge gratitude to Gabe Dumpit, Jen Bentham, kick-ass copyeditors Stacy A. and Kellie, proofreader Sarah E., and everyone at Lake Union who helped usher this story into the world in its best possible incarnation. Special thanks to David Downing for his sharp editing eyes.

For being my rock: my family. My mother would have been my biggest cheerleader were she still with us. She is such an enormous part of this book, as is my amazing, fierce, kick-ass father. I met with him outside, six feet apart, and masked in one-hundred-degree and twenty-degree weather alike until it was safe to meet inside again. Hugging him after a whole year and a half was a gift. My sister, Monica, was an early reader and my ride-or-die. My niece and nephew, Amy and Nathan, own my heart and give me endless story material. Sweet Serena and weird little Annie always lift my soul.

For being the best assistant I could wish for: my beloved Joey Cat. This is the last book written with his fifteen-pound weight draped over my left arm and his soft snoring providing the soundtrack to my writing life. Thank you for protecting me from the evil printer. You were a good friend. I was honored to be your human.

For welcoming me and my stories: my wonderful readers. I am so grateful. I love hearing from you. Your words of encouragement kept and keep me going.

For being the true partner I always wanted, for believing in me during the long drought, for your love and coffee deliveries: my dearest Jason. There is no one I'd rather be quarantined with.

BOOK CLUB DISCUSSION QUESTIONS FOR

MORNING IN THIS BROKEN WORLD

1. How was each of the four point-of-view characters already isolated and guarded before being forced into lockdown?
2. In what ways do the various characters emerge as their more authentic selves by the novel's end?
3. What are the different ways in which the characters help one another, both physically and emotionally? Luna says repeatedly that she is accepting Vivian's charity, but Vivian disagrees. Do you?
4. Why is it important that Luna invests in her ballet classes near the end of the story? She's never going to be a professional dancer, so why does she pursue this? What does it represent that was missing from her life before the novel's start?
5. Vivian invests a great deal of time and money in her garden. Why do you think it means so much to her? How does it parallel what she is growing and nurturing in other areas of her life?
6. Time with this new family changes how Cooper sees his potential future. What impact do Vivian and "the boys"

have on him? How does he change his relationship with and awareness of his father's shortcomings?

7. The Brood X cicadas are a strange natural phenomenon, emerging every seventeen years for a brief and *very* noisy life cycle. How do they play into the novel's themes? How does the process of their metamorphosis compare and contrast that of the point-of-view characters?

8. Luna often sees herself as weak. Do you think this is true? In what ways does she exhibit weakness, and in what ways does she exhibit strength?

9. Wren has very strong beliefs about the power of her "wishes." How does her belief evolve over the course of the novel? What important revelation does she have about her "superpowers"?

10. How did your own experiences during this strange time affect your reading of the novel? In what ways were the characters' experiences similar to or different from your own?

11. Could this nontraditional family have formed if it weren't for the pandemic? COVID is the catalyst that changes each of their lives profoundly. How have challenging experiences changed you, in both negative and positive ways? Were you able to keep any of those positive changes in your life as you moved forward?

12. Vivian's feelings about her own life and death change greatly from Chapter One to the end of the novel. What caused her to change? Do you think there was a specific moment that was the turnaround for her, or was it more of a gradual transformation?

13. Caretaking—for anyone—is important but exhausting. Both Vivian and Luna admit to neglecting their own health while they take care of others. You may have heard the expression, "You can't pour from an empty cup." How does that saying apply to both of these women? In what ways have you perhaps had to make changes so that you, as a caretaker, were taking care of yourself as well?

ABOUT THE AUTHOR

Photo © 2021 Alison Gambill

Katrina Kittle is the author of four novels for adults, *Traveling Light, Two Truths and a Lie, The Kindness of Strangers,* and *The Blessings of the Animals,* and one novel for young adults, *Reasons to Be Happy. The Kindness of Strangers* was the winner of the 2006 Great Lakes Book Award for Fiction. Katrina teaches creative writing at the University of Dayton and for Word's Worth Writing Connections. She lives near Dayton with her fella, cat, beagle, and out-of-control garden. Katrina has a thing for goats, gardening, and going barefoot and is addicted to coffee, pedicures, and Indian food. You can occasionally see her onstage in local community theater productions, and she is always at work on another novel. For more information, visit www.katrinakittle.com.